If
Wishes
Were
Horses ...

If
Wishes
Were
Horses...

Francine Pascal

Crown Publishers, Inc.

New York

The jacket artist has just opened the N.A.L.L. Foundation to promote art in all its expressions. Artist-in-residence programs are available in music, painting, and literature. The foundation is located in the south of France at 232, Boulevard de Lattre 06140, Vence. Telephone: 93-58-13-26.

Published by Crown Publishers, Inc., 201 East 50th Street, New York, New York 10022. Member of the Crown Publishing Group.

Random House, Inc. New York, Toronto, London, Sydney, Auckland

CROWN is a trademark of Crown Publishers, Inc.

Manufactured in the United States of America

Design by Jim Davis

Library of Congress Cataloging-in-Publication Data
Pascal, Francine.
        If wishes were horses . . . / by Francine Pascal.
        I. Title.
    PS3566.A7727I38   1994
    813'.54—dc20   93-25726
            CIP

ISBN 0-517-59682-2

10   9   8   7   6   5   4   3   2   1

First Edition

For my daughter, Jamie Stewart Carmen
and
my brother, Burt Rubin,
and
as always, for John.

If wishes were horses, beggars would ride.

Anonymous

If
Wishes
Were
Horses ...

FRANCE
June

When a great tragedy comes into your world, everything else shrinks to accommodate it. The new monster bullies its way in, filling all the corners, squeezing your normal, everyday life tight against the walls. And then it takes over and follows you everywhere.

It sits down with you at the table, turning every bite of food dry and tasteless; if you try to read a book, it blows the words around until they're an unreadable jumble; any work requiring more thought than lifting barrels or scrubbing floors becomes nearly impossible.

And it never leaves. It goes with you into the shower, walks alongside on crowded streets, pounding at your mind with the insistence of a panhandler who won't go away. And when you look in the mirror, it's already there waiting, carved into your face; it destroys your sleep and then rushes in first thing in the morning, flooding you again with its poison waves. It devours your life. There is no respite.

And you're not even the one dying.

It has been one hundred and thirty-seven days, almost five months, and it feels as if it could have happened yesterday. The sharpness of it never fades.

Unlike today, with its constant numbness like the pins and needles of a sleeping limb. I long to shake myself out of this hypnotized state, to find the energy and the courage to grab on to my life again.

But I need a beginning. A way to start.

It could be something small, even ordinary, as simple as a knock on the door or the ring of a phone.

Isn't there anyone out there thinking of me now?

What time is it in New York? Three in the afternoon, six hours earlier than here in the south of France. But they're all too busy. Besides, what would they say to me now, at the height of the day? Talking to the bereaved is something best done at night, after a couple of drinks, when their lives are quieter and more sentimental and the prospect of another ordinary evening looms before them. That's when it becomes more appealing. Call France, find out how Anna's doing. But it means so much less now.

I'm not there anymore. I'm not part of them, not the place they can go to at night or during the slow bits of the day to escape from their own lives into the exotica of tragedy. The best kind, someone else's.

But the phone stays silent. No one needs to be a wonderful person right this minute in the bright sunshine and excitement of a June day in New York.

Maybe later. *Tant pis pour moi,* because I need them right now. I need the sound of the phone, the connection with my real life. The life I so courageously fled.

None of these things around me, the furniture, the pictures, the small touches — the little collection of eighteenth-century porcelain angels grouped on a corner table, the wooden candlesticks, Italian, seventeenth century, on the hand-carved mantel, none of it — nothing in this strange, foreign villa, now my villa, is of me.

They all belonged to my predecessor, M. Carson, the American expatriate I bought it from. Actually, he had died shortly before, and I bought it from his estate. Intact. As is. Watchdog included.

The late M. Carson, my own personal Rebecca, will never know what an impossible challenge he has left for me. Not only did I buy his house and his furnishings, I also bought his staff; at least they chose to stay on.

Five months ago it seemed a perfect idea. I had to get away from New York, I was suffocating. I had the money, not the millions of the truly rich, but for me, a woman on the lip of middle age, enough not to have to think about using it up for a long, long time, unless I made a radical change in my life-style. Not a likely change to make overnight at forty.

The villa is small, inconspicuously tucked into two acres of terraced, wooded land. With its whitewashed exterior, crowned with the expected orange tiled roof, it is enormously charming, a gem overlooking the Mediterranean at Vallauris with a stunning view of Cap d'Antibes. It's just the right size to discourage guests, only two bedrooms and an office upstairs; downstairs, a small living room with connecting dining room, a tiny closet of a bar, and a good-size kitchen.

The dominant sense of the villa is warm, light, and delicate. The interior is done all in soft, aged Mediterranean colors of faded rose and quiet greens with touches of blues and yellows. Every corner seems touched with some thought, yet not too busy.

I'm sure I would have liked M. Carson, but if his staff is any clue, he probably wouldn't have liked me. His guardian certainly doesn't. She's so secure in her position, she thinks she can say and do anything. And she's right; with my halting French and culture-shocked emotions, I could never fire her. Kill her, maybe, but never the courage to fire her.

Odile Bareau, her name, never tires of telling me how it was an *équipe,* a team of wonderful people working together, including the patron, when the impeccable M. Carson was here.

I, on the other hand, am still too locked inside my own head to do anything but keep my distance.

Besides, I do struggle terribly with the language. Like bad hair days, there are bad French days and when they happen the language is no more comprehensible than beautiful, but unfamiliar music. On those days I can't help but think that I'm punishing myself unnecessarily being here. After all, it's been hard enough.

At any rate, according to Mme. Bareau, five months earlier, before I arrived, *l'équipe* was a unified, contented force, with a routine cast in cement. No wonder, too, it had been without change in twenty years. With the exception of the electrician, the new boy, there only twelve years, the staff—the guardian; the gardener; the plumber; and the *garagiste*—was the same. Only the guardian, Mme. Bareau, is full-time and lives on the premises. Her house is a small wing of mine, jutting out from behind my living room, with its own corridor and a separate entrance.

Now, I have arrived and I want changes: a new, modern bathroom with a lighted dressing table, an expanded kitchen with a double oven, a dishwasher, and all the other cooking conveniences available. A house for living, not just decoration.

My life is very different from M. Carson's. For one thing, I am a woman and he was a man; a gay, antisocial, neat-as-a-pin man of fifty whose only guest was likely to be a young Arab boy scooted into the house and onto the bed and given the one available ashtray in the house and probably not allowed to put it down on any of the furniture.

I know the boy smoked because he came by here shortly after I moved in and I gave him a leather wallet I had found in the house to keep as a memento of his former friend. In the few minutes he was there he chain-smoked and held the ashtray in his laborer's hand.

He asked to be able to work around the premises, he needed the money now that his benefactor was gone, and I agreed. Little did I know that he was not part of *l'équipe*. But I was quickly informed, at least four times in the first two days, by the guardian, the plumber, the electrician, the gardener—the team—that I had made yet another error. It took me three weeks before I worked up the courage to let Ali go. Of course with a five-hundred-franc note tucked neatly into his hand. No big loss, he was falling-down drunk most of the time, but I did squirm at being made to do it.

As I squirmed at so many other things they were making me do, things that had to be done exactly as they had been done before. I squirmed silently. Cowardly. They were a river in full flow, and I was simply sucked in and carried along.

I dreamed of damming their flow with my own body, stopping it dead and forcing it in my own direction. But I had to get my bearings first. Find my direction. And my courage. Would I ever get my courage back again?

I have developed a routine in my house. I get up at twenty to eight in the morning. First thing I do is throw open the shutters so that the guardian can see I'm not a layabout. Then I do my morning absolutions, six of these, six of those, four knocks, five taps, it's all done in under three minutes. But it does keep the devils away.

There are devils. And they're waiting for me. Some have already come and done their damage, and it was terrible, but there are others and I must keep them at bay.

Once I finish my morning preparations, I can safely take a shower and dress. Then I greet the dog. I say the dog, not my dog, since as I mentioned I acquired him, also, along with the house and staff. Every morning first thing I do is give him a treat, which he instantly snaps out of my hand.

The guardian, in her one bout with humor, warned of the morning I forget his treat.

Nonetheless, I give him his treat, then pet him. Many mornings I don't reach out fast enough for the caress and then he's gone. Just as well; as he lives outside he can smell a little strong. I find myself rinsing my hands after the contact, just like neat and precise M. Carson must have done. Am I growing like him?

Is it the living alone that tightens life so? You are for once in total control. Nothing you ever do is challenged. There are no other influences, no mistakes but your own. Simple things: if you leave the scissor on the night table one day, it is there the next and the next and the next. It still shocks me that my daughter or my husband hasn't used it and casually left it lying in some unexpected place that takes days to locate. But no one is here to borrow the scissor and so it stays in the one spot.

Like my life, unless I force myself to move it.

And that is the primary reason I have thrown myself into France. To make my life move once more. So far all my courage has not gained me an inch. On the contrary, it seems as if everything has been thrown backward, inward, into a corner of my psyche that hasn't been mined since childhood. That primitive part where language begins, that place from whence you take that first timid venture, frightened, head tilted meekly to one side, eyes aware of every shadow, belly exposed, out into the world to be accepted, to fit in — to find love.

God knows, I'm not even near finding it. In fact, I can truthfully say I have not one real friend in the entire south of France. Somehow that sounds like a boast — a feast of self-pity — but it's true. Not counting my *équipe* that is no longer an *équipe*, now just a group of malcontents, I know four other people: the real estate agent who sold me the property; the lawyer, but I can't say I really know her since I never saw her, everything was done by telephone and fax; and two friends of M. Carson, Pierre Rossi and Jean-Claude Martin, a gay couple who have lived together for almost twenty-five years. I spoke to Pierre on the phone a couple of times, and he was kind enough to invite me to lunch at a beach called L'Ondine on the Croisette, that magnificent wide avenue bordering the sea, in Cannes.

"Just look for the handsomest man on the beach sitting with an old queen and you've got us," Pierre told me, and left it to my imagination to decide which one he was.

Pierre turned out to be the "old queen," except he really wasn't. He was actually quite well built, a little too short to be traditionally handsome, no more than mid-fifties, with an instant sparkle and a quick and naughty sense of humor.

But he was right about Jean-Claude, who was about ten years younger and absolutely gorgeous by any standards. Tall, beautifully built, with platinum hair and striking blue eyes, he could have been an actor.

Most of our conversation was about the house. Jean-Claude was an antiques dealer and had helped furnish it. He was a fund of very helpful information about things like how to wind the grandfather clock, what products to use on the painted furniture, and the care of the tapestry. Pierre gave me the history of my new dog, whom I had to pretend I was mad about, and how to care for the miserable animal.

"You should have brought him to lunch. He loves it here." He told me that M. Carson always took him to restaurants.

Actually, that's the way in France. The dogs do go everywhere, and as a result I admit they seem quite civilized. They're always welcomed in restaurants, often served first with a bowl of water slipped under the table, if they deign to lie under the table. I have seen little poodles sitting upright on chairs, their chins at the plate, missing only a fork.

It was a three-hour lunch, and by dessert my head was dizzy with all the gossip. They seem to know everyone in Cannes. And everyone had a story. Though Tipi's would probably stay in my mind forever. You had to see him to appreciate it, and I was lucky because he was right there, just two tables away.

According to Jean-Claude, Tipi was the most popular, sought-after lover on the coast and had been for years. What was his secret? I asked.

Look for yourself.

I did, and what I saw was a rather ordinary-looking man of about thirty-five. Ordinary, that is, until he moved his left arm up to the table. The entire hand was missing. Cut off at the wrist. Long healed, the lower arm had thinned of excess muscle, leaving only a skin-covered forearm bone that seemed to taper slightly toward the end.

I could feel them watching me as I unfolded the puzzle and laid it out flat in my mind. When his "secret" finally hit me, I think I squeaked; I certainly looked away.

Of course, the embarrassment must have registered on my face because they both laughed.

Welcome to the Côte d'Azur. The work is done, the money is made, it's all free play time now.

We had a wonderful, comfortable time. Completely superficial. They didn't ask about my loss, and though I knew through Mme. Bareau that a dear friend of theirs had died of AIDS just the week earlier, I didn't ask about theirs.

The silent complicity of the wounded. Perfect friends for me. In fact, I made overtures to them; I invited them to dinner the following night, but they said they had a dinner engagement in St. Maxime, a good hour and a half west of Cannes. That's fair enough. I wasn't totally discouraged.

With nothing to do the next evening, I thought I might try to improve my French a bit and take in a movie. As I came down the rue d'Antibes, the main shopping street in Cannes, toward the theater, I saw my would-be friends buying tickets for the same film. I hid in a doorway, not wanting them to be embarrassed by their lie. I should have told them to shove it. Shoulda, woulda, coulda; my real language in France.

So strange. How did they know so fast that I was to be avoided? And why? Did they look into my soul and see the emptiness? Do people run from the lonely?

Fortunately, I am so involved in the simple day-to-day-survival existence among my enemies that I almost don't have time to miss having friends.

I miss him. That other part of me. Dreadfully.

And I miss ordinary things: a reason to speak English in my own house, another voice to break the silence; a voice that speaks of things I know, things we both know; a voice in on my secrets and my humor. I miss that terribly.

And there is so much politesse that most social overtures, at least those directed to me, are the Hollywood equivalent of "We must have lunch sometime." But needy as I am, I actually find myself waiting with napkin ready for the lunch that will never be.

I do so want someone to touch. I miss the touching. Not only don't you talk when you are alone, but you don't feel another human body. Sometimes in shops I pass close by another person just to touch them lightly on the pretense of moving them out of the way.

And to be touched. Strangely, that's easier. On a very superficial level you can buy that at the hairdresser. The best of that, the most intimate, is my new discovery, a massage. I had never had one, nor did I ever find the need for one before.

When I was a child my mother used to have a masseuse who came to the house once a week. Vanya was her name, and she was short and very dark, foreign, maybe Polish, and she lugged a heavy metal table that even in its folded state came up to her chin. I knew "masseuse" was a foreign word, but since my mother used it, I assumed it was Yiddish.

They would disappear, Vanya and my mother, into her bedroom for an uninterrupted hour: Do not even knock on the door! Terrible instructions for an eight-year-old. When I grew up and heard people, men in particular, talking with passion about massages, all I could think of was the little, dark woman and her huge table. I never wanted one.

My present discovery was accidental. I had been invited by Jean-Claude and Pierre for an afternoon on someone's Offshore. Coupled with the terrible snub of the last time (the invented excuse that turned out to be a lie) and the fact that I hate speedboats, it was a perfect opportunity to say no, but I didn't. The lure of company was too great. I accepted and paid dearly for the weakness. No one told me that to reduce the stress on the base of your spine, you must stand when the boat pounds into the waves

Of course, not knowing this, I sat while the moron cowboy who ran the boat yelped and roared as he smashed the prow into each wall of water at fifty knots. The end result was a terrible pain in my lower back that kept me on one cheek or the other for the next week.

I had to get relief, and the prospect of finding a chiropractor, asking for recommendations (from whom?), was dizzying. As for the Yellow Pages, even the French can't figure them out. Then I got lucky. One afternoon, later that week, quite by chance I parked my car on the rue Mace, a little street off the rue d'Antibes, in front of La Maison de Massage.

Since the suite number was 102, I assumed it to be on the first floor, which in France is equivalent to our second floor, except in this building for some unknown reason it was the third floor of a five-floor walk-up with six doors on each floor. I know all this because I went through almost every one of them before I found the right one, most of them grappled at in pitch darkness. The hall light was set at an economical thirty seconds.

Little did I know that I had entered on a monster called the *sous-sol,* the basement, which put the *rez-de-chaussée,* or the RC, the lobby, on the second floor, thereby forcing the maddeningly elusive first floor up one level and dumping it on what I would expect to be my third floor.

When will I learn that nothing is ever what I expect it to be?

At last, in a xenophobic fury, I found the right door. It was unlocked and I flung it open and stormed in, bursting with complaints. But no one was in sight.

I could hear sounds from inside, muted, and water sounds, powerful like a fire hose, a little unnerving, but at least there were no screams. And no sign of people.

I waited ten minutes, shifting from painful cheek to painful cheek, and still no one came. I was desperate, longing for the relief I knew awaited me. I waited another ten minutes. Hello? Hello? I called toward the back. Perhaps they hadn't heard me come in. No one replied.

At last a Playboy nurse appeared: a young, pretty woman in a mini-uniform stretched tight across her ample *embonpoint.* I asked for an appointment, explaining my emergency condition.

She arranged an appointment with M. Gilet at seventeen hours. I knew that meant five o'clock in real time (for further understanding of the term *real,* substitute "American"), but the computation doesn't come naturally and I must start from twelve and work my way to seventeen. By the time I realized I would have to wait another two hours, she had written my name in the book.

I had no choice. I had to find relief from the pain.

Down on the street, I bought the *Herald Tribune* and walked to a café nearby on the rue d'Antibes. For the price of one *citron pressé*—that's fresh lemon juice, water, and as much sugar as you can jam into the glass (they haven't conquered the melting problem yet)—you can sit in the cool of an umbrella undisturbed all afternoon.

Normally undisturbed, but that day a Gypsy woman carrying what appeared to be a tightly wrapped infant in one arm was working the street. She stopped at each table, her hand extended for a donation.

Do Gypsies really dress in these long rags and robes all the time? Or are those only their working clothes? I watched her cross the café. It struck me she seemed too old to have such a young baby. I would have continued to examine her, but she turned in my direction so I buried myself in my newspaper.

Without looking up, I could feel her presence. She was very close, close enough to intrude on that no-man's-land space between people. Her boldness was more than slightly aggressive, and it touched off my own leftover anger from the massage experience. I ignored her. Aggressively.

Wordlessly she put her hand out toward me, poking the dirt-lined fingers with their cracked yellow nails almost into my face. There was no pretending not to see her, so I looked up. It took effort to arrange a kindly look on my face, but I did as I shook my head, no.

She leaned down into my face and spat. A wad of saliva splashed across my cheek. I jumped up to attack her, but she held out the baby like a shield between us. I grabbed at the tiny, thin paper napkin under my glass, upturning my drink and spilling *citron pressé* across the table and down my leg.

"*Salope!*" I shouted the ugliest French word I could think of.

Her response was to throw back her shoulders, aim her chin at me, and watch smugly in silence as I fumbled to wipe her dripping spittle from my face.

"Disgusting! *Dégueulasse!* " I couldn't stop myself.

But all she did was walk off. Not one bit faster than she had come; in fact, she took her time, haughtily tilting her head and turning to make sure I watched as she boldly stopped at the last table on the rim of the café. Before she could extend her hand to the seated couple, the man jumped up and grabbed it, jamming some coins into her palm. Now she turned toward me and smiled, the ugly, gap-toothed smile of a Gypsy thief.

With the soaked napkin held against my cheek, I went straight to the toilet. To wash up and to cry. Stupid things like that upset me far, far more than they should. Anything that might ordinarily garner any emotional response, happy or sad, brings me to tears. That's just the way it is now.

I'm weak, defeated, I have no heart left to withstand the smallest bump. In defense I try to keep my interior state as close to silent and empty as possible; the goal is to allow space to only the most superficial maintenance considerations: houses, cars, paperwork (not my real work, which is also done on paper, I'm not ready for that yet), the study of French, and, most mindless of all, shopping. Buy another pair of boots, another jacket, another anything. Keep buying. Bring home something new wrapped in crisp tissue and slipped into a shiny shopping bag. Something that wasn't there before. That wasn't part of that awful time.

And it works for surprisingly long periods of time — sometimes almost a whole day. But then from behind some hidden corner of thought, touched off by a half-heard word, a note of music, a sign, the lightest tap, a push, a knock, a touch of skin, and the silence is invaded, the emptiness is flooded with feelings. Control is unhinged. Nerve endings snap and shoot the leap from zero to a million hysteria points, bursting through the top in rage and confusion and terror and spilling out in tears, and tears, and more tears. . . .

I want him back!

If I could scream, I would scream the same words, always the same words: It's more than I can bear! More than I can bear!

I left the restaurant and hurried up to the safety of M. Gilet's waiting room.

And there I waited until seventeen hours, at which time the massage king himself appeared. Wordlessly I followed M. Gilet into a small room as clean and shabby as the reception area with two shadeless windows. The only sign to its purpose is the 1950s vintage massage table. Only Vanya was missing.

Monsieur, my savior, fixed a folded sheet over the black leather table and stood back, waiting. It took me some seconds to realize that I was supposed to undress. Even a doctor gives you something for modesty. But there was no towel or robe in sight. The sunlight that washed every angle of the room made hiding impossible. And my back was killing me. And it was France. That's the way it's done. I guess.

Wiped out by the overexpenditure of anger and frustration, reduced to a beggar by my pain and longing for relief, I turned toward the corner and began slowly to unbutton my shirt, desperate for some magical way to strip, get to the table, and lie down all within the same split second in a kind of larger, all-encompassing, hand-is-quicker-than-the-eye method.

No way. I steeled myself, unpeeled my clothes, and forced myself to walk calmly, measured step after step, stomach held in tightly, to the table. There I stopped, mere inches from M. Gilet, waiting, stark naked, for him to tell me how to lie down. Oh, the power of the clothed.

He did, and I dove gratefully down stomach first onto the table. And waited, my head buried in the fragrant sheet with the not unpleasant odor of somebody else's body.

He poured some coconut-smelling oil on my back and began lightly to massage the side near the offending hip. Even his light touch gave pain. I moaned, and the touch became heavier. I groaned.

"*C'est nécessaire,*" he said.

I bit the side of my thumb, be quiet, this is going to help.

The strokes were longer now, from the top of my thigh up to my waist, each stroke pulling flesh in a wake behind it. And as it pulled the gathered flesh in its path, I could feel that side of my buttocks parting. From my thigh and up, down and up, in a steady movement plowing a road through the supple flesh. The pain was replaced by an accompanying surprise — no, shock — of the open feeling in that very closed place between my legs. And worry. Was this medicinal? Of course. He was, after all, crossing that painful area I had shown him in the back of my waist.

French medicinal.

Now with both hands he began to work another path that led this time on a slant across my buttocks to the upper side of my waist, thus pulling open my buttocks even more shamelessly. Of course he had to see all that was happening; it was full daylight and he was only inches away. But there was no reaction in his touch. It was steady. By turning my head toward him, I could see half his face as he leaned back slightly on his heels. It was implacable.

But, of course, I told myself, I had never had a massage before. And this was, after all, another culture, another method; this was France.

His fingers dug deeper into my skin, moving closer toward the apex where thigh and buttocks are joined. The flesh road became longer, stretching up to the center of my back. Each stroke engendered different tingles of feelings as it moved along its path, the most shocking at the beginning where the pull began to open me, and as his hand moved higher the tingle as my buttocks slipped closed, the two sides touching, sending a spasm along those nerves that travel into the deep reaches of longing. Over and over again, mesmerizing all feeling into that one action. The opening and the sliding closed.

Somewhere in the back of my consciousness I heard his voice. For the instant it made no sense, and then I understood. I was to turn over. Hypnotized as I was, still the cold and clear reality of his demand hit me. Turn over and be totally exposed, my face as well as my body.

He stood back, waiting, a small smile on his placid face. He was untouched by what had happened. Look at him. Just the masseur doing a job. Obviously my own reactions were the only things out of line.

I closed my eyes and turned onto my back. And when I opened them I could see nothing out of the ordinary in this very ordinary man's face. It was obviously all in my own filthy mind.

I watched as he poured the oil over my belly and rubbed it down my thighs. My God.

Was I being stupid, naive? No. I told him I had a problem, and he worked on it in his way. That's the way it had to be done. That I was aroused was my problem or pleasure. Not his.

But my back doesn't hurt in the front. Perhaps this will be the massage part. But it wasn't.

His manipulations followed the same path as on my back. Only in front the apex of the thighs and groin were even more vulnerable. I must have been out of my mind; surely I had fallen into the hands of one of those wonderful, quiet, boy-next-door rapists. The only thing to do was get up from the table, excuse myself, give some phony reason, late for this or that, and leave.

These thoughts worked furiously in my mind while the rapist worked his magic.

If you put a frog on his back and rub his stomach, he will be paralyzed. You can stop and he won't move for almost a minute.

I was the frog. So pathetically needy.

I lay still as his strong fingers worked the line from deep beginning to ending on either side of my belly. The only moment possible for escape was the instant between the time he lifted his hands from my body and the moment he brought them down to begin again.

The instant passed and passed again. I didn't move. I could feel all the juices pouring from those deep, swollen places.

The shame was deep, but I no longer cared.

In my mind's eye I could see the deep pinkness of the parted lips, feel his eyes, the daylight, the very air itself, touching me.

Now he moved to my inner thighs, separating them slightly; and then, using three fingers on each hand and starting from just inside my knees, he began carving a deep line into the flesh toward the top of my thighs and then beyond, brushing, feather lightly, against the outer side of the labia lips now drenched in a thick, viscous juice, whose drops slid down between my buttocks to the sheet below.

He continued tracing his slippery path onward through wiry, wet curls to end on the swollen mound, his fingers hesitating hardly a beat before they rose once more up into the air.

All this in a graceful hand ballet. Deep in and up into the air. I could feel my flesh reaching for his hands as they rose up.

The spasms within my body throbbed, but the outside was still.

Or perhaps it wasn't. Perhaps he could see. He had to know his effect on me.

He stood near my breasts, leaning into the side of them, reaching down to begin the long stroke again. I felt him against me; was it his penis or his hipbone or what? I couldn't tell.

I was suspended in a preorgasmic ache from which no clear thought could emerge.

Were those strong, long fingers going to slide inside me? This time? Next time? What time?

I was lost in a sensual madness.

Now he abandoned one side and concentrated only on the other.

Flying as I was on that wild road, spinning that arc through the air and down, swept into the tunnel with only one exit, rushing along at speeds that only a crash stop can halt.

He stopped.

I crashed.

That was it? One lift of his hands and they never came back. My eyes sprung open, it was over. He had stepped back. I could feel my nostrils expanding, sucking the air. My body lunging for equilibrium.

Don't show him.

He smiled and waited. He wanted his last piece of torture.

Shakily I stood up, propelling myself to the corner where my clothes hung as I had left them on the edge of a standing scale. I grabbed them to my body and turned to face my tormentor with some last bit of dignity, but M. Gilet had already left the room. Not walked out, more like disappeared.

Nuts, I thought. I'm nuts. I'm not in France, I'm down a rabbit hole, trapped inside my head, and crazier because I've surrounded myself with this creation that's only imagination.

Or am I just so very hungry?

Outside in the waiting room, I took a seat. There were amenities to be served, I had to wait for M. Gilet to pay the bill.

I had to stop trembling.

I wasn't there two minutes when M. Gilet appeared, as cool as if our appointment had never happened. Except that he was ready to be paid.

I paid the son of a bitch.

And made another appointment.

NEW YORK CITY
1973

I t could hardly be called a newsroom, yet it was a real newspaper and this was the room where it was put together. In truth it was the front half of the first floor of a brownstone — and still looked like somebody's living room without the furniture. Outlines where pictures once hung, darker paint along a wall that must have been home to a couch, and near the window an outline almost like a shadow where a tall lamp once stood shielding the long, thin bit of wall from sunlight.

No attempt had been made to make the room appear more like an office; that didn't matter. All that mattered was that the *Westside Word* got out every Friday and was distributed by six P.M. the latest so that it would be in lobbies from West One Hundredth down to West Forty-second Street in time for the people coming home from work to grab a copy. It was free, a giveaway.

Because most of the staff of five had graduated from college within the previous three years, there was much more headstrong idealism, innocence, and sophomoric humor than this genre of newspaper, a glorified but very successful advertising sheet, normally engendered. Also, because the owner didn't give a shit what articles went into it as long as there were the right number of ads, the staff had true autonomy and they used every bit of it.

This week they were running a devastating interview of a fairly well-known no-talent, a Broadway musical director named Marvin Charnel. The man had a good start on arrogance, but by the time *Westside Word* reporter Anna Green, new to journalism, Vassar '72, finished with him the reader would have spit if he'd walked in the room.

In the theater Charnel was known as a credit hog, having

invented a spurious category known as "concept by," a device by which he as director could hog extra credit as an originator. Writers are always so hungry to get their plays produced that they made easy pickings, and on almost every play he had successfully added his new credit line. And this time he also claimed the lyrics, which Anna believed were idiotic enough to be truly his.

Additionally, Charnel had gratuitously condemned her friend's first off-off-Broadway musical in the nastiest manner and now, when the phone rang during the interview, had told Anna to answer it and tell his wife he was out. Just like that he gave her the order. Of course, she wouldn't do it and simply handed the phone back to him. But bastards like that are lucky, and it wasn't his wife, it was his girlfriend.

Anna had the most fun describing his hair. Oh, the power of the press, especially when, like Anna, you had just acquired it less than three months earlier and were still tossing it around like a new toy. Charnel, the victim, was obviously terribly vain about losing his hairline in the front. Actually, it was hard to tell because he had compensated by combing all the hair from the center of his head, and from the looks of it at least four other heads, forward and down to his eyebrows. And then teasing it. And spraying it. It became a lusterless brown hair hat. And then there were the sunglasses — at seven in the evening, in the house. Of course, she couldn't resist.

Anna had a talent that was nearly completely obscured by the passion of her ideals. It would be another two years before she could cool down enough to let it flourish.

"You better watch your own hair when he reads this." Barbara Glassman, best friend, ex–Vassar roommate, fellow worker, and niece of the owner of the paper, had just finished reading Anna's piece.

"You like it?" Anna asked.

"It's great. I wish I could write like you." And if total truthfulness were possible, Barbara would have said that she wished she could be like Anna in every other way, too — look like her, dress like her, eat like her (she never gained an extra pound), and be getting married in less than two months just like Anna.

In fact, Barbara Glassman has been wanting to be Anna since they'd met in high school some nine years earlier. From the first time she saw that long, thick, deep brown hair with the mad profusion of curls — not tiny, frizzy twists of wire, but soft, round curls, curls that flashed a fiery auburn in the sunlight — and the dark blue eyes and the white skin with just enough freckles splashed across her nose to soften the seriousness of the beauty, Anna Green became her ideal.

Their upbringings had been comparable; though the Glassmans had more money, the Greens had enough to enjoy all the same privileges of upper-middle-class Jewish families in Manhattan — a large Central Park West apartment, good private schools that fed into the right colleges, specialized summer camps (art, music, or horseback riding), liberal politics, social activism, overcautious parental overdirection, and therapy when necessary.

But Anna was blessed; even at fourteen she had had a perfect figure. It was all Barbara had ever dreamed about, but at five two and 130 pounds, with her thin, straight, dark blond hair and sallow complexion, she couldn't even work up a bad imitation. Barbara wasn't jealous, she truly loved Anna. Loved looking at her, loved being her friend.

"Thanks, I was pleased with it. Thought I nailed him." Anna said, comfortable enough with her best friend to show her pleasure and her pride. "What time's what's-his-name showing up?"

"Devlin. Soon. Supposed to be before four."

Nick Devlin was the new editor-in-chief of the paper. That sounded better than it was. The last three people who had the job had quit, the longest staying almost a year, because the work was far too demanding for one person.

Of the five-person staff servicing the thirty-page weekly, two were ad salespeople, two were part-time reporters (Anna and Barbara), and then there was the editor-in-chief. He was responsible for all the editing, the weekly columns, the layout, and anything else the others didn't handle.

Plus on Thursday nights he had to take the paper down to the print shop and hang around there until nearly dawn to make sure the cut-rate printer didn't spill too much gin on it. The pay for all this was commensurate with a Woolworth's trainee, but there was a never-ending supply of young journalism graduates who would do anything to work on a newspaper in New York, any newspaper. The latest was Nick Devlin.

According to Nick's résumé, he had graduated with a master's in journalism from Columbia three years earlier, had worked on small papers in Billings, Montana, and Forstoria, Ohio, and had just turned twenty-seven a month earlier, in June. Until he found his own apartment, he was staying temporarily in Brooklyn with his parents, and according to Barbara, who had seen his picture at her uncle's, he was not gorgeous but looked intelligent and modest, maybe even a little shy.

At exactly 3:45 P.M. Nick Devlin, who indeed looked exactly as Barbara had described him, walked into the office, took one look at Anna Green, and fell deeply in love.

It happened just as he opened the door, and it threw him so badly that all his carefully made preparations were blown right out of his head.

He had been planning this moment for days, practically written it out like the scene of a play, right down to exactly how he would greet his staff. How he would walk into the room, not too fast, not too anxious, smile, catching the right balance between chief exec and friend, and in as deep a voice as his Sinatra tenor would allow, greet them.

"Hello, everyone."

That was the winning phrase out of about twenty possibilities.

This planning had been going on for days. He had referred to his staff so many times at home that his mother with her sharp Irish tongue had compared him to his uncle Louie, a family ne'er-do-well bullshitter. After that he stopped talking to his family about the new job. But he himself was still impressed and kept thinking about how he was going to handle his "staff." The first and only comparable arrangement had been when he was editor of his college newspaper, but that wasn't a real staff, just a lot of buddies and some pains in the ass.

Of this group, he was most nervous about the two ad people. They were in their thirties, and it was important that he not look like an inexperienced kid to them. He had decided the best way to handle them was not to be too friendly right away. He wasn't so worried about his writers, two young women who were both under twenty-five. He could handle writers because, more than an editor, he was a writer himself. And he usually liked writers.

The door wasn't even fully opened when he caught a flash of the dark-haired girl sitting across the room. She was leaning way back in her chair, her miniskirt almost totally lost under her thighs, her long tanned legs up and crossed with her heels leaning on the edge of her desk. He didn't catch all that at once.

His first glimpse was of a mass of dark curls and the most beautiful face he'd ever seen. Then his eyes found the rest of this extraordinary sight — the T-shirt and the little piece of jeans skirt, and then the legs. . . .

By then Devlin was well past a third of the way into the room, well stunned, his plan already blown. He hadn't even looked around, given the practiced smile, or uttered any one of the twenty different possible first greetings.

The best that could be said for Nick's entrance was that when he fell on his face, nobody saw it because it was all in his head. They just thought the confusion was because he'd stumbled into the wrong office.

Except Barbara, who recognized him from his photo.

"Hi, are you Nick Devlin?" she asked gently, pleased at how well he translated from the two-dimensional to the sweet warmth of reality. At the sound of his name he froze. She got up to shake his hand, not so much to greet him as to calm him down before he bolted.

It worked. Her sensible little hand was the magic touch to bring him back to reality.

Was it too late to give them the practiced smile? Yes, it was. No one would believe it, but he had to say something and "Hello, everyone" was the first thing he could grab. Unfortunately he still hadn't come down enough to look around, so he said it directly to Barbara.

"Barbara," she said gently, all maternal juices gushing to the surface for this poor lamb, and then introduced him to the others.

"Roger Wein, Adam Hawkins, and Anna Green."

He was fine with Roger and Adam, but when it came to Anna, he fell apart again, and this time everyone knew what his problem was. At least everyone but Anna. She just thought he was one of those nervous people who seem to dive into your face when they meet you, a type she had come across before. Sometimes it heralded a crush, but often it was just a severe lack of confidence. She hoped it was the confidence problem because in no way was this slightly too tall, slightly too thin, ordinary-looking young man of interest to her. And he looked so midwestern, an absolute pejorative in New York, in his casual outfit, which was in reality his Sunday suit without the tie and with the white shirt open at the collar and a sports jacket instead of the suit jacket that went with the pants.

Actually, he had a nice face. And maybe not so ordinary. Now that he was breathing again, the eyes had begun to look more normal, sort of crinkly, the blue a little too light, but kind of sexy. Anna liked the nose, strong, bony, like her father's. An intelligent nose. And very nice lips, the top one a little more prominent than it should be.

Anna thought she was going to like Nick Devlin. Definitely. Unless, of course, he was in love with her.

Of course, Barbara saw it all right away. But why wouldn't he go nuts for Anna? She was always surprised when any man seemed immune to Anna's charms, to that beautiful face with its haze of curls, that face Barbara herself could watch for hours on end.

Barbara loved Anna. And with her warm nature she often felt an overpowering need to hug her and to hold her hand and tell her how much she meant to her.

Barbara was a toucher, it was the way she talked. Lightly, she would reach out and tap your arm as she spoke. After a while the listener would move his arm closer, waiting for that sweet, rare contact that had become more important than the words.

Barbara Glassman was a young woman caught in the vise of the sixties sexuality that had by 1973 become something of a burden. She was tired of going to bed with too many unimportant attachments, she wanted to be in love and marry and have her own baby in one of those carrying sacks strapped to her chest, pressed against her breasts. Again she wanted to be like Anna, getting married. At least that's what she thought she wanted.

Not that she wanted to marry Steven Buchwald, Anna's intended. And she was about the last person in the world Mr. Gorgeous would even date. He never dated anything but beautiful women. Even at twenty-eight he exuded such confidence and poise that when he and Anna walked into a restaurant they would immediately get the best table. Of course it didn't hurt that Anna was so spectacular. Still, Steven could get it on his own.

He had his own qualities. Aside from his good looks, his powerfully developed body gave him a strong, solid presence that people respected. He could be a little boorish, his humor was primitive, repetitive, but he had a charm that softened the flaws. For Barbara, his worst flaw was that he was an anti-intellectual, bemused by Anna's radical views, but treating them in a way that said they were unimportant. Not to be taken seriously. Soon enough Anna would be eased into her true métier, wife and mother. Barbara couldn't understand Anna's blindness to an attitude that was so obvious to her.

Or perhaps Anna understood that he was right. After all, Barbara herself wanted those things, too. But she also wanted the progress the sixties had won for women. And she wasn't going to choose a mate who didn't understand that. Steven didn't, she was certain of that.

He wasn't crazy about her, either. He wasn't that comfortable with unbeautiful women. The only thing Barbara had going for her was family money. That was as near to beauty as she would ever get for Steven.

Not that he was a star fucker, someone interested in toadying to celebrities or people with money; no, his interest in money was more a fascination with its properties, where it came from and how to get it and then, once gotten, how to use it. And for such a young man, he was remarkably good at all aspects of it. He had been given a good head start by his father, who had made a quantum financial leap during World War II by dismantling water tanks and selling the used steel to the government.

In the late forties, the elder Mr. Buchwald moved his family into a luxurious old apartment on Sixty-eighth and Central Park West and invested wisely in real estate in suburban Long Island. Those investments set the family up comfortably and saw the three children into a well-advantaged adulthood.

With that kind of background, his good looks, and his own talent with money, Steven Buchwald was very desirable, a local prince. And Anna Green, something of a princess herself, was a natural choice for him.

Still, from Barbara's point of view, it was a bad mistake, one of the few she had seen Anna make. Well, it wasn't made yet. It would be six and a half weeks to the mammoth wedding at the Pierre. Barbara was to be her best friend's maid of honor. Despite the one concession to the revolution—they would write their own vows—it was all very old-fashioned, as if the sixties had never happened. It was a subject she and Anna couldn't really discuss.

Anna knew that her friend disapproved of her fiancé. In some ways she did, too. She knew he lacked wit, the quickness to take a thought and turn it inside itself. That delightful trick her father did so well. But she could make him laugh. So Barbara was wrong; he was not without humor.

But then there were bad days when she didn't know why she was marrying Steven. Days when she thought she would call the whole thing off—break the news to her parents, swallow the embarrassment, and take off for Europe. Except first she would have to write a note to each guest, canceling the wedding, and then return the gifts (and many had been received) with another note, some kind of minimum explanation. The prospect of her parents' pain overwhelmed her, and each note became a written admission of her inadequacy and their disappointment.

Even the simplest part, rewrapping the presents, was too diffi-cult to consider. She never should have thrown the boxes away. Sometimes she thought that might have been her last chance to call the whole thing off. If only she hadn't thrown out the boxes.

Still, there were things about Steven that were exciting. Sexu-ally he was much more sophisticated than anyone she'd ever been with. She'd had her first orgasm with him two years earlier. She was twenty at the time and had been having serious sex since eighteen, but mostly with other inexperienced, fumbling eighteen-year-olds. Before eighteen it could hardly count, being mostly a here-and-there experimentation, much of which was terribly unsatisfying.

People talk about the sixties as if it was a whole decade of revolution when in truth the early part of the sixties was just as hidebound as the fifties. It wasn't until later, 1968, when Anna was seventeen, that it really exploded.

That year, like the rest of the country, Anna had watched the Democratic convention take the revolution to the whole nation, showing them all as clearly as a movie who the villains really were. Then the shouting began, and the momentum was not to be stopped; the noise became an action that swept everyone along. No one could resist it, at least no one under forty. They said thirty, but it was bigger than that. Forty. No one under forty.

Change was flourishing. The ugliest part was over. The whole country was loving it. TV, movies, young, old, everyone was kicking up his heels at the new freedom. And, in the full bloom of the seventies, they thought they had all the time in the world.

So Anna Green was going to marry Steven Buchwald on Sun-day, the thirteenth of September, in the year 1973.

Unless she could find the boxes.

"Hey, Devlin"—Roger Wein put out his hand—"nice to have you here."

Nick savored the moment to look at them as strangers because he knew that once he knew them he would never see the raw reality of them again.

Physically, this was what they really looked like: Roger Wein, soft, capon-looking, brown hair, brown eyes, brown suit — all faded looking. He would certainly need direction. And Adam Hawkins, short, smart, knowing a little bit of everything, but not enough for the long haul. Probably his tenth job in as many years. A huckster in training who would never make it. Hot for Anna or Barbara, or anyone who might fuck him. Nervous, with the foot that never stops tapping, but lightly. If it's under his desk, you don't even hear it.

Nick didn't expect to have trouble with either of them. He'd just let them move on their own. He didn't know shit about advertising. He had told that to Resnick at the interview, but the guy was so busy trying to place a bet on the third at Aqueduct that he'd have hired anyone. Luckily Nick got the job before the results came in. Danish Dancer was a long shot that promised to be even longer the next time.

Barbara was nice, a sweet nonthreatening face; somewhere along the line she had taken on that extra malted and still couldn't get rid of it. But her hand was soft and round with a friendly, helpful grip. He knew she'd jumped up to save him. He knew she'd seen what had happened.

But Anna . . .

Oh, my God, Anna.

By the third week it was obvious that Nick was one of Resnick's better choices. In fact, everyone agreed, his best. Resnick's friend, Abe Rosenthal, at the *Times* sent Nick a message to come see him when he was ready for a move. Of course, Resnick never delivered it.

Nick was a good chief in other ways, too, a good editor, quick to pick up anything he had to know about the advertising end of the paper, reliable and fast. But his true strength was in his writing, his columns. It was obvious this young man could have a brilliant future in journalism or possibly even fiction. His prose was impeccable; it leapt into life with an originality that was stunning. No question but that Nick had a unique talent, with one drawback, his timing. It was excruciating to watch. He was never late for a deadline, but never a minute early, either.

You could be sure to catch him on Thursday nights agonizing over the last of the columns and rewrites. By then everyone else had long gone home and Nick would be sitting draped over the typewriter next to an old chipped ten-inch dinner plate that used to catch the water under the one living plant, now jammed with cigarette butts, some of them crushed out and others still holding on to their fragile, burned-out ashes. Two packs' worth, at least.

And then there were empty beer cans, always Budweiser, lined up along the edge of the desk or stuffed into the overflowing wastebasket. A perfect 1930s newspaperman.

By the time he got everything down to the printer and waited around there, he would be drooping from beer and exhaustion.

Those were the only times he felt some relief from the torture of his unrequited love. But he could barely enjoy the respite, because time, the clock of his life, was spinning around at a terrible speed. In less than a month Anna Green, the very point of his existence, would be another man's wife.

And unless he could win her over, his life would be devastated. He would never love anyone else the way he loved Anna. Simple. That whole, magnificent joy of life would be totally lost to him.

It was almost like a disease the way it had overtaken him, not just his mind, but his whole body. He felt sick from it sometimes. Nauseated, his stomach swirling at the thought of never even having her. Never feeling her love. Why couldn't she love him? He loved her so.

Quickly he understood that she was avoiding him. It was obvious. She made certain that they were never alone together in the office. If there was a hint that they might be, she would instantly scoop up her giant leather purse, fling out some excuse, and flee.

Nick was convinced she hated him. Perhaps he should think about quitting. Some days he thought that the painful awareness of her sitting barely six feet from him was too excruciating to bear. No less to work under.

Still, he knew that no matter how negative her response, it could never hit anywhere near the deep river of feeling, that powerful current of love, that was coursing through his system. Nothing he did seemed to quiet it. It raged day after day. Even on days he didn't see her, pounding, pounding, never letting up.

He loved his Anna Green, the one with the soft voice, the sweet smile that creased the line above her upper lip, the smile that started deep in those crayon blue eyes, the smile so apparent in every feature that if you didn't see her mouth, you would still know what she was feeling.

But as the days passed he came to understand that he was wrong, she didn't hate him. She didn't even care enough to feel anything that strong about him.

A lot of his feelings weren't even sexual. But a lot were. Especially in bed at night or alone at his typewriter on Thursday nights. Just the nights he didn't need the torment.

But they were there trapped in his head: her full, silky breasts with the faded rose nipples, the narrow rib cage that dipped smoothly under, all in one line, to swell out and around the hips.

Of course, since he hadn't seen her naked, these were all his own creations; but the legs, he could see the legs, he knew them intimately, the freckles around her kneecaps, the sometimes hairless shins (usually close to the weekends — shaving for her intended?), and the feet, the small, high-arched feet with the perfect toes caught in the worn leather straps of her sandals. Straps that emerged between the large toe and the one next to it, that seem to hold them spread open, waiting. . . .

If he could only take those toes into his mouth. Taste her skin, rub his lips along the underside of her curved instep and then up, up, all the way until he was resting his cheek on her thighs and then burying his face in the warmth of the nakedness between her legs.

He wanted to take everything of her into his mouth.

All a nearly impossible dream since she barely spoke to him. She was polite and sweet but almost seemed to be fleeing from him. If she caught herself alone in the room with him, she grabbed her papers, mumbled some excuse, and fled.

The most encouraging thing to be said for Nick was that he seemed to have unnerved her. Was there hope after all?

Another Thursday passed in the same excruciating pain. Now there were only twenty-seven days left.

*

Barbara tried to talk to Anna about Nick. Something was happening, but she couldn't figure it out. She could guess what was happening with Nick, but Anna wasn't herself. Maybe it had nothing to do with Nick; he was just coincidentally there while this other thing was happening in her life and it looked as if they might be attached. Was it possible? Anna and Nick? No.

Anna and Steven. Even bigger no! And yet there it was.

Barbara could have liked Nick, perhaps more than just liked, but she would have to wait a long time for him to get over Anna.

"So . . ." Barbara made a stab at it. Who knows, maybe it was all in her head. "What do you think of Nick?"

"Almost nothing. I wish it were reciprocal. He makes me jumpy the way he's always staring at me. He looks like he wants to eat me up. Doesn't he know I'm getting married in three and a half weeks?"

"He can't help it."

"Of course he can."

"Not if you're hit by a lightning bolt."

"I hope not. It would be a waste because he's such a good writer and so smart. . . ."

"So you do like him."

"Sure I like him. I'd even like to be his friend, but it would be like playing catch with a grenade. I can't go near him."

It's so out of balance, Barbara thought, all those men in love with Anna and here I am . . . Is it just this moment? Will it be different later when they discover that she doesn't love them and they have to move on to someone who will? Someone like me? When will that happen? Do I have to wait years, or will it be different when Anna is married? No, they'll still love her. Why shouldn't they, I will.

"Why don't you try to talk to him?" Barbara asked. "Sort of diffuse him."

"Maybe I will. It's so uncomfortable this way."

"While you're at it, you could put in a word for me."

"No kidding, Barb, you like him?"

"Yeah, I do. I really do. And I think he's a brilliant writer."

It made Anna stop and think for a moment. She'd been so intent on discouraging Nick, on escaping, that she really hadn't taken note of the one thing they could be friendly about. His work. It would give them something to be comfortable about. Change the air between them. Lighten the tension, make it easier. Right, that's just what she'd do. And soon, like today.

As for Barbara's revelation — it seemed to have slipped right passed her.

Today was the worst day for Nick. It seemed every time he looked up, there she was looking at him. Normally she avoided him, blatantly, but today it was as if she were purposely trying to make contact. It was what he had dreamed of for the last three weeks and now it was happening and he couldn't handle it, didn't know what to do, where to turn and where to look.

Not only would she catch his eye, she'd smile, too. That glorious smile, and just for him.

He'd been sitting over the same line in the column for fifteen minutes now, and at the piece since the late morning and only a quarter into it. And that quarter made very little sense. He'd have to find the courage to meet her eyes, give her the opening to say what she wanted. Obviously she had something to ask him.

With his luck it would be some technical question. All this agony of expectation for nothing.

He looked up. And there she was, looking at him, smiling. So he smiled back.

"How's it going?" she asked, sweet and friendly as possible.

"Slowly."

"Why don't you take a break? Get a fresh start." Either she was going to ask him to have coffee or a beer with her or she was just giving medical advice.

With his luck it would be neither. Probably she just wanted his seat. Whatever, he was going to give her a chance to do something.

"Maybe you're right," Nick said as nonchalantly as his interior madness would allow. In his head he casually flipped off the typewriter and with easy cool stood up and turned to her and smiled. "Join me?"

In reality he slammed off the typewriter, missing the button the first time, and fairly leaped off his seat, spinning toward her with the expectation and readiness of a puppy.

This was it, the moment to make contact, if only he had had one millimeter of courage. She'd certainly given him the opening. But he froze, he couldn't do it. He couldn't bear the refusal.

And then, just like that, after three weeks of watching his excruciating longing, his bleeding, in a voice as comfortable and friendly as if it were an everyday occurrence, Anna Green invited Nick Devlin to join her for coffee.

That same inner person, the goof inside Nick's head, who had fallen on his face so badly that first terrible day, this time leaped into the air, kicking his feet together and shouting, "Yes! Yes! I love you! I want you! Marry me! Marry me!"

The outside person managed to keep the inside nut boxed in while furiously digging around for a clever acceptance retort. And when it wouldn't come, defeated, he mumbled that he'd love to. But his breath failed him so that the words came out so softly, she didn't quite hear him and had to ask a second time.

This time he summoned as much strength as he could, over-shooting the mark far enough so that his "Yes!" jolted heads around the office. No matter, he wasn't enough aware of anything else to be embarrassed. In fact, in his excitement he even pulled out a smile.

They walked together toward Columbus Avenue. For some reason he couldn't seem to walk next to her in a straight line. He kept arcing out toward the curb so that she had to turn to see him. And each time she turned he jammed his hands into his pockets. A couple of times he missed with the left hand and had to make a rerun.

Anna hadn't expected such a violent reaction to her invitation. Maybe she should have just continued with the jump-and-flee policy and not started anything. Well, now it was too late. She had to go through with it. She certainly couldn't back out now. No telling what he would do. She wondered if he would be able to talk coherently in the restaurant.

How could she have such an effect on someone? Someone who didn't even know her? Someone she wasn't even attracted to?

At Columbus and Seventy-fourth they turned into the doorway of Damius, one of four billion such New York coffee shops. But this one had a double entrance, probably to keep out the drafts in the winter, making the passageway so small that Nick had to plaster himself against the wall to make room for Anna to pass. There was no way to avoid their touching.

It was the first time they had touched. They had never even shaken hands at that first clumsy introduction, and there was no other time that they had been close enough to even brush against each other accidentally.

Excuse me. Excuse me.

As soon as Anna moved into Nick's body space, she felt his heat. Granted it was August in New York, but it happened to be one of those cooler days that look and smell like autumn. Faux fall. So it wasn't the air, it was Nick. There was a warmth rising from his skin that formed a heavier-than-air heat mass around him, and when Anna entered it she felt it radiate against her own body.

Once inside the restaurant, Anna walked toward the booths in the back. It was well past lunchtime, and the place was nearly empty. She slid into the last booth, one with a seat that wrapped around the table. He moved in next to her, a shy distance away.

A terrible silence ensued, until at last the waitress broke it asking if they wanted a menu.

"No," Nick said, "just coffee." And then to Anna, who was suddenly struck shy, too. "Right? Coffee?"

She nodded and the waitress jotted down their order and walked away, abandoning them to their awkwardness. Like two strangers who wake up in bed together and can't remember why or what happened and feel strangely intimate, in their shared yet uncomfortably distant arrangement.

For an excruciatingly long few seconds neither could find the thoughts to form the words to start a conversation. And then, of course, just as in a movie, they both recovered at the same moment, their words clashing together incomprehensibly and then stopping at the same time, leaving them both in silence again. But this time the silence was amusing, and when they opened their mouths to speak again, they both laughed.

And a tiny tendril of friendship had begun to sprout.

"I like your columns," Anna said. "That one about that guy who's going for a job interview and his car breaks down at the airport and he's going to pick it up on his way back except he gets the job and never comes back for the car. I loved it. I laughed out loud. How'd you ever come up with that one?"

"It happened."

"You mean you know someone who would actually do such a crazy thing?"

"Intimately."

"Not you?"

"I just finished paying it off last month."

It was nutty, Anna thought, but somehow charming. And unexpected. "You're a terrific writer."

Then it was his chance to say how much he liked her stuff and especially her style. "Got a nice edge to it," he said.

And then she said what do you think of Adam and Roger and he said they were okay, but he really liked Barbara.

And that stopped Anna for a moment. Maybe he was interested in Barbara. Should she say something, let him know Barbara had asked about him, encourage him? Wouldn't that be a neat answer to everything. Barbara and Nick.

Not bad, she thought. I'll do it.

But then she didn't.

And Nick waited because obviously Anna had some comment on what he had just said. But the moment passed and she didn't say anything, so he went on describing his meeting with Mr. Resnick and how Barbara wasn't anything like her uncle, who was a real hustler type. Hardly what he expected from a publisher.

Before it was too early to bring Barbara into it, she told herself. And now the moment had passed and it would be awkward. It had to be done delicately; timing was everything.

Bullshit. Something else had stopped her.

The conversation moved from the *Westside Word* to other newspapers; he had had his heart set on the *Herald Tribune,* but when that folded it left only the *Times.* And then on to stars like Russell Baker and Scotty Reston, Johnny Apple; a dip into politics, they agreed that Nixon was dangerous; literature, Garcia Marquis was great, James Gould Cozzens was overrated and unread, *The New Yorker* was dipping, enough with the pointless Pakistani slices-of-life pieces.

And with the coffee. They'd had three cups apiece and were near floating. Nick seized the moment and suggested going next door for a beer. And Anna agreed. There was something so warm and comfortable about the day that she didn't want to give it up. And there were things about Nick she wanted to know. She'd had a peek into his head, and she wanted a better look.

In the past three weeks she had created her own Nick Devlin, and naturally he wasn't that interesting, being made up of all her leftover prejudices and expected reactions dropped into ordinary pigeonholes. The real Nick Devlin was totally different. And she was surprised how little about him she had guessed right. He wasn't nearly as square as his appearance; in fact, his clothes seemed to be some unimportant holdover from childhood. Something he hadn't considered in years. He'd probably be surprised she noticed them since he didn't.

They left the coffee shop and walked, still deep in conversation, to the bar next door. The atmosphere was afternoon neighborhood bar: all-purpose dark, jukebox but not too loud, corner pinball machine in use by two bony, raw, nineteen- or twenty-year-old boys, out of work or out of school or both.

Three people sat at the bar, one middle-aged woman, her short, muddy-brown dyed hair coiffured stiffly into artichoke layers that framed her face like a hat. Obviously she was a steady by her comfort and friendliness with the bartender.

The other two customers were men, definitely not together. One was potbellied and older, maybe late sixties, retired to full-time but not the serious, passionate drinking of earlier years; and the other was a younger man, slim and gray looking, a runaway from some local accounting office, a bookkeeper with an afternoon drinking problem. With one foot on the ground, he kept looking over his shoulder, ready to leap if someone from the office happened to come in.

They all seemed to be looking over their shoulders a bit. Guilt in the afternoon.

Nick and Anna took seats at the far end of the bar, away from the others. A slight thrill of playing hooky fed their comaraderie, and once they were seated a beer seemed too tame and too slow. Anna ordered a vodka tonic, and Nick joined her.

Then they both fell into embarrassed silence while they waited for the drinks to save them. Fortunately they arrived quickly, and both dove into them. An instant alcohol jolt took them back to the ease they had begun to feel in the coffee shop.

"Are you living at home now?" Anna asked.

"Not by choice. I'm desperate to find something I can afford. Or a roommate. Anything. Know anyone who wants to share an apartment?"

"Me."

"You talked me into it."

"Can you believe it, I've never had an apartment of my own.

Sure, I shared dorm space up at Vassar—with Barbara, actually—but that's not the same. I was going to get one after I graduated, but then it seemed silly to go to all that trouble since I was going to get married in a few months anyway. So I stayed home. With one thing and another, the months turned into almost two years. And now it's too late.

"Of course Steven and I are going to have our own apartment, but that's not the same. I feel like I missed out on an experience."

"You could postpone your marriage and try it for a year or so. I'd share it with you. Be nice, like the office, with each of us pounding away at our typewriters."

"I love that sound, don't you? And the feel of everyone working together."

For Anna, deep in that first heat of being a real writer-for-money writer, doing that impossible thing, getting paid for something you would pay to do, it was total fascination.

"It's like some kind of a trick, isn't it?" she went on, smiling with the excitement of telling somebody who understood just the way you did, "and all of us are in on it; we know how to mold and shape our thoughts into an arrangement of words that magically turns blank paper into our own message. I'm just starting out, and it's quite possible that a few thousand people are reading me already. How come that isn't as powerful as it sounds?"

"I don't know. Considering most of them believe everything they read, it should be very powerful. But you're right, it's not. Maybe it's the transience of papers, in front of your eyes one minute, around the fish the next, maybe that's the built-in safety factor."

"Or maybe it's just the avalanche of words every day that simply inundates itself," she said. "Whatever. It's still the best place in the world to be. Isn't it?"

"You're asking me on the wrong day. I have to put this thing to bed tonight."

"Ingrate." She laughed. "Have you forgotten what you would have given a year ago to be in the position you're in now? I would have given anything."

"Yeah," he said, "I remember exactly what it felt like being on the outside. I remember thinking, There's no way in. It seemed like there were at least a million rules guarding every door, and I didn't know any of them. Naturally every spot inside was taken, all kinds of brilliant and capable people in front of you, and no family contacts you could use to even sneak in.

"And then one day you find something that matches something else and you're in. With me it was a piece of luck. A newspaperman's dream. I happened to be in a theater when the male lead dropped dead in the middle of his dying scene. I mean literally died. Poor bastard. I went right home and wrote it and took it into the local paper. They used it and I was in.

"And then once you're in, of course, all the rules are suspended and you can do whatever you want because you're a writer. Maybe not a good one all the time, or ever, but you're a writer and that's that."

How could she have avoided this great guy all this time? Anna thought, We could really be friends. She didn't want the conversation to end.

"And then"—she kept it going—"when someone asks you what you do, you can say, Writer, and not feel like you're pretending. God, I love it! Do you love it?"

Nick felt embarrassed. It sounded like such a girlish question, but truth was he did love it.

She was waiting for his answer. So he told her the truth. Well, almost. He told her, yes, he loved writing and newspapers just about more than anything else in his life. What he didn't tell her was what he loved most in his life at that minute.

"You always hear about writers after a while complaining how much they hate to write," she said. "How it's such agony to drag themselves to the typewriter every day. Is that what's going to happen to us? I can't believe that I won't always love to write."

"It's probably unnatural to love your work as much as we do. Certainly nobody else does. Except maybe painters and musicians. That's probably why most of them aren't taken seriously. They like it too much and it shows."

Another drink and they moved in closer to each other. Anna would have liked to touch Nick in a friendly manner. Reach out and put her hand on his arm. Instead she made contact with her smile.

Of course, she told herself, it's the drinks, but maybe there was something there all the time and that's why she'd been running. Impossible. First impressions were the clear ones, and there was nothing from the start. This was vodka attraction.

Nick's head was swimming with love for Anna. His body was on fire. All the symptoms of love were alive in him. With any luck he wouldn't have broken out in a rash all over his burning face. Surely he must be flushed. She had to notice, but she seemed so cool and comfortable, and all her guards were down.

Then Anna bent down to pick up the little napkin that had slipped off her glass, and she grabbed his arm for balance. She let go when she got back up but stayed close.

"Are you really getting married next month?" The question had been shooting back and forth in Nick's head, bouncing off the inside of his skull, looking for a way out. The vodka gave him one.

"Of course I am. Unless . . . unless I can find the boxes."

"What boxes?"

"Long story."

"I'll help you. I know this liquor store they always give me the empties. How many do you need?"

"Hundreds, and they all have to be shiny white."

"Give me a chance. I can start now. How much time have I got? Twenty-seven days? I'll have them all, I swear."

"Twenty-seven days!" She seemed surprised.

"Didn't you know?"

"I guess I did. After all, it is my wedding, but I don't know, somehow I thought it was longer."

"Remember, we got a deal." Nick stood up between the stools, his body almost touching hers. "All I have to do is find the boxes." With that he leaned in and took her face in his hands, bent slightly, and kissed her lightly. His lips stayed softly on hers. She didn't move away. He pulled her in to him, and the warmth from his body spread its heat and his kiss became more demanding. Anna moved off the high stool and slid down along Nick's body. Both were standing now pressed tight against each other. Her soft lips opened, and his tongue slipped into the warm, sweet, wet interior. And the transition from taste to taste sent out aches of passion.

They stood together in this public bar, clinging shamelessly, Nick's hands moving up and down the side of her body, tracing the line from thigh to rib cage and then across the back and down to her buttocks to press them into him, and his hardness into her.

Anna adjusted her legs so that she could feel the muscles of his thighs pressing tight against her. And the ache between her legs hungered for more closeness.

The serious drinker at the bar had no interest, but the woman and the younger man watched. Hungrily. The pinball players stole glances, wanting to stare but, being young enough to be on the brink of arousal at all times, too embarrassed to watch.

It was dark enough to keep the lovers feeling almost private in their hazy space, removed from all by a fuzzy half-drunken passion. For Anna, from out of nowhere, for Nick, an explosion of feelings barely kept under control these two long weeks.

I love you, was all Nick could think of, could feel, I love you, and then the words escaped his lips: "I love you, Anna." His secret that never was a secret was out.

"Oh, God," said Anna. And he braced himself for losing her, but she didn't move away. She stayed attached to his lips, his body.

Finally they parted, each sitting down on his own stool, their hands still touching, caressing each other's thighs, arms, face, anyplace that held them together.

Now she said all the things people in such surprising situations say — This is crazy, I must have had too much to drink, It's mad, This can't be, and all the many protestations her hands and body made lies of.

Nick could barely speak. Nothing he could say would improve

his situation. Only harm it. So he stayed silent, loving her with his eyes and hands. Dreading her recovery. Waiting for her to flee.

And then he heard it start to happen. She gained strength from the blame she heaped on herself. And at last she found the power to say the dreaded words, I'm sorry.

But he couldn't let her escape so easily. He'd touched her. Their bodies had made contact, he had a chance. He knew he did, but he mustn't screw it up by being weak. Loving is not begging.

"I admit it," he said, "it hit me the first time I saw you. You knew it."

"Yes, I'm sorry."

"Why are you sorry? Because you don't love me? That's okay. We have time."

"No, we don't." A touch of an edge was in her voice. Her hands withdrew. He was losing her.

Do something. Say the right thing.

He did. "That first day I saw you . . . You can't imagine how many times I had practiced that entrance. Christ, you knocked everything out of my head. You saw it, didn't you?" He took a chance and another chance and smiled.

It worked. Everything lightened, and the direction was changed. They were friends again.

And sober and a touch uneasy.

"I guess I'd better get back," Nick said, beating her to it by an instant. But it was important that he say it first. Everything he did was going to be important now. If he had any chance to succeed, he had to do it right. And he had to win because she was all he wanted in life.

How did this happen? A month ago he was in total control, feeling great, excited, ambitious, clear, strong, confident: all the things you feel when you're not in love. Now, everything hurt. Sometimes he felt as if he could barely speak. And he was trapped in the longing day and night, and not even knowing what he was longing for. At least not until this afternoon. Now he knew, and it was even more desperate.

Twenty-seven days. That's all he had, and then she would be lost to him forever. He wasn't going to lose her. No matter what. Twenty-seven days starting today. And today wasn't a bad start.

※

It was hot outside in the street, and the hard glare of the late afternoon sun made the air heavy with a true August weight to the day. Nick and Anna walked abreast, leaving a wide avenue of space between them. Even Nick needed the distance. He would have liked to be invisible, just leave her with the memory of the feel of him. Not let her see what an ordinary, everyday-looking arms, legs, elbows, no magic person he was.

Suddenly he felt hopeless. How was he ever going to win her? What was he doing loving someone like Anna? She was out of his league. Damn it. Well, maybe not entirely, he did have talent, he knew that. Everyplace he'd worked he'd come in as nothing special and in a couple of months shot to the top. He had it. He knew he did.

It had always been that way with writing. No matter how plain he was in other things, that's where he shone. He wouldn't have given that up for anything. Till now. Till Anna.

God, she thought, what a stupid thing I've done. The whole point of the meeting was to try to find some comfort in an awkward situation; now that was impossible. She might have to quit the paper.

Anna looked over at the man; could she really call him a man? Steven was a man. That's the way everyone thought of him, even though he was only twenty-eight. It wasn't so much that Nick was younger, it was his awkwardness, unfinishedness. Besides, he was too slim to be a man. He was the sort of person who developed later, probably stayed boyish well into his thirties. She'd never been attracted to the boyish types. Too frail, she wanted someone solid. Someone who made her feel small and delicate.

Remembering the feel of Nick at the bar, how her arms had gone around him too easily. She could feel his spine and the bones that held up his shoulders; they weren't padded with muscle like Steven's. He didn't feel anything like Steven. Even his erection was different. Somehow more alive, more anxious to reach her, more disconnected.

Anna Green, the erection authority. All half dozen she had been intimately involved with over the last four years.

She knew Nick was in love with her. Did she really mean to discourage him, or did she want his love? Perhaps only to give him a taste, a soupçon, of what was possible, to insure that his feeling stayed alive.

Was it cruelty to encourage someone she didn't care about to love her? Or by allowing him to love her, did it make her care? Was it Anna's way of directing him toward the route to her heart?

This had happened before, this unasked-for love, in fact more than once, and it had always unnerved her. And she claimed to hate it. But did she really? All that precious passion existing only to be lavished on her alone, no substitute would do, surely that couldn't be dismissed lightly, or possibly not at all.

That person who loves you, want him or not, belongs to you in a way. A responsibility on the one hand, on the other a bonus of love to your life. Another choice.

These unknown possibilities had begun to create a temptation in Anna to connect with Nick, to explore further this man who loved her so passionately, so unexpectedly. She recognized that these might have been the feelings that kept her from running earlier that afternoon.

Tomorrow, with Steven, she might feel guilty and regretful. Today, the trickle-down emotion was only embarrassment. Enough of it for her to make some excuse as soon as they got back to the office, grab her things, and head off.

Back to square one, thought Nick. She's fleeing from me again. But it wasn't so. They could never go back to square one, not after this afternoon.

FRANCE
June

If wishes were horses, beggars would ride. A proverb from my father's childhood. I'd always seen that beggar, galloping at top speed, rags flying behind him, wildly ecstatic. His wish had come true. But I was too young to understand that just the opposite was meant.

But maybe they were wrong.

Recently I heard a story about a friend . . . well, she's no longer my friend, but I'm still historically connected to her; I've known her since graduating college, eighteen years ago. Anyway, she loves espionage books and she's lonely and unloved and a widow in the worst way, her husband committed suicide, and the other day she was at La Côte Basque in New York when whom should she see but the foremost writer of the spy genre, William de Chardiet.

On a lark she sent a note over to him that quoted a line of his usually found in some fashion in all his books, and he wrote back and invited her for a drink at the bar after lunch. She shooed away her lunch partner and met Chardiet at the bar.

Let me digress a little; in the four years since her husband's ultimate rejection of her, she probably hasn't gotten laid more than half a dozen times; that's only a little more than one fuck a year. Now she's in love. And he's captivated, too. Out of nowhere.

There's my old galloping beggar. You see, sometimes they do ride. Well, just enough times to make it seem possible.

I'm waiting.

And while I wait, time collects. In my mind I can see each day being detached and sent drifting like the leaves of a calendar in a movie transition, unused and untouched, onto the discard pile. Well, I do use them for eating, sleeping, and all those other necessities of survival, but I never crack them open, dig into them with my hands, squeeze them through my fingers, smell them, lick them, taste them . . . I don't do any of the things that people who are alive do.

Not anymore.

Like tonight. Here I sit in a local restaurant over a dinner of roasted chicken as yet another leaf from the calendar floats away. And to complete the inanity of the picture, it is a very ordinary chicken. Even in France dinner can be ordinary. I asked for the *cuisse,* the thigh and the leg, and now I sit, with no appetite, staring down at the food on my plate, at the shiny brown skin stretched tight over the fat part of the leg, and at my teardrop as it rolls over the skin and slides down into the crease and disappears out of sight.

And I remember another time, so many years ago, in childhood, when I sat and stared at my tears as they collected on the hard skin of the oatmeal that was my daily breakfast. That time I cried because I was being made to eat something I detested and I was too young and too powerless to change the situation.

Tonight, all that time later, I'm still too powerless to change anything. Even the election of my own memories. They take over, insist on being heard; they jump into my mind and force me to remember the worst of the pain. To re-form again in my head that horrible April day in New York when we first found out the inescapable.

We walked home, my husband and I, from East Sixty-third Street toward Central Park. We were silent, stunned people. The news was so overwhelming, it hung in the air exactly as it had been given, undigested, unrationalized, the devastation so out of place, with no way to fold it into the calmness of that ordinary afternoon.

When we got to Sixty-third and Fifth Avenue, he turned toward the wall of one of those massive old gray stone buildings, put his head against cold stone, and wept. Then anger overcame him and he pounded on the wall with his fists like a baby in a fury. Later that night the sides of his hands would be raw from the rough stone.

I stood watching, unable to control my own tears. I remember only one feeling, horror at his impotency, his powerlessness.

It had been a mild, bright spring day, early enough in the afternoon so that there were many people on the street, probably coming back from lunch, but I actually can't remember anyone outside of us. Though later, when I thought about it, I thought how people must have turned to look at him. In New York even a sneeze is sidewalk theater, and this was a well-dressed man in his forties, obviously not a clochard or a nut, showing emotion in public.

The cut-stone wall of that building is implacable, unchangeable, and though I've walked past it many times since, at all hours, in all seasons, that corner will always belong to him and to that terrible day. Of course, there is no trace on the stone of where his head touched or his fists pounded, or his tears fell; there's only the heavy silence that knows, that remembers.

When my mind leaps back to the fright and pain of that day, the thoughts are muddled, confused by shock, but the certainty was there, right from the beginning, that a trap had closed around him, iron bars had slammed down, locking him off from the sweep and movement of life, locking him in a trap from which he would never escape. Holding him there alone and emptied of hope.

And leaving me on the outside, the free side, the safe zone. Grateful and guilty.

Never again would I be truly close to Nick. It's hubris to think you can share someone else's dying.

Once I heard a description of Paris as a marvelous party to which you are not invited. All of France, without the language ability, is that same party. But I am determined to conquer it. People have assured me that it will come if I keep exposing myself to it. Absorb it, they tell me, into the ears, into the brain. And I do. Every day. No one at the villa speaks a word of English. Many times, of course, they don't speak a word of French to me, either.

I have been told it comes, the language, almost like a revelation. You work, you work, and then one day all the babble transforms itself into words. Words you understand. Incredible! And you don't even know how it happened.

Last night I had another in the long line of incidents unique to my French experience. I had gone to bed rather early, about ten, and was listening to a French talk show. Fill the ears, fill the brain, and so forth. Somehow I must have drifted off—they are very talky people, the French—and as I awakened I became aware of a man's voice.

In my semiconscious state I knew it was the television, and I knew it had happened at last. I ripped myself from sleep and jumped up out of bed, elated. The babble had transformed itself! Magically, I understood every word that was being spoken!

And no wonder. The program had changed, and they were speaking in English.

I could have kept my sense of humor about it if I'd had someone to share it with, but though Mme. Bareau was probably still awake, she would never have understood so complicated a story told in my convoluted French. As for my French friends who dumped me for a movie, I'm sure I'd have caught them in the middle of a huge party to which, like Paris, I was not invited.

Damn them all. I won't be defeated. At least I've seen how spectacular the moment of revelation can be—even if it was faux, I still had it for a flash.

Besides, life has perked up. There's new hope. I've gotten an invitation. One of those "you must come to lunch" things, except this one was real. It was from a count and countess de Willenich, an important couple from Paris. He had been in the French Senate, and she was the daughter of the duke de Culluary.

When the invitation first arrived, in my excitement I had thrown the envelope away and had to scramble about in the garbage to make certain it wasn't addressed to M. Carson. Or to Occupant. Neither, it was meant for me. Mme. Anna Green-Devlin.

Indeed.

The lunch is called for Friday at one o'clock in Grasse, a town about forty minutes north of the coast.

In New York I would wear my usual sort of casual, hanging, longish skirts and loose-fitting silky top and long beads. A touch romantic, hippy *ancienne.*

But here in France the style is very different. It's pretty and neat. Bright colors, short, well-fitting, pert. Nothing limp and hanging. The question: Do I wear what they wear to try to make them like me, or do I wear what I like to be as I am?

The answer: Endear myself, of course. My kingdom for something pert, but at the moment there simply isn't anything like that, so I must make do. I choose the closest thing in my closet to French clothes, a beige silk skirt and blouse, all hang a little too much, but shorter than most of the others and more conservative, with a color that fades comfortably into backgrounds.

The Villa des Flores, home of the de Willenichs, is magnificent. More formal than a country house, with a circular driveway that sweeps past carpeted lawns up to a fortressed entrance leading into the château. Either side of the interior road hangs heavy with huge old bushes, deep, dark green from age, and unusually high and full from years of pampered good care and perfect south of France weather.

Each side of the approach is a perfect mirror image of the other, right down to the bougainvillea at the entrance arch forced flat against the wall and trimmed to bloom in identical fingers of purple across from each other.

Before I can find a place to park the car, a little man in a black suit with white gloves rushes out of the doorway and over to my side of the car. He opens the door and greets me. Obviously he will park the car.

As I get out of the car, I reach back for my purse and the bouquet of flowers I have brought, in the process knocking the purse off the seat onto the ground. I bend down, he bends down, I get the purse and he catches the sunglasses that have slipped off my nose. I smile, he smiles. And then I rise, sweeping his face with the bouquet and leaving a line of dark yellow from the stamen of one of the star gazers on his cheek from chin to eye. Eventually someone will tell him. Certainly not me.

I haven't even formally arrived yet, and I'm in a sweat. Do I really need this? What makes me set up these terrible agonies for myself for no gain?

But there is a possible gain: the gain of a new life. One I need so desperately. And marching into these challenges is the way you go about creating it.

Surely Nick would cheer me on.

My first sight of the room stuns me, then warms me with its beauty: soft, delicate blues and greens and rich roses with touches of gold. Everything, even the people, seems to blend in to form a picture so perfect it could be a painting.

But I can't look now because, magically, though I am exactly on time, all ten other guests have already arrived, which is truly amazing because the French are always late. Have they rushed just to watch me squirm? They're in for a good show.

The men leap to their feet, the women barely look up. Since this is an invitation through an American friend of my publisher, I don't know my hosts. Mercifully quickly they make themselves apparent. He, the count de Willenich, is wonderfully handsome, not at all the effete, French look, but a rugged, almost American appearance. And looking at least fifteen years younger than his eighty-odd years. She, his wife, is slim and elegant and at least another fifteen years younger than that.

Quite unexpectedly they are both very welcoming. I'm stunned. The countess takes my hand and introduces me to the other guests, whose names never even make it inside my head. Even if I weren't so nervous, I never could have remembered any of them. They were so hopelessly foreign to my ears. All the men take my hand and kiss the air above it. Well above it. The vestiges of a lost formality.

The women shake my hand. In France everyone shakes hands, even small children. The women's French hands feel small and delicate, slipping in and wiggling out of my big American paw in one graceful movement.

Suddenly the little man in the white gloves is at my elbow with a tray of champagne. Gratefully I take one and dare to look up at his face.

It's still there, the dark yellow line.

"You're a writer?" asks a small, turtle-headed man in perfect English. "Anna . . . ?"

"Anna Green-Devlin," I answer, giving him my friendliest smile. Obviously he has my problem with foreign names.

"Would I know the name?" he asks.

His question comes at a lull in the general conversation and seems to grab everyone's interest. Writing can do that.

When they hear I am a poet, an American poet (a French poet, okay, but an American one — practically an oxymoron), they don't leave the room, but they do the next best thing: they turn back to their French conversations and that's the end of me.

I don't tell them about being a rock lyricist. Nor do I tell them of my great, serendipitous success. Quite accidentally, Wicked, a well-known rock singer and composer whose real name is Jake O'Malley, came across one of my poems and put it to music. It worked brilliantly. If I had written it originally as a lyric, it couldn't have been better. Since then I have allowed him to put music to five other poems and written seven new ones for him. That's what keeps me in the south of France. And keeps me very well indeed.

Nonetheless, since I don't know how this group will respond, and since I've become so timid, I don't tell them this other piece of information, and they quickly lose interest. With the exception of the turtle. Since I am new to the area, he would be happy to show me around.

I have learned very quickly that no matter how lonely you are, it is better to sit home and eat a boiled egg than go to the finest dinner with someone as unappealing as the turtle.

Though of course I am in the market for friends. . . .

Two more glasses of champagne improve my French and bring out some social graces I think are delightful. So, apparently, does my host. Enough to put me on his right at the table. He chats on, ignoring his other guests, wanting to know all about me, outpacing me in champagne and then in gorgeous wine.

I am certainly a little drunk, but it doesn't matter because I know I probably will never see anyone at the table again, at their election, though the turtle would be at mine. And I'll probably never see the table again, either, since the count is paying far too much attention to me and his elegant countess is getting more and more annoyed, and on top of that he's drinking too much and somehow it's my fault.

I excuse myself, ask for the bathroom, *toilette* in French, and take myself off in that direction. Though I don't have to visit the bathroom for practical reasons, I do need the respite. Surprisingly, the door is exactly where my hostess promised. The first thing in France I have found without asking four times.

As is common in France, the *toilette* is indeed just that, the utility set in a room all its own, the sink and other facilities located in an adjoining room. This one is just big enough for a toilet and a small counter with a mirror above.

I run a comb through my hair, refresh my lipstick, catch a few relaxed breaths, and turn to leave when my eyes fall on the toilet.

The seat is up and there is the most unfortunate stain on the otherwise gleaming white porcelain. Unlucky for me, but I certainly can't leave it like that. Needless to say, last one in must take the blame. And my social position can hardly sustain the blow. I flush. It remains.

I wait for the tank to refill and flush again. No change.

It won't be the first time in my life I've cleaned a toilet, though never in someone else's home. Nonetheless I can't go out leaving it in this condition.

With the failure of the flushing system, it's become what they call a "hands on" job. So what. Being a Madame PeePee (as the French refer to their *toilette* attendants) is not the end of the world. In fact, it's probably good for the soul.

Using sufficient tissue I attempt to clean the bowl. Nightmare time: it's not a stain at all; it is, instead, corrosion — rust.

It may well not be the end of the world, but at this moment, locked in this little room, with all those wonderful, elegant French people waiting out there, and my entire social life at stake, it feels damn close.

The choices seem simple. I can stay here, safe in the little room for the rest of the luncheon. Certainly after a while someone would be sent to inquire after me. They will tap gently on the door. "Is everything all right?" they will ask.

"Yes," I will answer, and give no further information. Being polite people, they will accept my response and go back to the table. After a bit longer, they will return to ask again. This time I might add an excuse. Perhaps a tiny upset stomach.

Again they will go away only to return some minutes later. This time a touch more concerned.

The door is jammed, I might say. By the time they get the butler or whoever unjams bathroom doors, perhaps most of the guests would have left. Or not left.

I would hear them outside the door, working on the lock. Of course they would be wonderfully sympathetic, whispering soft encouragements, courage, courage. All the while I would be hanging on to the inside knob with my entire body weight, my feet wedged firmly against the door.

Eventually they would be forced to abandon the lock and take the door off its hinges. Just at that moment, the very instant they heave the door free, I would jump down to the floor, releasing my weight and sending the six feet of solid hundred-year-old wood slamming back onto the entire group of guests, who would then be pinned under in exactly the positions in which they were seated at the table. All knocked unconscious, of course, or possibly killed, whatever works best for me.

With all of them out of commission, I would make my escape unseen.

The other choice is to simply walk out and pray that the next person to use the toilet is either the host or hostess, who damn well should know what cruel punishment they have inflicted on their guests.

I arrive back to the table covered in sweat. I watch each guest at the table, trying to decide which one I would want least to leave the table next. Without question it is the young and handsome baron de Buisson, who I think has been studying me in a rather friendly way.

I throw down two big glasses of wine, not too difficult considering it's a 1978 Châteauneuf-du-Pape, a silky, slightly smoky Vieux Télégraphe; I'm sipping the third as I await my doom. Until I can wait no longer and seal it myself by telling my one French joke—in French.

They all listen, confused by my French and my bad taste. I know as I am telling it how wrong it is, but I long for a speedy self-emulation; the wine is beginning to smooth the hard edges of survival.

When I get to the part in the joke where they were all standing up to their necks in garbage, I begin to feel adorable.

Beware feeling adorable.

The count certainly thinks I am. He laughs the hardest at the punch line, even though I have managed to screw it up hopelessly. I laugh the second hardest to keep him company. Everyone else looks politely perplexed.

Just at that point, the gorgeous baron de Buisson excuses himself and heads for the bathroom.

Of many such small, disastrous events is life made up of, I tell myself, longing to wrap that dangling preposition tight around my throat and pull hard.

Nonetheless, rather than just sit there and curse the darkness, I light one tiny candle and join the others for coffee in the magnificent summer salon.

The salon is a large room with floor-to-ceiling sliding glass doors that lead out to a patio flowered in impatiens, a pastel mélange of colors cascading down the sides of tall, hand-wrought ceramic jardinieres.

On the interior walls the garden continues. This time it is Monet. I recognized all three from his garden collection called "Arceaux Fleurs."

There they are. All within reach. In the house. Not in a

museum. Someone lives with these paintings every day. They come down in the morning, look at them, dust them, arrange the lights above them, any excuse to touch them. Because touching a painting is touching the genius itself.

I have a terrible longing to make contact, to feel Monet, to touch his mind, but there are too many people.

I take my coffee and wander out into the hallway, and there, to my good fortune, at the end of the corridor over a Louis XV console, is van Gogh's "Sunrise." And nobody is watching.

I sidle up to it like a thief about to snatch it. And then I do it. So lightly my fingers barely graze the surface of the hard, thick paint. It's almost as warm as my hand. I pull away quickly, but I am still alone. I go back for another touch. This time only over the fires, touching the vibrant oranges and reds and then the raised yellow and white lines of wheat. There is a contact that excites me and makes my heart pound harder.

Now I have to smell it. See if it still carries the odor of its creation.

The sound of a soft creak in the floorboard behind me makes me turn. It's the little butler who had welcomed me originally. Luckily I'm not touching the painting, only smelling it, which could look like a normal close-up examination since no one would be smelling a painting to begin with so he couldn't possibly know. And if he did it doesn't matter; he's had my number from the beginning.

Additionally, I would never be coming back. I smile at the little man, relieved to see that the yellow line has been cleaned from his cheek.

I return to the salon in time to be part of the exodus. Lunch is over. Unlike American lunches or dinners, where people tend to drift out individually, in France they leave as a group. And usually without any warning that I can discern. First they're there, all sitting, enjoying coffee, and then on some unheard signal they all rise and in a chorus bid their good-byes and, almost on the instant, disappear.

I insert myself in the middle of the parting knot, the dance of the thank-yous and good-byes. But my host stops me. I had mentioned the beautiful calla lilies that border his lower garden. Would I like to take some home? he asks.

Indeed. I'd love to.

In that case Jacques, the butler, will get me a clipper and I can cut them myself.

At that moment my hostess bids me good-bye, but I explain that I'm not leaving just yet because I'm waiting for a scissors to cut the flowers.

"I know that," she cuts me off, not impolitely, "but I'm leaving. I have a bridge game in Mougins."

I was not to worry, the count would be here. Obviously any jealousy she felt wasn't enough to cut into her bridge game. Or maybe it had only been my overstimulated imagination.

And then she's gone.

While the count is seeing the other guests out, Jacques brings me flower clippers and shows me the way to the garden. And leaves me to cut them myself.

They are truly magnificent, the calla lilies, creamy satin-white flowers on broad, green, leeklike stalks that rise up from thick masses of shiny leaves and then gently swoop in a graceful arch over and out onto the path. Each flower presented at its moment of perfection.

I cut ten perfect flowers, all low on their long stems. It makes an enormous bouquet in my arm. I hope I haven't been too greedy, but there are hundreds of these beautiful flowers and they are irresistible. They look so lovely resting on my arm, their translucent white heads thrown back and their long necks dipping gracefully over my elbow. If romance were tangible, it would be these lilies.

I walk back through the salon, where Jacques is waiting for me. I hand him the clippers, thank him, and turn to leave. But he stops me. "The monsieur would like to see you. Please follow me."

He leads me into the majestic front hall dominated by a circular staircase that sweeps up and out of sight to the second floor.

He dips behind the staircase, and I follow him into a narrower, arched-ceiling corridor hung with small Chinese prints, a corridor that twists and turns into another wing of the house. And a closed door.

He knocks, and I hear the count from within. *"Entrez,"* he says. And Jacques opens the door and steps aside to let me enter.

The minute I set foot in the room, the door behind me is closed, taking with it the outside world and the little butler.

It is a bedroom: large and magnificent, with an enormous crystal chandelier hanging low over an equally oversize bed. And on that bed, nestled in among all the satin and silk, is the count himself. Holy shit!

Across the room on the TV a crowd is roaring as a low-slung car screeches around a dangerous hairpin turn, skidding on its two outside wheels. Millions of people, plus me now, are watching the Montreal Grand Prix.

I stand there clutching my lilies, staring at the sight — the count, the television, the bedroom, everything.

"Come in, Anna, come in." He slides off the bed, careful not to spill the deep amber liquid in his glass. And stands there, barefooted in his dark blue silk robe, smiling at me. Obviously while I was innocently gathering flowers, he had jumped into the Scotch bottle and drunk his way down to the bottom. And now here he is, all eight decades of him, standing there not three feet from me, completely sloshed.

Would I join him in a drink?

I mutter something about getting home, but he pays no attention, simply makes his way over to the trolley that holds the crystal and the liquor and holds out a glass. "Scotch?"

"No, thank-you, really I—"

"Gin?"

This is a perfect example of what Nick was always telling me. Open yourself more to new experiences, he used to say. Take more chances. If it's uncomfortable, as a writer you can always remove yourself and drop back into the observer's mode. I can't really imagine why I'm so worried anyway, this man is well into his eighties. Even to myself I'm beginning to sound like some kind of virgin schoolmarm who thinks everyone is out to seduce her. I mean surely, I'm not that irresistible. Additionally, by now even the irresistible is probably impossible for him. Moreover, where am I rushing to? I don't have to be anywhere until winter.

"Vodka," I say.

And sit down on the small Empire chair, still clutching the flowers.

More excitement on the television, more screeching of tires, roaring of crowds, and the announcer goes wild. I try to watch, but for me it's what I always hate: a car chase without a plot.

The count hands me my vodka, easily enough to put away a stevedore. I smile a thank-you and take a sip. He watches me with pleasure. Encouragingly. I'm a good guest. I take another sip.

And another. I worry that he's going to watch me through the whole glass, but when he sees I can manage on my own, he leaves me and goes to curl up on the bed again.

After all, there are worse places to watch the Grand Prix from than the count de Willcnich's gorgeous bedroom in one of the most beautiful villas in the south of France, comfortably ensconced in a Louis the Whatever chair, sipping good vodka out of Baccarat crystal.

Besides, I like him and obviously he likes me. So few people seem to these days. Another couple of sips and I'll be in tears about all the people here who don't like me and the one at home who loved me and then abandoned me.

Left me at the moment in my life I needed him so badly. And I loved him so deeply. Loved him with all my heart. . . .

I clutch the lilies tighter to my body. The tears are beginning to rise.

"Avez-vous déjà fait amour avec une autre femme ou peut-être deux hommes à la fois?"

The French takes me unawares, forcing me to rip myself from the slightly winy, warm pool of self-pity I had been sloshing in and snaps me back instantly into the old translating mode.

Have I ever made love with another woman or two men at

once? Can't be. No, I'm screwing up a verb somewhere. Damn it, I hate this language. I'll never learn it.

"Encore, monsieur, s'il vous plaît," I ask, smiling to stall for time. *"Doucement."*

"I asked"—he speaks in English this time—"have you ever made love to another woman or, perhaps, two men at once?"

My God! I understood perfectly. And fast, too. Practically as fast as English. Okay, I forgot the "perhaps," but I really am learning. I am learning!

The elation fades as quickly as it came. This son of a bitch is coming on to me. This hundred-year-old creep is reliving his ruttiness on me.

I clutch the lilies tighter to my body. And start to rise to make my escape.

Is this really happening in my elegant, delicate, unattainable France?

Now he moves closer to me and tries to put his arms around me. I pull away, gently; he is aged and I am after all a guest.

"Please," I say, backing away, two snapped lily heads dropping to the floor. "I'm sure you don't mean this. . . . I mean, there must be some mistake."

"You are adorable." He smiles at me and advances again. "Let's fuck!"

"You just stop this!" Fascination is gone. Furiously I glare at him as I back up well out of his reach almost to the door, knocking into another chair.

"How could you! And me a grieving widow. . . ."

I can't believe I said that. That's a cliché no one has ever used. Obviously I don't slide that easily into the observer's mode. In fact, now I'm crying. And I can see the count is truly shocked. And sorry.

Meanwhile, though blinded by tears, I find the chair I almost fell over and still clutching the flowers, my beautiful, broken flowers, sit down. With my free hand I search in my purse for a tissue. Of course there are none, but then one is proffered to me. I accept it.

"I'm so sorry, my dear Anna." The count is of course behind the tissue. He taps my shoulder lightly, compassionately. "Would you like another drink? Do; it will relax you."

I don't even look up. "No."

"No?"

"No, thank-you." (Early training is forever.) I wipe my tears and blow my nose and get up. And hear myself start to apologize for leaving. That upsets me almost more than what has happened.

"Please, sit down," he says. "It's truly a wonderful race, you know. Come, my dear, you sit over there and I'll sit here way far away and we'll watch it together. It's so much nicer to watch a sport with a friend, *n'est-çe pas?*" And as promised he goes over to the bed and sits down.

For one stupid moment I actually consider staying. After all, I tell myself, there are no rules about this sort of thing. You do what you want, it's certainly not dangerous. Maybe he could be a friend. Besides, no one is watching.

Then sanity returns and I manage a polite smile and bid him au revoir. His French elegance has returned despite the bare feet as he sees me to the bedroom door, where the magical Jacques appears to lead me out of the house.

I suppose the butler knows everything. M. de Willenich probably does this all the time. Maybe Mme. de Willenich is in it with him. Maybe she sets it up — bridge, bullshit, she's probably hiding in the closet.

Suddenly the heat is stifling, and I'm aware of a sharp coolness where my dress, wet from perspiration, touches my skin. She surely was in the closet. I can hardly wait to get out of this house.

The walk back through the corridor to the front hall seems much longer than before, and I look around to check I'm not being led to some basement prison. But, no, there is the massive front door. Of course, Jacques rushes to it and, banking his weight against it, pushes it open, and I burst out into the sunlight and freedom.

Someone has kindly pulled my car up to the door. Jacques races around to the other side to help me in. I thank him and then remember hearing that often guests tip the servants. But I don't. Sorry, honey, it hasn't been a good day for anyone.

Except maybe Mme. de Willenich.

It's almost four and the sun is still very strong, but my car had been considerately parked in the shade, and slipping into its coolness revives me.

An hour and a half to get home. Most of it spent just getting away from the villa. No matter what road I take I keep coming back to the villa. I hope they're not looking out the window.

I ask four different people for directions. I have asked up to a dozen at other times. It's not the asking. That's easy. It's the answer that throws me. But, like the news program "France Info," which repeats the same news all day long, eventually by late afternoon, after having heard the same thing ten times, I have a very good idea if we're at war or not.

Same with directions. After hearing the exact words each time, I feel the knot begin to unravel and I can figure it out.

Actually it took me two months to understand what "Fransonfo" was. Eventually I realized that it stood for France information ("France Info"), which makes brilliant sense since it was a news program.

Finally I make my way to the main road, which is jammed with end-of-the-day traffic. I'm in no hurry. I have no one at home waiting to hear my marvelous story.

Or was it sad? Have I been treated like a fool?

Now that the confusion and nervousness of the moment have passed, I feel an emptiness in my stomach. Lost and alone. Another failure.

Or perhaps it really was a wonderful, funny story I'll delight in for years. No, it can't be, because I don't have Nick to tell it to.

Nick, the rat, who would have laughed with me and then, right under my nose, sold it to some magazine. Nothing was ever beyond the reach of the free-lance monster. Not even our daughter. She would come home from school with some delicious piece of gossip, just bursting to tell it, start talking, and then screech to a stop midway, realizing that the enemy was listening.

"You can't use this, Daddy," she would beg him. "I'll get killed if you do."

But he was like a jackal on the prowl. Nothing was sacred when Nick was on deadline. We all knew that.

So much has changed in this last year. The unexpected twists and turns that Nick would take with the vagaries of life, his magical sleight-of-hand tricks that could change appendectomies into humorous and totally original adventures; that talent is wiped out, gone with him. As for me, I could only hope to approach his genius when he was right there behind me, pushing, cajoling, encouraging me to take a chance. Get free! Soar!

With Nick gone, I've retreated to a secrecy inside my head. And when I do look out, the perspective is distorted by the distance. Too far away to see the truth of anything.

But I'm afraid to step nearer. All decisions are agony. And I stay the disembodied observer, the invisible narrator, in what feels like someone else's story.

NEW YORK CITY

A live! They were soaring with life. With love. That the paper got out at all in those next two weeks was amazing. Nick never worked so hard or so fast in his life. The less time he had to spend writing or editing, the more he could spend with Anna. And they were together almost all the time.

At first surreptitiously, always as if by accident. Anna needed that. Nick knew it and played along. But it caught fire, and then they dropped all pretense and that was all that was happening in the world. That was all either of them wanted to do.

Central Park was a block away, and they sat there, on their special bench, for hours, talking, touching, loving each other.

And there was always another revelation they couldn't possibly live without. Another revelation to leave them breathless.

Closer and closer they moved to each other, until at last they were too close for words. They couldn't let go, Anna and Nick. The outside world disappeared. They didn't know where they were. And they didn't care. They only knew what they were; they were each other. And people who saw them from the outside would sometimes be touched by their own nostalgia and have to turn away.

Their lives existed only when they were together. But together was still limited to the office or the park, or the bar where they had spent their first hours; their first touch.

Nick didn't press her. But he was pained. How could she go home every night to Steven? Did she become someone else when she left him? (She did.)

As for him, the minute she was out of sight he collapsed from total exhaustion, from having every nerve and fiber in his body wired with electricity and then suddenly unplugged.

And it wasn't just that he was working like a madman, loving and working every waking hour. It's that there was nothing left afterward. Nothing to care about. Nothing mattered, not food, not people, not cold, not heat. Nothing. He might have been walking in his sleep.

Sleep was the one thing that did work. Getting into his bed at night, alone, where he had her all to himself. He savored those brief moments before he drifted into sleep. Those moments alone with Anna, his mind's Anna.

He knew he couldn't make any demands on her. It was all so fragile, the thinnest crystal that could shatter from just the sound of the wrong words. It was a chance he daren't risk. And so he never asked. And she never offered.

How could she have? How could she have explained about the other life, the one that was separate and alive, filled with familiar people and purposes and feelings she knew so well? Another life with other values, totally distinct, but a life that understood its history and its directions.

A life she could see all around her. A life lived in her parents' house, in the world of friends and school and ambitions. In a world of the future, of marriage and children. Of houses and cars and money. Of limited vision, perhaps, but how could Anna, with her own limited vision, know that? She was young enough to think she could see it all.

There were no open questions in that other world, in the one she really knew, and if there were questions, you didn't ask them. Could she just simply step out into something she had never felt before? Could she trust herself? She, who when she made that rare spur-of-the-moment decision would look back a week later and see its foolishness?

She had always complimented herself on her ability to learn from her mistakes.

If she were playing a part, the being in love, she played it so well that it might have been true. True enough to fool even herself. But if it wasn't a part, then how could she be so superficial that she could be loving one man so completely and marrying another?

Which was the real one? Not the real love, the real Anna.

Nick would wait with her for the subway. She could have walked home, but then she wouldn't have been comfortable if he walked with her, near her house. So she took the subway, and it was a bonus, extra time together while they waited for the train.

Anna thought she never wanted that train to come. And when it did it was as if she were leaving for another country, another world, not just a station away. Not just for overnight.

The excitement of these new emotions was addicting. But there was that moment, that instant every day, in the beginning of each meeting, the flash when they were strangers, when they both felt the panic: was it gone? It had appeared so suddenly, it could disappear as easily.

But it never disappointed them.

Each time their simple proximity to each other would produce a shell of heat that would separate them from the rest of the world, that same pulsing excitement and desire that would course through their bodies, building up power until it released in a rush of love. Of desperate need.

Over and over again they created these sensations. Almost like a game, a feat that would be tested anew each time. And it always worked, and they ran with it and took it up to its penultimate moment and then gently retreated.

And even then it wasn't over; now the good-bye became a creation of its own. A separate, excruciating, delicious entity that had its own beginning, middle, and ending.

But one day there would be no good-bye. Or so Nick dreamed. But something had to happen; it had build up such steam, it either would go forward or explode.

Or perhaps both.

※

It happened that famous Thursday night, the night at the print shop. Anna had never stayed beyond six in the afternoon. But today he heard her tell Barbara that she was going to help him at the print shop.

When he heard that he nearly swooned. Though he barely knew what he was doing for the rest of the day, he did it well and fast. Best he had ever done. He had to. He needed all the time for Anna. Fuck the paper. But the only way that could happen was if he could finish his work quickly.

Frantically he raced to finish up all the editorial work, wrote a dozen headlines, and laid out as much of the paper as he could in the office. That left his last worry, Walter, the printer. Normally they had a few drinks together and shot the breeze while they worked. Maybe Walter would see the picture when he met Anna. Everyone else seemed to.

But it turned out when they arrived at the print shop that Walter didn't want to see anything that would ruin his Thursday night. At almost seventy, the retired printer had very little else to do with his time, and he looked forward to his night with Nick.

To Walter the kid was special, smart, and talented and still in love with his work. It gave putting out that little paper all the same excitement of the deadline and comaraderie of the old days at the *Herald Tribune*, the newspaperman's newspaper, where the journalists cared about their words and so did the printers.

He'd always loved newspapers, Walter had. And thought if things had been different for him, if he'd had finished high school, if his father hadn't gotten him a shot at the union, and maybe if someone he knew, some friend, had done something different with his life from what his parents did, maybe then he would have known he could also try. Maybe if that had happened, well, then, he might have been a newspaperman himself.

Things were happening on newspapers. If you were on the outside, you thought it was only a conduit for information, a machine that pounded action into words, but if you were closer, if you were inside, you knew newspapers were a world unto themselves, an entity not unlike a religion with codes and rules and gods, and at one time or another everyone who worked there believed in them with all their hearts. Walter had seen that and envied them.

And he had spent lots of daydreams fantasizing himself as a reporter. Of course, he never told anyone that, but as soon as Walter Jr. was old enough, he started to talk to him about being a reporter and take him down to the paper every chance he got. Walter was a foreman then, so he had contact with the editorial staff and they were very kind and patient with his little boy.

When Walter Jr. was in high school he got him a summer job in the pressroom. But it didn't stick. The kid didn't even want to be a printer. All he cared about were cars. And that's how he ended up — selling used cars. It was okay. It was a disappointment, but the kid liked it and he was good at it. Now Walter was concentrating on his grandson.

Meanwhile he had this Thursday night thing with the give-away paper. And Nick. He really liked Nick. With Nick he wasn't just the printer, he was part of the team, doing layouts, makeup, even making some editorial cuts when they needed the space.

Nick wasn't just being nice. Walter knew newspapers, and he could really help. Still, there was always too much to do, and it took most of the night, sometimes till as late as three in the morning. They'd be near sloshed by the end, Walter on gin and water and Nick on beer, but they always made it. And it looked pretty good. Of course, they weren't always in the best condition to judge by then.

So when Nick walked in that Thursday night with Anna, Walter wasn't pleased. He was pleased enough to look at her, she was so beautiful, but in half a minute he knew the score. He was shut out. He might just as well have been a plain old printer. Or better still, the machine itself.

They were nice enough to him. Polite, well-brought-up kids, but he could have been the pope and it wouldn't have made any more of an impression.

So he decided to just do the work and watch.

The watching was not bad. It was obvious that they were hot in love, but there were complications. And they were hard to figure out. They touched a lot, every time they were within reach, which was often because the room was small and they had to work together over the layouts. But the touch was tentative. Not the way two people who knew each other's bodies touched. And they were both so skittish, nervous, catching each other's glances, holding them and then snapping away. In two hours Anna made three phone calls, each one whispered and urgent sounding.

And then the work itself. In the four weeks Walter had been working with Nick, he had never seen him so well prepared. Or so sloppy. If a story didn't fit, he'd snip it off like a barber or lift out a whole paragraph from the middle. Walter felt sorry for him and tried surreptitiously to fix up the stories. He needn't have been so careful; Nick never noticed.

But the real tip-off for Walter was Anna. Every half hour or so she'd announce that she was leaving, gonna grab a cab, they could manage without her, okay? Unless. . . .

And then she'd find her own unless . . . and stay on.

For some strange reason these two people who were so obviously in love had just as obviously never slept together, and Walter was sure tonight was the night. It was that simple.

Now that Walter had figured it out, he liked it even less. He was embarrassed. Not by Anna and Nick, but by himself: his own thoughts. He was beginning to conjure up his own mental pictures of the two of them making love. He wished they'd leave. Their sexual heat was getting to him, right to his own crotch.

Nick could see that Walter was getting uncomfortable. Of course, he couldn't know why. But he felt guilty about the old guy. One more thing he couldn't handle tonight. He had to finish the job before she took off. He had to leave with her. But he was never going to make it. Anna would never last two more hours, and that's what it would need, even at top speed just ramming things through, to put it to bed. Now even his own words were making him crazy.

"Nick . . ."

This was it. This was what he was dreading. She was leaving.

"Maybe I better be going . . . you don't really need me. I mean, you can handle this yourselves. . . . Okay?"

His heart dropped. There was no hope. She meant it this time. She was really leaving, and there was no way for him to go with her. It was tearing at him, this need for her. And now he was losing her. Like gossamer, she was floating on a breeze, away, out of his reach.

"Sure," he said, for what could he say?

"Really nice meeting you, Walter. Take care. See you again, soon." She shook his hand.

Poor Walter couldn't even look at her. He turned his beet-red face down to the work in front of him. Go, already.

"You know"—Nick couldn't stop himself—"I could probably get this thing finished up in about, I don't know, what do you think, Walter, an hour, hour and a half?"

Walter shrugged and said he guessed so. He wanted to help Nick. The night was ruined for him already. Even if she left now, Nick was too far gone to pull it together. He was doing shit work, and it wasn't going to get any better.

Actually, he wanted them both out. They were making him feel shitty about himself, old and dirty. What was it? Dirty old man. That's what he was.

And on top of that, he didn't need them. He could finish this stuff up himself. It was nothing, a joke, a giveaway paper. Why was he pretending it was a real newspaper? Suddenly Walter felt lousy. Like he never wanted to do this again. When you retire, you get out. What was he hanging around for? This was kid stuff, and he didn't belong. And they sure didn't want him. Maybe they were even laughing at him. Yeah, he felt bad. And it was their fault.

He wanted them out.

"Tell you what, Nick, you did all the hard stuff already. I think I can handle the rest myself."

Nick didn't even say "Are you sure? No, I couldn't stick you with all this," or anything like that. All he said was, "Great. Thanks a lot." And he grabbed his stuff and the two of them were out the door.

Now that they were gone, Walter didn't feel so bad. In fact, maybe he'd been too rough on them. Actually, it was kind of nice, the two of them so hot for each other. Made you remember.

And when you remembered, you had to smile. Nobody but people in love make it so hard for themselves. Well, maybe that was all part of it. Whatever. It turned out okay; after all, it gave him his big chance. Here he was, Walter Finster, a newspaperman at last. Editor-in-chief. Nice. Better than nice — fantastic!

Almost as good as their fuck. Well. . . .

FRANCE
Late June

Jake, better known to the world as the rock star Wicked, called me this morning. He's got a big tour in England and Ireland coming up this September and needs two new songs from me.

I haven't written anything in almost eight months.

Of course, he knows that. We're close. And I know he's putting pressure on me not just because he really does need some new material, but because he thinks it's good for me to work. I think so, too, but nothing happens.

It's not as if I sit at a blank screen; I never even get there. I haven't turned on my computer since I arrived in France. But he leaned on me today, and I promised to have something for him by the end of July. He said he'd come down here himself and pick it up. That gives me almost a month.

Jake is more than just my composer, he's my dear friend as well, and he loved Nick, too. And Nick, who hated rock music, was crazy about him.

They were both about the same age, maybe Jake is a couple of years older, but their references were the same. Irish Catholic fall-aways, sixties city kids who loved all kinds of games, especially basketball. Directed people who knew what they wanted to do right from the beginning.

I remember the first time we all had dinner together. That was almost three years ago, just after Jake had bought the first of my poems. He'd released it in late June, and within five days it had hit the charts. And big, too; we were number two that week.

Jake was living with some actress at the time, and one night we were working late and he suggested I call Nick and we all grab a bite together. We went to one of his local bistros off Ninth Avenue, Cafe des Sport, and Nick met us there.

Unless you've ever been out anyplace with a rock star, you can't imagine what a huge fuss people make over them. I was a little concerned about Nick. He never was good at being noticed. And when you're with a celebrity like Wicked, there's no way to avoid it.

And there was another worry, a vague one, about my collaboration with Jake. A collaboration carries with it a strange kind of intimacy; though limited to one area, it can be very intense. Additionally, it was so stunningly successful, I just wasn't sure how Nick really felt about it. Though, as usual, he had thrown himself into my work, instantly becoming my editor, and I found out somehow he could play that by ear, too. Still, he was yet to meet the collaboration face to face.

When we, Jake, his current, Dena Steinberg, and I, arrived at the restaurant, Nick wasn't there yet. They had a table for us way in the back that was slightly more private, but not enough to keep the staff from excited whispering and giggling.

There was an audible buzz from the other patrons as we passed by on our way to the table, but Jake handled it nicely. Long ago he had mastered the ability to keep a friendly face yet discourage contact. It usually worked for most of the people, but there were always a few who had to have that autograph no matter. Even those he handled with patience. Jake, star that he is, is also a very nice guy.

Nick had to like him.

I was facing the front of the restaurant when Nick came in. But we at the table were involved in ordering a drink, so there was that split second between the time I first saw him and actual recognition, an instant only long enough for that unique flash of unshaded truth. But I remember it. I remember thinking: Nice-looking. Young guy.

Young. But already ending his life. Only we didn't know it yet.

My main concern that night was that these two men get along. It seemed so important at the time. Even crucial.

I introduced them and sat back to watch. The initial jockeying that ensued could have been taken from a wildlife documentary. They smiled at each other, more open than I had ever seen either one of them. Too open, for Nick, anyway. Then they sort of jabbed and tested and tried very hard to be nice, but there was very little real communication.

I was worried. It wasn't going to destroy my working relationship with Jake, but it would taint it.

Then the openness dissipated to formality, and I stepped in. I put forth horrible conversation openers like "Jake can't stand those whatevers at the whatever" or, to Jake, "Nick thinks you're right about doing the something concert."

I did that for what felt like five days, and then, mercifully, dinner was over.

Despite the comfort I thought the wine would bring, dinner was a failure. Not that they hated each other, they just didn't make contact, and in the end I felt like an interpreter struggling with very nice deaf people who had no common language.

The four of us walked together to Eighth Avenue, Dena and Jake to walk home and Nick and I to find a cab and head down to the Village. At that moment I remembered I needed some milk and Jake said he wanted a six-pack of Pepsi, so we went into a Korean market.

I paid for my milk and turned to find Nick, but he wasn't there. Then I spotted him with Jake and Dena in the back of the store near the frozen food bins. They seemed to be very involved in conversation. Suddenly Nick grabbed one of those long grabber poles and leapt up on top of the sliding doors on the bin.

"What's happening?" I asked Dena.

"It's a bet," she answered, her eyes still on Nick. "Jake bet him forty dollars he couldn't get one of those Poland waters down with the pole."

She was referring to a lineup of huge bottles of water on the top shelf a good nine feet above the refrigerated counters.

"Nick, what are you doing? They're at least three-gallon bottles," I said.

"Five gallons," he answered me from halfway up the wall, one hand clinging to a narrow shelf and the other waving the pole.

"He can't do that with the pole," I said to Jake. "Besides the fact that the bottle is too heavy, deft is not his strong suit."

"I'm counting on that," Jake said.

Suddenly it was after business hours and Jake had changed allegiance. I was out and Nick was in.

Nick won. Nick, who could barely carry a cup of coffee without losing half, clasped that pole around the neck of the bottle as if he had worked in grocery stores all his life and slowly lifted it off the shelf and carefully lowered it, inch by inch, to the floor.

There was applause all around, and the start of a wonderful friendship. Wonderful right to the end.

Jake sat with me in a lot of hospital corridors over that last year and a half. He knows my loss, but he's outside it now. When Nick died, the net that held us all together opened and everyone else escaped. Everyone except me.

It's almost five months now, and Jake's life has gone on. To be expected. And my job is writing lyrics for his music. Either I do it or he has to get someone else. It's only fair.

After the phone call, I'm troubled all day. I keep thinking what a fool I'd be to lose this, too. I've lost Nick; if I lose my work, I lose myself.

I have four weeks. If I start now, I could do it.

By nine o'clock at night, after almost thirteen hours of agony in front of the computer, of panicked sweat that spread to nausea and didn't bring even one usable word and not more than a dozen unusable ones, I turn off the machine.

I'm just not ready. My automatic response is resentment toward Jake for forcing me to face my inadequacies. But then, once away from the pressure of the monster machine, cooler thoughts prevail. Jake cares, that's one of the reasons he's putting the pressure on me. But he can't know how far back in the struggle I am.

I make my decision to stick to the original plan. The small and simple start, the modest step forward. Preferably using an approach I'm familiar with, something I've handled before. And then I find my small start.

I have always been a list maker. For me writing everything down on paper changes endless, mundane chores into organized time. You simply read the list and follow the directions; there's no thinking involved. Oh, how I've come to love "no thinking."

The lists I begin keeping are strangely reminiscent of those smeared scribblings of nuts who write down all their twisted plans for the world on lined paper in little school notebooks. But, of course, mine are quite different. Besides the fact that they always use soft number two pencils and I'm writing mine in pen, I am not crazy. Yet I admit, at the core there is a small similarity, hubristically, at least, for I, too, have written down lists of plans for my life. Only instead of "Murder the Jews," I have "Make friends."

I wonder often how people I meet in stores or restaurants would feel about being my friend, coming to my house. It would be interesting for them to spend time with a foreigner, an American. The world seems interested in Americans. They might not like them, but they are interested.

And when I talk to men in these same stores or restaurants, I wonder whether I should try to sleep with them.

Do it. Get it over with.

Demolishing the sexual barrier is right up there on the list. In fact, it has become my litmus test of life. What stronger beginning is there than the connection of human beings at their most elemental, their deepest form of mingling? And I desperately need a beginning.

Usually the men I consider for this semiskilled labor are around my own age or older, and sometimes much older men. They ought to be easy. And grateful. After all, I'm a good-looking woman, obviously educated, with class — just look at my clothes, my bearing — and of course I must have intelligence and imagination; why else would I be asking someone that old and undesirable if I didn't have an interesting mind?

I plan to run my list in a highly disciplined manner. No leaping around finding the easy ones. Starting from the top, as soon as one thing is accomplished, I'll check it off and move on down. So far, no checks yet. But the first chore seems eminently attainable and actually quite reasonable for such a mad list.

"Learn French."

I long to make my first check.

They say that the best way to learn a language is in bed. Fuck your way to fluency in three short months. Since there is no one in my bed, French or otherwise, I have done the second best thing. I have enrolled in a school.

And today is my first day.

I feel about ten years old. I have a notebook and newly sharpened pencils; all I'm missing is the lunch box. How I do torture myself.

Important question: What does a forty-year-old woman wear to her first day in a class where she is entering three months late in the term, twenty years the senior of every student and at least ten years older than the teacher? I know all this because I peeked in the classroom before I signed on. The answer is obvious. She chooses something as close to the color of the chairs and the walls as possible.

I leave the house my normal hour, early, a festival of taupe. Mme. LeGrange, the headmistress, has given me precise instructions on the route I am to take. Because of the sea everything is simplified. I've worked it out perfectly. If the water is on my left, I'm going toward England; if it's on my right, I'm going toward Russia. It's impossible to lose my direction. This morning I am going toward England.

I was at the school for enrollment, but that was last week and I went by taxi. Today I have my new car and I'm on my own. The car has five gears. *Malheureusement,* I grew up automatic.

It was the translation that got me. Actually, there was no translation; that was the problem. Not one person at the Citroën showroom spoke a word of English.

At first I asked the *garagiste* lots of questions as best I could, pointing to this and that: all mostly for show, since the amount of horsepower, the health of the carburetor and the spark plugs, and any of the other interiors all have very little meaning to me in English.

Naturally he answered me in French, thereby compounding my confusion; his responses required far too technical a vocabulary for my overextended comprehension in any language. But at some point in the conversation it was simply too late to admit to not understanding. When that happens I fall into a terrible habit — pretended fluency.

I've gotten very adept at it — in fact, so facile that it has become a language all my own. I know just when to smile and nod my head, I even know how to add those cute little body comments that make everyone feel so friendly. There's no way to tell that I'm not native born. Naturally they love it. And that feeling of success is so seductive, I can't stop myself.

Unfortunately, the price for such pleasure can run high, sometimes in the neighborhood of a lime green car with five gears. And forget about exchanging it.

In the United States nothing is ever too old or too worn to be returned to Saks. In the French merchandising system the concept simply doesn't exist. You buy it, you don't like it, you eat it.

Though we are two Western countries with enormous communication between us, I have found surprisingly deep cultural differences.

For example, I have noticed fewer walls, fences, and warning signs here. The French seem to feel that competent adults don't need cordons at the side of every road, the edge of every cliff, or the top of every building. If you're dumb enough to go up to the roof and hang off, that's your business. The government isn't your mommy. In the United States sight-seeing areas are treated like hangouts for the suicidal.

Here, there is an earlier involvement in the food chain. Chickens still have feet with toes, and pictures of fat, contented animals decorate the butcher shops. And not as pets, either.

Convenience is lower down on the list of necessities. Supermarkets don't deliver; they don't even load the bags for you. And until recently didn't even give you bags. You brought your own.

But they're not deterred, the French shoppers; they support stores sometimes bigger than some small villages. And stack their carts with the desperation of prenuclear attack panic.

On the other hand, they treat their food so lovingly. Even in supermarkets the people behind the counters respect the products. I saw a young woman packing a live Dungeness-type crab with claws big enough to snap off her fingers. But with such loving care did she fold down its gigantic menacing pincers that it practically licked her.

And French dogs do not choke on chicken bones.

All this is part of my new life plan to torture myself so completely that it wipes out all other emotional pain.

For some reason I must have misunderstood the class time, for the lesson has already begun. I slip in quietly and take a seat as far in the back of the tiny room as I can. There are only seven other students.

Mme. Feddis, the teacher, kindly stops to greet me and introduce me to the other students.

Though we are well into June and it gets very hot in the sun, the classroom is in the shade and made entirely of stone and tile and is surprisingly chilly. Actually, cold. Naturally everyone else is dressed properly in sweaters. I am in a T-shirt and barefooted in leather thongs.

I find by moving my seat a little, I can catch a sliver of surprisingly strong sunlight that cuts across the end of the room. While I'm busy trying to capture a little warmth, Mme. Feddis is trying to get my attention. She reprimands me gently. Two minutes in the class and I'm already being naughty.

And that's just what it feels like. All the years of maturity and the respect that comes with accomplishment are wiped out. I'm a little girl again. And then, like the new little girl in school, I am asked to tell everyone something about myself.

It has to be the most basic things, because that's all I'm capable of saying. And I find no one is interested. I'm not sure if it's because I am too old to be interesting to eighteen-year-olds or because my French is so poor or because I'm boring.

It's unbearable to be so reduced. It's insulting. Such disesteem. And painful, too. I'm desperate for attention. I do something right in there with my new ten-year-old age. I brag. Now I tell them how I write songs. I name a few (in English) that they know, and they all start to listen. I don't even tell them I don't write the music, just the lyrics. I don't care. I want them to be interested in me.

The bell rings, and it's time for a break. Everyone heads out to the garden to stand in the sun and drink coffee. It's a lush garden, with huge, dark green ivy covering the walls intermingled with thick, deep purple bougainvillea and white jasmine. Pink geraniums overflow large earthenware pots and drip down their sides. It's not that the garden is so well tended, it's just that in the south of France with the warm sun year round and the rich rains, the foliage can hardly be stopped. That kind of ease of nature must have an effect on the expectations of people.

For some reason I assume they all speak English. All the world speaks English, right? Well, all except my *équipe* at the villa. And, it turns out, this class.

To my horror I find that six of my classmates are from a school in Stuttgart and don't speak but a few words of English. The seventh student is from Eastern Europe and has the fluent command of about twenty English words, most of them from songs. He even knows the first line of one of my most popular ones.

At first everyone seems friendly, but unfortunately we have severe communications problems, and eventually they drift off together to talk and joke in comfort. You are not what you eat, you are your ability to communicate. After that maybe it's your credibility, but first someone has to understand you.

Again I'm on the outside.

The seventh student, the Transylvanian or Romanian, has no choice. I have latched on to him, and I can't let go. He's all I have. I try to speak French to him, but he's actually worse than I am.

Normally I enjoy speaking French with foreigners. I find their pronunciation so refreshingly clear, and because it's a late learned language the syntax isn't French and therefore very understandable. I never have the trouble the French seem to have understanding foreigners who speak their language.

Hundreds of times now I have had the experience of saying a word, a simple word—*au secours*—or any one of dozens of other words and the French person will look at me baffled, then lean in and cock his head, *Comment?* I repeat, *Au secours.* Still they don't get it. Again I say it in my clearest, best accent, giving the *r* all its proper rumble, *Au secours.* And again. Still it doesn't seem to make sense. And then suddenly it hits them: "Ahh"— they smile, the dawn—*"au secours!"* Just exactly as I said it.

Unfortunately, that word means *help!*

I always mean to do that back to French people when they speak English, but I'm too kind. At least I used to be.

A bell rings and we all march back to the classroom. Glu Gla—I know it's not his name, but that's what it sounds like to me—escapes back to his seat. As the afternoon progresses, I begin to feel a strange comfort. The comfort of a ten-year-old's world. There's a certain welcome security to its limitations. For me, a person who has been on the edge of sheer cliffs for so long now, it's very pleasant not to feel the danger, the danger of responsibility. I don't want to lead anyone anyplace anymore. I want somebody to tell me what to do. And how to do it. And then it will be their fault if it goes wrong.

I relax, sinking into my rediscovered childhood; in fact, I get so carried away that I raise my hand to leave the room. That turns out not to be necessary.

I like taking notes on my new, clean spiral pad. And just like years ago in the beginning of the school year, I start off perfectly neat and organized. No doubt I will deteriorate into the usual casualness as the term progresses and by the end will have scribbles and pictures all over the pages. That will be nice. I try a doodle and find it's automatically the same profiles of cartoon girls I used to make in grade school.

The bell rings, and all my new friends disappear instantly. I pull my books up tight against my chest, just as I used to do as a teenager, and head out for my car.

Green has its surprising advantages, especially this bright, lime green. You can instantly pick your car out of any parking lot.

In the French manner I have parked my car with the two side wheels up on the curb. It's a little more difficult to maneuver it out of such a spot with my new shifting abilities, but I always feel good when I'm learning something new.

The French have lots of new tricks to teach me about cars. They are marvelous at parking. They use a method I call creative parking. There is never a place too small or odd-shaped to accommodate the average Frenchman's car, whether it's got one side on the curb or is jutting out halfway onto the road. They never seem to worry about other cars scraping them as they pass.

Driving home today is easy. I think I have a touch for this shifting thing. I like it. It makes me feel—I have to whisper it even to myself—French.

At the bottom of the hillside that leads up to my villa there is a beach. You can't see it from the road above, because it is well below, but you can see all the cars parked along the side. I've been meaning to stop and take a look, and today's bright sunshine makes it seem a perfect day. It's also on my list under "Participate in French activities."

I find a French spot for my car, halfway into the side of the hill, halfway out into the road, and do a crash course on incline parking. Not perfect, but damn good for a first time. And safe enough; the van behind mine will absorb any blows from passing cars.

There are two ways to get to the beach. You can either cross a very dangerous road where cars zip past at terrible speeds (I'm not that French yet; it would take me weeks to get across), or you can take the second way, which is under the road by way of a rain sewer.

That is another example of differences: at home public beaches are well controlled. There's always proper parking areas and lots of gates and signs of instructions for dos and don'ts. You would never enter a public beach in New York by way of a sewer, even if it is only a rain sewer.

Actually, it's not as bad as it sounds; on the other hand, it's not what you think of as the perfect entrance to a beach in the south of France. From the looks of the number of cars parked, though, it must be a very popular beach.

Gingerly I descend the steep iron steps that lead into the sewer and then walk carefully along a wooden plank that bridges the little river of rainwater running down toward the beach and from there I guess into the sea. It's a dark tunnel and longer than I anticipated. If it was New York, you could be raped three times before you got to the other side. That's how long it is.

I walk it fast.

When I get to the middle I see a man coming toward me from the other end. He's walking on the same plank as I am; so he's coming directly at me. I'm not pleased, but I'm too far in to turn around and run; besides, it's rude. Sounds foolish, but that's often a consideration of survival in New York. Do you get into the elevator alone with a delivery boy who could as easily be a mugger-killer as a hard-at-work young man? Or step aside and risk insulting him by mumbling some excuse about forgetting to water the cat and flee, thereby making him feel like shit since he knows you're running only because he's a male black or Puerto Rican between the killer ages of sixteen and twenty-four?

I don't know if I sense less violence here because I'm a foreigner and not familiar enough with the life or it really is less violent. In either case, I feel less threatened, so I continue on. As the man comes closer I can see he is an Arab — the French equivalent of the Puerto Rican or whoever the latest, poorest immigrant happens to be. I'd like not to get on this elevator, but it's too late.

Of course, he couldn't be more polite. He even steps off the board and onto a wet rock to allow me to pass. Now it's I who feel like shit. I continue on without looking back. I suppose the only way to assuage my feelings would be if he whacked me over the head.

A few more steps and I'm out again into the blinding sunlight. My first impression is that the beach is much smaller than I expected and far more crowded, probably sixty or more people on a piece of beach no more than fifty by fifty and closed in on either side by steep cliffs of rocks that climb high up to the road above. The next look tells it all.

It's a nude beach. Absolutely and completely. Penises and breasts and fishy white or fiery red rumps as far as the eye can see. But mostly penises, because it's predominantly a gay beach.

Well, I'm here. And it is France, I tell myself, and all part of the experience, the adventure. Besides, I can't do that tunnel again so soon.

Timidly I make my way down to the water. It's actually a very clean beach, and the water looks lovely. Too early in the season for me to swim, but warm enough to wade a bit.

I take off my thongs, which I will never wear again in that freezing classroom, roll up my taupe-for-disappearing-into-walls jeans, and walk down to the water. I'm aware of dozens of eyes on me. I am an interloper. And no wonder, I'm the only person dressed.

First thing I do is drop down to the sand quickly. I'm less noticeable that way. Now what?

The obvious, of course. Undress.

It's nearly impossible to find an area big enough to lie down in because not only is the beach small, but the tide is way up, cutting the little that remains to just two triangles of sand on either side of the riverlet that runs from the sewer pipe down to the sea. Many people are forced to find places on the rocks.

There's no way I'm going to get up and move again, so I carefully ease myself down onto a sliver of sand between two sunbathers and very slowly start to unbutton my shirt.

I've been struggling with the last button on my shirt for about as long as I can. Now I must move on.

I feel an enormous sexual excitement about exposing my breasts even though it's very ordinary here in France. Watching the women on the Croisette beaches in Cannes, women of all ages and proportions, has accustomed me to the sight; still, the difference is great when it is you and the first time.

Actually, I've thought about it for quite a while. Thought about it with a certain longing. Sometimes when I'm in my bed in only my underpants, I try to imagine I'm on the beach. I promise myself I will try it next chance I get. Not on the Croisette, but at some small, unimportant beach where I am certain not to see anyone I know. A place where people don't easily drop by, ideally someplace you have to get to by a rain sewer.

I don't wear a bra. Haven't in years. So slipping out of my shirt does the whole thing at once. I have less of a problem than I anticipated. In fact, I have no problem at all. I like it. I like the feel of the sun on my breasts and the excitement of the nudity. Next time I'll take off the rest of my clothes or maybe even later today. Right now, strangely enough, I feel more comfortable than I have since I arrived in France.

I don't feel anxious, I don't feel like crying. I'm not nervous, uncertain, or scared. I'm part of a group. I'm in its safety. I belong.

I am participating in French activities.

I may have earned my first check on the list.

One of my fellow sunbathers, the man on my right, gets up and starts to gather his belongings—a towel and his clothes. I look at him and smile in my new-felt comfort, and he returns the smile as he stands up. Then he says something to me I don't quite hear, so I sit up, shielding my eyes from the glaring sun, and say, *"Pardon?"*

He bends down toward me, his purply penis swinging perilously close to my shoulder, and repeats his words.

"Now you have more room," is what he says. This time in English. How did he know I wasn't French? Was it because I didn't take off my jeans? Or the way I said the word *pardon*? Was that his clue that I was trying to pass? And if it was, why not let me slip through if that's what I wanted? In one sentence, for no gain, for random malevolence, this stranger has uncovered me as a fraud, an interloper, and wiped out all my pleasure.

I don't even nod in response; I just lie back down. Let him think I'm Chinese.

Now at least I have enough room to uncross my legs and spread out a bit. But not for long. This time a young Frenchman squeezes in beside me. By now my other neighbor has eaten up a little more room for himself, and all the newcomer can find is an odd-shaped swatch of sand that starts alongside the middle of my body and extends behind an adjoining rock.

"*Bonjour.*" He smiles an adorable twenty-year-old smile. *Voilà,* I'm French again.

He's very friendly, with a strong Calabrian accent that is quite common around Nice, though a little hard for me to understand. But his questions are easy: What is my name? Am I alone? Where do I live? Assorted nosy questions I answer as it suits me. Of course, as soon as I speak he knows I'm not French, but he's not sophisticated enough to know what I am from my accent. So I tell him I'm Swedish, because that suits me. There must be some dark-haired Swedes.

All the while I'm sunbathing he's up on one elbow looking down at me, his free hand pretending to brush sand off my hip. Now I feel his fingers creep to my waist and pull playfully at a belt loop.

He wants to know why I don't take off my jeans. I think he says he'll help me. I smile and continue taking the sun. But I don't take his hand away. With my eyes closed his touch feels soothing, uncomplicated.

Now he begins to ask me something too difficult and heavily accented for me to understand completely, but it has to do with being Swedish. From the little I catch, it's not the lack of blond hair that's confusing him, it's the fact that I'm not taking off my clothes. Swedish was a bad choice.

So I say, Not Swedish, Spanish. I'm having a very good time. So, it turns out, is he. So good that he moves closer and whispers that he wants to come home with me.

Instantly I feel the lightness leave me. I look around to see if anyone is watching or listening. This is exactly the kind of situation that has separated me from my imagination all my life. Just this sort of choice. At the end of my life this is the very thing that is going to make me scream that I shouldn't have held back. What for? For whom? Nick is gone. Look at the things I could be missing. The feelings that might never be awakened.

How many times do I have to learn that no one is watching my life, no one is keeping score?

Just for the moment pretend I say yes. We get up, Jean-Paul and I, gather our things, and walk off the beach. Just like that. Again the crowd looks up. He is young; maybe twenty was pushing it. So maybe they smirk or giggle—who cares.

He gets into my car. No, let him follow on his motorbike. The point is to make the choice and then take it where it goes.

Most probably there's been a plumbing or electrical emergency at the villa, there always seems to be, but even if the full *équipe* isn't there, certainly the stars are—the gardener and Mme. Bareau. And they're not blind and they're always suspicious anyway. So now they have it.

I can create a hundred different acceptable reasons for Jean-Paul to be there, but what's the point of making this choice if I'm going to try to squeeze it back into the shape of my old life?

The whole point is to let the madness in. Or out.

All right, now we are in the house. I can't give him a drink because who knows how old he really is. Besides, this isn't a party. It's a mission. In that case we go directly into the bedroom.

All through these ruminations I have been lying flat on my back, my eyes closed. I can feel Jean-Paul moving closer. His penis is stiff and pressing into the side of my leg. The sun is very hot, and the combination of the other naked bodies around me giving off their own heat brings its intensity near to crackling. I feel myself responding to his touch. I will certainly take him home with me.

I lift my head up slightly to tell him my decision, but he's far too involved to hear me. There he is, this disgusting little creature, rubbing up and down against me like a puppy.

I try to move my leg away, but there isn't room. And besides, he's holding on to it. I push against the top of his head with my hand, but it doesn't stop him.

I quickly peek around to see if anyone is watching. No one seems to be, but surely they can hear him scraping against the sand and feel the motion. We're all so close it's as if we're all in one big bed together.

Is this the madness I was looking for? I don't think so. I would like to smash my fist against his head, but that would be too noticeable. Too embarrassing.

How many times have my actions been ruled by the fear of embarrassment? I hate this fool in me.

I've allowed this to start; I encouraged him, played with him, and now I have to see it through. Surely he wouldn't have tried this with anyone else. It must be written on my forehead — Mr. Southern's Candy comes to the south of France.

And then it's done. Hideous to think this asshole has actually ejaculated against my leg. And I've permitted it. Thank goodness I'm wearing jeans.

I refuse to open my eyes when he gets up to leave. He's all jolly and says he would like to see me again. I don't answer.

Finally he's gone and I unbutton my jeans and nearly rip them off. My underpants at the same time. Now I am naked. My body is burning with the heat of my fury.

Is this what my new life will feel like?

NEW YORK CITY
June

Making love. Feeling his naked skin under her fingers. Holding his thin frame against her and feeling her breasts touching his chest. That's what she wanted so desperately. To make love to Nick. Her desire for him was unbearable. Devouring her very life, morning, noon, and night. Though she had sex with Steven, it was never Steven, it was Nick. Always Nick.

As they entered the Empire Hotel on Sixty-third and Broadway, Anna had scrambled to arrange herself for a presentable appearance, but there was nothing she could do about the flaming red of her cheeks or the mass of damp curls that were sticking to her face. And Nick, too, was a confusion of disarray.

Neither said a word as he took her by the arm and led her into the lobby. She hung back a bit when he stepped up to the front desk to make the arrangements. It was the first time she had ever gone into a hotel like this for the express purpose of making love.

The guilt she felt was enormous. The betrayal of Steven was almost as strong as if she were married to him. And indeed she would be in less than a month. How could she do this? Or how could she do the other?

Together they moved toward the elevators. The doors responded instantly to Nick's touch and opened. It was empty. They got in.

All three walls were mirrored, which left them no choice but to look at themselves. If they weren't locked into this cage, Nick thought, she would certainly flee. He could hear her breathing speed up and sense the growing panic.

He reached out and took her hand. She let him and smiled a

small, brave smile. It was hard for him to understand what kept her so frightened. Why she seemed so ready to bolt all the time. He knew she loved him. What was holding her back?

He kept his distance in the long ride to the fifteenth floor. "It'll be a great view. We can probably see the office," he said.

"And no one can see in," she answered.

He thought she was kidding, but the look on her face told him she really was relieved to be so high up. Nick was worried. What would happen? Would she go through with it? She had to.

They found the room quick enough, but he sensed her hanging back. And he ignored it. Don't ask anything, he told himself. Don't speak and turn it all into reality.

It was an ordinary room, clean but dreary. He was suddenly scared. It looked too real. Real enough to break the spell for her.

Anna came in behind him, but she didn't close the door. Open, it was an option to run. Nick looked at her, and she thought she saw hurt in his face and leaned against the door, closing it.

They were where they longed to be. All those times in the park, or in some bar, or waiting for the subway, all those times trying to shut out the people watching. Now at last they were truly alone.

Nick looked like such a boy to Anna. His rumpled jacket, his hair sweetly disheveled, and those eyes, those longing blue eyes with all the questions in them. Eyes that looked right into her soul, saw through all the layers of disguise and knew her. And loved her. How could she resist him?

And then they were in each other's arms. Squeezing their bodies together and ripping at their clothes to uncover their skin, the better to feel each other.

They didn't know they were at the bed until their bare legs touched against it, and then they sank down and lay back, still joined together.

There was no separation between them save for the moment he withdrew his hips slightly to slide himself into the heat between her closed thighs, soft flesh that spread easily at his touch, opening gently to allow him entrance into the warm depth that closed around him, pulling him farther and deeper into her. The sound of her wetness and their racing breath matched the rhythm of the bed as it bounced under them. Their speed grew as they climbed to their apex, racing along with exactly the same movements, gobbling up the road ahead of them and then crashing off the cliff, first Anna as she flew out into the opening, slamming her body up against him, and then Nick as the lightning bolt shuttered through his limbs.

They didn't move, pasted together as they were by their sweat and by the juices of their bodies.

"I love you," they said.

"I love you. I love you. I love you," was all they could say.

And then they came apart, and each flung themselves back flat upon the bed, their bodies gasping for the cool air.

And there was no sound in the room except their breathing. And they wanted none. They needed none. It had all been said and done.

The terrible temptation to ask Now what? was refused, and they lay there encased in perfection and silence.

Nick pulled the sheet up around them, for the shock of their temperature drop made the coolness that had been so welcomed now feel sharp against their skin. Anna turned her body into his and put her arm across his chest, her head buried into his side.

Anna woke first. She was curled up against Nick. She opened her eyes. She had never seen his back before. They loved each other, knew each other's faces, every mark, every contour, but she didn't really know his body yet. As he didn't know hers.

Anna traced her fingers down his shoulders, over his hipbone and down onto his flat stomach. Still he remained turned away from her, but his stomach fluttered slightly at her touch. And she laid her open hand over the area until the fingers slid into the hair around the base of his penis. He was hard, and the shaft of his sex had risen from his stomach, leaving room to run her fingers underneath. She could feel the length of him touching lightly against the back of her hand.

He was so still that she had the sensation that he wasn't breathing.

Now her fingers encircled him, pressing his swollen hardness in her grip. With her other hand she pushed his hip down until he was lying flat on the bed. His eyes were closed, his arm crossed over his face as if to hide from her.

She pulled her body up and moved across him until her face was inside his aura but not touching. She could feel his heat, and the odor of her body was still on him. Her lips brushed against the head of his penis. Lightly. Barely touching, she moved them across his silky skin, back and forth, until she could feel him rising, reaching toward her. And she opened her mouth and took him inside, deep down until he touched the back of her throat. He moaned in exquisite agony and held her head down on him until she gasped for breath.

And then he lifted her up and pulled her to him, sliding the length of her body over his until her face was up to his chest and then beyond, until the triangle of her soft wetness was directly over his penis. Gently, his hands holding her under her arms, he brought her down onto him until he could slide easily into her, and she came to rest against him, his penis deep inside her.

They made love like that, barely moving. And when they came again, it was slow and luxurious.

Finally it was time to speak. First they said the things that they had to say, the feelings that were spilling over, bursting from their hearts. Feelings of the body, of the imagination, of the soul. And then the mind: reality had to be dealt with.

And for Nick that meant only one question. "You're not going to marry him now, are you?" And before she could answer, he said, "You can't."

She said nothing; and the power of that silence stunned him, turning his stomach. He couldn't believe she could even consider such a possibility, not after this night. Clearly there was some place in her that was closed to him. A place his mind couldn't seem to reach. He had been quiet all these weeks. Now he had to hear her answer.

He pressed for it. "Why?" he asked.

And she answered that she didn't know why, but God knew she'd barely thought of anything else for weeks. "But, you see," she said, "I haven't stopped it yet. That must be some kind of reason."

"That makes no sense. That's like saying because it exists, it's right and should continue to exist."

His voice was uncharacteristically hard. He had never spoken to her like that, and she was surprised. She looked at him. "I won't be forced into anything. . . ."

He spun away from her, sat up sharply, and reached for his clothes. She lay on the bed watching him. Not moving.

He stopped, one sock in his hand, and looked down at the floor. He felt he had lost. In that one moment he had lost everything. Perhaps everything he had never had.

Anna couldn't bear his pain. "Please try to understand," she said. "I've been going in one direction all my life. Following some invisible plan and not even knowing it. I only know it now because it's being challenged. And I'm having difficulty abandoning it."

"I'm in love with you, Anna. I want you in my life. Ask me anything and I'll do it."

"Wait."

"I'll wait."

And he turned back to her, and she moved into his arms.

I had an accident in the car this afternoon. Not a terrible one, just a dented fender, mine, but it was clearly the other driver's fault. He tried to cut across me from the right lane to make a left turn. Naturally he hit my front left fender.

The French motorist has brilliant manners as long as he stays in his car. This one got out and he yelled at me. Of course he yelled in French.

This is what I couldn't say to him: You dumb bastard, you cut right in front of me. We both could have gotten killed. Are you drunk or something? How could you do such a stupid thing? You wait right here, I'm calling the police.

This is what I didn't say to him: Give me your license.

What I did say was: *C'est pas vrai. C'est pas vrai.* About ten times, until at last he threw his hands up in the air, got in his car, and drove away. Whereupon the other drivers shouted at me for blocking traffic.

I learned a valuable lesson. Never argue in a foreign tongue. Go directly to your own language. No matter if no one understands you, at least you can express yourself. And it's far less of a disadvantage than being handicapped by lack of words or, worse, saying the wrong thing, and it has the added value of being somewhat intimidating for the opposition, not being able to understand what's being shouted back at them. Well do I know that.

Though the accident was unimportant, just some minor damage to my fender and my psyche, still I was very upset driving home. This unhappiness I carry with me (actually, "unhappy" is a bad choice of words, as it seems to connote a temporary departure from "happy," while I am in fact well into "quite miserable"), dogs me like an affliction, a limp that makes me feel heavy and out of step and never lets me forget its existence. And that's only the quiet times I must live with every day.

Then there are other times, times that strike without warning. In perfect calmness, sometimes in company with people quite unrelated to my life, while I'm sitting and talking about something comfortably ordinary, even dull, suddenly that hideous scene in all its terror and fury comes screeching into my mind, that time when I first heard that Nick would die.

And then the scene disappears, quick as it came. But I'm left battered and often can't continue listening, certainly not talking. Sentences spoken to me lose their meaning, and I feel as if I'm trapped in a familiar language where I know every word when they stand alone, but string them together and it becomes an incomprehensible jumble.

And then other times, instead of passive pain and sadness, I get angry: irrationally, pointlessly angry. I try to hide these feelings, but I can see that they show and other people are confused and wonder what they have done.

But when I'm alone with that anger—not in the house, but in my car—I scream. I close all the windows and scream. Over and over again until the rawness rips at my throat and one scream runs into another, taking off with a force of its own, until I'm outside the sound, a listener, and it frightens me. And then at last it stops.

The car has become the most private place in my world. Not my house. If I scream in my house, Mme. Bareau would surely come to help me or at the very least call the police; but in my car, alone, if someone should hear me, they wouldn't pay any attention. Car people are transients and no one's concern or responsibility.

In an attempt to discipline these bizarre feelings, I've tried to confront the diverse elements that contribute to them, starting by recognizing the essentials of living alone. It's a very new state for me, a person who has shared her home always, first with her parents and sisters and then with her husband and child.

My child, my eighteen-year-old daughter, Lily, is far away on the other side of the world. She has chosen to do her junior year abroad in Japan. It had been a dream of hers since high school. No matter what my needs, I felt her plans should go on. I had to adjust to my new life by myself.

Very new for me, only five months, this living alone, this unknown territory. Certainly I have friends who live alone, but I don't really know what their lives are like when I'm not around. And to ask them the questions I would have to ask would be too invasive. Perhaps show their weakness, a vulnerability better kept private.

So, for me, this brand-new world is empty. Not just of people, but of rules and form and shape. How do I cope? There must be a million magazine stories with just that information. But I'm not a user of other people's lives and methods. I always have to invent my own.

First thing is to identify the enemy. That's simple — it is a disease called loneliness. Not to be confused with aloneness. Nothing wrong with that, aloneness, if you use it the way you want. If you stay in charge. But as the months pass I can see how subtly that power can be stolen from you. The thief works from within. It is smart and hungry and so natural you don't even know it is devouring you.

At first you think it's just plain old self-pity, and God knows you certainly deserve some compassion and who better to give it than yourself? After all, who knows your pain better than you do?

That's how it starts. An early warning symptom.

And then one morning you wake up with tears that choke your throat. Too tired to fix that robe that has been hanging half off its hook for days, or close the other part of the drapes despite the fact that the sunlight glares in your eyes, or do something about that pile of clothes on the chair, or simply buy something to put in the refrigerator, something you might even cook, or, finally, bend down and tie that fucking shoelace.

And that's the top of the hill. As you descend, life becomes nearly primitive: it's somewhere between five in the afternoon and ten at night and you are in your kitchen, leaning against the

stove, holding an opened can of anything; it could be corn nib-
blets, beans, or some other inoffensive bulk food that doesn't
even have to be bought, it just appears in every house, in every
pantry. This is still early in the sickness, so you're not eating it
cold. You've actually cooked it. Well, not exactly cooked, more
like heated and right in its own can. And now you stand there,
spoon in hand, eating your dinner.

How pathetic.

But what difference does it make? You're all alone. Nobody
will see. Nobody cares, anyway.

When those words arrive, that's more than just a symptom,
that's the full-blown disease.

I fight that disease every day of my new existence. My weapon
of choice is challenge. Never insurmountable, always difficult,
surely unfair and unjust, self-created, homemade challenge. So far
I've found the energy to attack it, but I don't think I've made forward progress except to keep the disease monster from my door,
most of the time. And when I do feel it creeping into the hallway,
I create yet another impossible challenge that calls upon a fury of
energy and race out there to trounce it.

I know what to aim for and what conquest feels like. I know
triumph. I had it once exquisitely in a battle with a wasp years
ago in happy times, on a tennis court. It was deep August, New
York hot, middle of the afternoon, no branch or roof or awning to
bring the slightest shade, to cut the full spread of sun. It was a rare
time when no one else wanted the Central Park courts. All eight
of them were empty.

It was the very beginning of the tennis rage. I had successfully
avoided learning the game as a child and now had to pay the
price. Learning anything as physical as tennis in adulthood is a
killer. But the city was playing tennis, it was in the rebirth of
New York and Central Park, and it seemed my duty to participate,
to give my support.

It was through the largess of Nick, who agreed to play with me
when no one else would, and of course, being a writer, he knew
that anything, even a game of tennis with a nonplayer on a fierce
summer afternoon, was better than writing. Dripping in sweat and

frustration, I had missed and chased a thousand balls and was beginning to think, Fuck the city with its tennis, I'm not doing it, when a wasp, a gigantic country wasp, flew at me.

I jumped back, but the beast came at me for another attack. I brushed him away and danced this way and that to avoid him. But he was relentless. I'm a city person, with little wasp experience, and I'm afraid of them. I retreated in fear, shrieking little-girl shrieks, but he followed me. Finally he made the mistake of driving me over the fear line and into my courage.

I turned the attack on him, with my most perfect swing of the afternoon—indeed, of my entire tennis career—a swing so sure that I could hear the *whoosh* of the racket as it sped through the air and feel the impact of the monster smacking right into the dead center, what they call the sweet spot, of my racket. I could actually hear its body crack against the strings, see its dark little pellet form shoot up into the air. Reloading my swing, I charged after him and, catching him on the descent, sent my racket smashing into him again. And again, this time with my most brilliant backhand. All the while shouting and grunting a terrible war cry.

At last I allowed him to drop to the ground. And with one last triumphant leap I landed with both feet solidly upon his back. Yah!

It was one of my finest victories. It gave me such a magnificent sense of winning, an exhilaration I will always treasure. The taste stays and will always define to me what a goal reached should feel like.

When I finally looked up I saw Nick just standing there watching me. He applauded. Happy because I had won the battle and happier still because he knew it was all over. There would be no more tennis. Nothing on the court would ever equal that triumph. And he knew me well enough to know I would quit while I was ahead.

And quit I did, but I will always carry that taste of true victory with me. It is perhaps what fuels my energy to triumph over this tragedy. Though this time without Nick.

I see it.

The wasp of my challenge.

NEW YORK CITY

Now there were only eighteen days till the wedding. A little more than two weeks to that dreaded Sunday. It was crazy. Nothing had changed between them, nothing had lessened, and yet the wedding plans kept chugging along, like a steam engine, heavy and powerful.

She'd said, wait.

He'd said he'd wait.

For weeks he'd been in a waiting posture, and no one seemed to notice. At least no one said anything to him. They had to know what was happening between Anna and him. There was no covering it up anymore. It leapt from their bodies like fingers of flame and filled the room with its fire, backing everything else into the corners. But even Barbara was silent about it. Friendly enough in other ways, except that he thought she looked at him with a certain sadness that disturbed him. What did she know?

And it seemed out of character for Adam and Roger to behave so discreetly. Was it possibly all in Nick's head? Under his skin? Was everything just as normal as it had ever been? Was this ache he thought so overwhelming just another part of the soap opera of everyday life?

Even if it was that for the rest of them, for him it was all-encompassing. Well, almost. He still had his work.

Sometimes his inner turmoil actually helped him, freed him to take risks that might have frightened a person for whom life was in normal balance. He did some of his best writing because he wasn't worried about who would like it (except perhaps Anna) or him for writing it. He had the boldness of the insensitive with nothing more to lose.

Resnick, the owner of the paper, Barbara's uncle, phoned him.

"Congratulations," he said, "I like what you're doing. It's got a little spirit there. But keep it contained. No reason to run over the thirty-two pages."

There was no way in the world he would spare enough time from his handicapping to actually read the paper. But he certainly could count.

"I thought that interview was so strong," Nick tried to explain.

"Thirty pages unless you can pick up more ads."

"Okay."

"But I like what you're doing. Tell you what, instead of a bonus I'll give you the pick six today at Aqueduct. How's that?"

Everyone knows winning the pick six is about the same odds as hitting the lottery. But Resnick gave him the names of the six horses and made Nick write them down and said he was going to lay out fifty bucks for him for the race.

Nick pitched the paper with the names in the garbage, but one stayed in his mind: "Gottawin."

Then Resnick called back later to say that he wanted Nick to go out to San Francisco for some kind of three-day meeting of throwaways, the name given to ad newspapers for obvious reasons. He wanted his paper to be represented. Of course, it fell on Nick's days off. He'd have to leave on Friday afternoon, this Friday, and it was Tuesday already, and he wouldn't be back until late Sunday night.

Actually, the idea of representing the *Westside Word* at a meeting with other editors was exciting to him. It made him feel like a real newspaperman. It was hard to feel professional working on a throwaway, a murky area that's slotted somewhere in that wide distance between a college weekly, a pure ad sheet, and the *Daily News*.

Besides, he'd never been to San Francisco. Only it wasn't going to work. He couldn't lose three days. He'd be nuts to chance it. That would leave him only fifteen days before the wedding. He'd have to tell Resnick he couldn't go.

When he called Resnick, he caught him in the middle of the

stretch call. That's a special phone number you dial to hear not only the winner of the race, but a rerun of the horses coming down the homestretch.

"I got no time to listen to why you can't go," Resnick told him, "I want you there. If you're my editor, you're there. If you're not there, you're not my editor."

Nick was momentarily taken with the phrasing. It was his mind stalling for time. He had to stay close to Anna.

"So?" Resnick asked, nudging Nick out of his reverie.

He grasped the empty air for an excuse and plucked a quick family death, an aunt. Then he changed it to an illness, and then he chickened, fumbled some more, and finally said, "Maybe she'll be feeling better by Friday."

"I thought you said she was dead."

"Right. Can I call you back in a few minutes? I just have to check with the hospital."

"Call me back after the ninth."

That gave him two hours to make up his mind. How much harder was it to do the impossible in eleven days than in fourteen? Gottawin.

That's when he got the brilliant idea to ask Anna to go with him. Alone together for three days. Better than that. It would force the decision, the commitment. Right now Buchwald was on the calendar, embossed in black and white and real, while Nick was some amorphous dalliance that made no demands, gave only pleasure when there was time for that. Buchwald really existed. Everyone knew he did. He was the moment she was concentrated on. It was to Buchwald she owed the choice.

Now he had to make her owe him one. A weekend with him.

It might not have the power of a marriage, but it might have the power to undo a marriage.

Later on, at two o'clock that afternoon, when he could wait no longer, he phoned her house. Her mother said she had left a half hour earlier. She would be coming into the office any minute.

But Barbara came in first. He was very tempted to talk to her. Maybe she could help him. Why bother? Either Anna was going to go with him or she didn't love him. He was beginning to sound like Resnick.

He knew she loved him. But he couldn't count on it. How was that possible?

There was Barbara doing it again, looking at him with that "poor baby" look.

"Something wrong?" he asked her. It was more of a challenge than a question.

But she didn't take up the gauntlet. Instead she smiled. It still had a trace of pity to it. "Are you going to San Francisco? I just left my uncle."

"Well, I don't know," he answered, disarmed by his need for her help. "You see, I have this problem, sort of an illness in the family. . . ."

"Yeah, he told me. Your aunt?"

"It's a lie."

"Anna?"

"Maybe she'll come with me." This was sort of a dry run, trying it out on Barbara. She didn't looked shocked, just interested. "What do you think?" he asked. "Think she can get away?"

"I hope so."

God, Nick thought, Barbara is so nice. Maybe it's a sign.

"By the way," she said, "you lost the pick six."

Fuck signs.

"Every horse except for the third."

"Gottawin?"

"Yeah, a forty-to-one shot."

Definitely had to be a sign.

The situation had to be handled carefully. Certainly not in the office. Maybe in the bar on Columbus Avenue, the one they went to that first day.

Twenty agonizing minutes later, Anna arrived. It squeezed his heart the way she looked; she was so beautiful. Her auburn curls were piled in a mass on top of her head with long, soft ringlets, really only stray wisps of hair, that had worked themselves free of the pins and danced up and down around her face when she walked. It was at least ninety degrees outside, and her cheeks and lips were flushed deep pink.

She was wearing a silky, sleeveless, light blue dress that slid lightly along her body as she moved, grazing now the side of her hip or shifting to outline the pointed nipples of her breasts and changing color constantly with its shimmer.

In its still state, the dress hung deceptively loose, a demure distance from her body, and, like the fashion of the day, stopped just above the middle of her thighs. Beyond that were those wonderful long, long legs with the freckled knees and the ever-present thong sandals whose leather straps wrapping around her instep made her foot appear even more naked than a bare foot would look.

It was not possible for Nick to be within any distance of Anna and keep from touching her. Even if it couldn't be the length of his body leaning against hers, at the very least it had to be some part of his skin feeling her skin. Perhaps nothing more than reaching out to put his hand on her arm to get her attention. He did that, and she turned, covered his hand with hers, and smiled at him.

"I have to talk to you," he said." Can you take off for a few minutes?"

"Sure." And in one motion she swooped her big beige suede bag off the back of her chair and started for the door. "Barb, can you pick up my paycheck when you get yours? I'll be back in about. . . ." She turned to Nick.

"I don't know. Maybe an hour."

"Take your time," said Barbara. "No trouble. I'll get them."

God bless Barbara, Nick thought, she was really on his side. And the nicest part about her was that she understood everything. From Nick's part, at least. For her part, she watched the lovers leave with a terrible but kind envy.

This time when Nick and Anna emerged from the building into the glaring summer street, it was all very different. This time when they walked down Sixty-eighth Street, they walked close together, their hands and fingers entwined, their shoulders nearly touching. This time they were shamelessly comfortable with each other.

They were almost halfway to Columbus when Nick changed his mind. The bar was the wrong place to talk. They needed the clarity of the daylight, the hard truth of sobriety. There was too much room for the abstract in a bar; vodka blurred the details and made promises easy to make and easy to break.

He steered her back toward the park.

They walked directly to their bench. In these last two weeks a single bench somewhat secluded from the others, the slats on one end badly damaged and awaiting repair, guaranteed their privacy, had served as their special spot.

They sat down, and Nick took Anna in his arms. She slid her hands under his arms and around his back and held on, pressing her body tightly against his chest. She turned her face up to him, and they kissed. Deep, warm kisses that concentrated all their longings into their mouths, their tongues searching and pushing deep into the taste of each other.

"Oh, God, I love you. I love you so much," one said, or the other, or both. "So much . . . so much. . . ." Faces pressed together, bumping against each other, mouths racing over cheeks, lips burrowing into damp crevasses hidden under chins, necks and ears, words muffled, buried deep in sweet-smelling hair.

Barely able to pull apart, to come up for air, to end the passion, Nick had at last to wrench himself from her. He had to. He had to ask her. He had to know.

Anna could see by his expression, the serious, controlled set to his features, that he had something important to say to her. Something she wasn't ready to hear.

"Resnick wants me to go to San Francisco this weekend for the American Weeklies convention. . . ." He hesitated, praying she would help him, but she remained silent. "I have to leave Friday."

"When will you be back?" She asked the safest question, but it didn't work, he wasn't going to back out now. He had already leapt off the diving board. He was in midair. Either the water was there or he was dead. Resnick.

"Come with me."

"Ohh. . . ." The word ended in a sigh as she turned away. But he took her face in his hands and turned her back toward him. And held her there where she had to see his face. She had to answer him. There would be no escape.

"Come with me, Anna. Please. . . ."

Now she tried another ploy. This time she put her arms around him and buried her face in his chest. But he wouldn't allow it. He couldn't.

With both hands on her shoulders, he gently moved her back so that she was facing him once more. "I have to know. Now."

Anna looked into his face. She saw the terrible need in his eyes, the pleading. She heard the silence as he held his breath waiting for her answer. Ernest. Innocent. True.

She loved his face. At this moment she loved it more than anything in her life. If only everything else would disappear. Go without a trace, without a whimper, no sound, no call, no cry. And certainly no questions.

Do it, her heart screamed. *Do it! Go with him!* Where was her courage?

"Anna. . . ."

And then she found it. "Okay." Easy as that.

"Okay?" Did he make it up?

"Yes," she said. "Yes. I'll go with you."

❧

Nick insisted on making the arrangements then and there. They couldn't drive out together to the airport because he would be coming from home, from Brooklyn, but they would meet at the Delta terminal at ten A.M., which would give them an hour before departure. Everything was settled. Nick didn't dare say anything more. They left the park and returned to the office. They were gone less than an hour.

Barbara saw them come in. She was dying to know what happened but couldn't tell from Anna's face. It was totally empty of expression. Unusual for Anna. And then she looked at Nick. He looked terrified. But when she caught his eye, his face relaxed into a wonderful smile. My God, thought Barbara, she said yes.

A better person would be happy her dear friend had made the right decision. A better person would be immune to the charms of her best friend's lover. Barbara felt a nip of guilt that she was neither.

Nick stared at the copy in front of him. The page might as well have been blank. Anna was taking up his whole mind. Counting the rest of today, there were two and a half days till they left for San Francisco. Together. He had won. Buchwald was out; maybe he didn't know it yet, but he'd lost. It was Nick Devlin, Gottawin, the long shot, by a lifetime.

The imaginary fool inside his head, the one who usually fell on his face, had a triumph this time. There was no stopping him now. He leapt onto the desk, threw out his arms, jumped in the air, and shouted for joy! The sound of victory reverberated silently through the room.

No one looked up.

Meanwhile, on the other side of the room, light-years away, Anna was in torment.

The decision she had been agonizing over for the last two weeks had been made in two minutes. Was it right? Did she really want to change her whole life? Give up Steven? Run off with Nick? Was she ready?

She wasn't married to Steven. Not yet, and maybe not ever. She was still free. She could go where she wanted and with whom. So why did she feel so tied to him? Why did it take such effort to break away?

Because it wasn't just Steven the man, it was Steven the life. Her kind of life, a life marked by familiar parameters more felt than named. Within them there could be boldness and choices, but of a certain sort. No one was running off to Bucharest. Paris, maybe, but even that was iffy unless it was done properly, properly meaning that she and Steven could go to Paris, maybe even live there for a year, and then come home and go directly into their real life; that was okay, but Bucharest? Bucharest was absolutely outside of the parameter. And in a way, for Anna, Nick was Bucharest. Even in Paris.

There was a frightening freedom to Nick. He planted no stakes in the ground to mark out his life. Nothing to hold him back. He was bursting with energy and talent and all the boasts of the sixties waiting to be lived. If she could just let go, he might lift her off the earth.

"Let go!" he'd said to her, "I'm fearless enough for both of us. I swear it!"

Or crazy enough.

As these thoughts terrorized her brain, Nick turned and smiled at her and he looked strong and certain, not like a kid anymore. And she said to herself, I want him.

FRANCE
July

In these last five months in France I have found things to be happy about. I'm happy they are such a deeply private people that they would never hold hands when they walk together down a street. Or sit in restaurants with their arms resting on the table, fingers intertwined, staring into each other's eyes, ignoring the food. And they certainly wouldn't sit in those same restaurants working on great ideas for screenplays or knockout twists for novels or even a good handle for a magazine piece. And outside of kissing a million times in greeting and parting, they rarely kiss in public.

Which is all wonderful since I don't want to watch any of that.

Additionally, thanks to my latest villa catastrophe, I don't even have to think about it. The new horror is so all-encompassing it doesn't leave me a minute for my true misery. Of course, that was the point of the whole adventure.

I see the new problem as a legacy of M. Carson: the revenge of the previous owner.

For me construction in France is one man in shorts with a hammer. And now it seems I must call him because my septic tank is clogged. Since the villa is downwind of the malfunctioning *fosse septique,* I don't have to understand a word to know this to be true.

This problem must be solved in time for my first dinner party, which in itself was a nearly impossible feat for a friendless person to assemble. But I managed to scrape together six people to come to the villa for dinner two weeks from Saturday.

The credentials for being a guest to this dinner are simple. No dead people. And you don't have to be my friend to get invited.

Two of the guests were the very surprised owners of a gift shop in Vallauris, and the other four are friends of my New York agent's who are scheduled to be in Cannes for a lawyer's convention next week. No matter how marginal this dinner is, it's to be my debut. In two weeks this place must be odor perfect.

I would have thought the plumber could handle this problem, but I am told it is so severe that I will need a specialist. It turns out that the mason, M. Frency, is just such a specialist.

I happen to know that M. Freney overcharged M. Carson hideously to build a very ordinary gazebo. And I've already had my own bad experiences with him. I was barely installed in the villa three days when he approached me with at least six absolutely necessary jobs that I must do instantly.

He gave me a separate handwritten *devis* (estimate) for each one. *Devis* is hardly the proper description since all it did was name the job to be done and the price. No further details. And in the usual French method of payment, part by check and the other part *espèce,* which is cash without tax.

The first on this list of absolutely essential work was six thousand francs to treat the wooden pillars that hold up the carport. He showed me how the *punaises,* I guess a French cousin to termites, had eaten into it.

When I asked him what the special treatment was, he seemed a touch insulted. Was this a lack of trust? But my friendly smile assured him it was only American curiosity, and he was kind enough to give me a complete explanation, staring most of the time at Georgie, the dog. I've noticed that French construction workers often seem more comfortable dealing with males than females no matter who the male is.

Three days later I accidentally came across the very product Freney had mentioned in the *droguerie* (hardware store) and found out that the special treatment was simply slapping on some chemical that would protect the wood against the dreaded whatever bug. Slapping it on, I might add, at the Freney cost of more than two hundred and fifty dollars a pillar.

Additionally, the man at the *drougerie* was kind enough to

offer the services of his nephew, who could do it for me this Saturday. The cost? Six hundred francs. A hundred dollars for all four, including the material. A day's work.

It was at that moment that I made up my mind M. Freney had to go. Unfortunately, as patron, I was the one who had to send him. Somehow I would have to garner the courage to tell him his sinecure had run out. But I was in no hurry. I had planned to wait until the house fell down or something clogged the septic tank.

Now it had happened. And I had to believe that if four pillars cost a thousand dollars, a septic tank would cost at least a million.

Try as I might, I was overcome with cowardice and would have given up completely and rehired Freney, the thief, if suddenly serendipity hadn't thrown Rene Hillaire into my life.

It happened on a Thursday. I had stopped by the Crédit Lyonnais on the rue d'Antibes to put some dollars into my account and pick up a new checkbook. The woman who usually takes care of my account, Mme. Terrier, was busy with a client.

She's a nice woman, and since I was in no hurry and they seemed to be enjoying the conversation, I offered to come back later.

"No, no," she said, "M. Hillaire is just waiting for his cash. And I have your new checkbook." And then she introduced me to Rene, saying he, too, was fairly new to the area.

In perfect English he told me he had come from La Rochelle, on the Atlantic coast, a little more than a year ago. He seemed very interested in the fact that I was American, and when Mme. Terrier excused herself to take care of another client, we continued talking.

We ended up having coffee in a nearby café, sitting over that for nearly two hours and then moving on to wine at the Festival on the Croisette. Rene owed his perfect English to having lived in Malta for five years. Surprisingly, we seemed to have uncovered an endless vein of interesting things to talk about. Perhaps some of the mutual attraction had to do with both being strangers to the area. But, of course, La Rochelle is hardly being my kind of foreigner.

Rene looked about forty-five and, with his earnest blue eyes and dark hair, was probably part of that black Irish strain of

Frenchman whose ancestors crossed the Channel with William the Conqueror. There was nothing romantic about Rene, at least not for me, but there was something else I sensed immediately, something I knew to be rare and valuable: the instant feel of friendship.

From our meandering conversation I picked up a strong renaissance quality to his interests, but what really fascinated me was his instinctive understanding of anything man-made. He knew construction and architecture as if they were his mother tongue; additionally, he could even talk about furniture and designers, landscaping and computers. No machine seemed beyond him. When I mentioned my sewer problems, sight unseen he showed an instant grasp of what had to be done.

I touched his arm to make sure he was real.

How unlike my darling Nick Rene was. Nick, who with all his remarkable talents had a milewide mechanical gap in his brain. If he had a flaw, it was that he refused to recognize that technologically speaking he was locked into the late-fourteenth century.

I remember once, early in our marriage, I found him in the kitchen trying to fix the toaster. He was at it for hours and had disassembled the appliance almost down to its atoms. At least fifty separate pieces sat on the counter in front of him. I watched, awed by the engineering brilliance of my husband. He studied the pieces for a long time and then, without a word, went into the other room and came back with an empty shoebox. Placing it just under the counter and using the crook of his arm, he swept in every piece, then dumped the whole thing in the garbage. He offered to fix my watch, but I hid it.

And another time we had the most annoying shower drip in the rarely used small bathroom next to our office. Nick always felt he could handle these ordinary problems, and that nothing, except perhaps love, was immune to the intelligent approach. Besides, again, as all writers know, anything is better than writing.

In the case of the annoying drip, he solved it simply by tying one of Lily's balloons to the end of the shower head where it silently caught the drops of water. It worked, and we had perfect quiet for nearly three days until he went to check the repair work. He opened the bathroom door to find the tiny room jammed with the balloon, by now swollen to horror movie proportions.

Now here was Rene, who knew all those mysteries and was ready to share them with me. Better than share them, he was ready to take them over all by himself. Though we had only just met, I felt an instant trust. Rene was a man of unusually strong ideals, perhaps a little too demanding in that he insisted others, too, maintain the standards he set for himself. Probably an impossible demand, more suited to theory than to ordinary life. Perhaps it was naiveté, but it charmed me.

In a matter of days we had become like old friends who could talk about anything. We were not lovers, so there was no danger of mistakes, which left us free to examine life and religion and politics, ethics and morals, and any idea we opined, no matter how provocative.

Rene was uncompromising in his beliefs, even somewhat intolerant. He became outraged and even hurt when he suspected someone cut corners. Nick would have been a little impatient with such innocence. Even I felt a bit jaded next to Rene.

Still, he was my savior. My friend. He marched in and took Freney in hand, *devis* started to look like real estimates, and when there was a difference, he dumped Freney and brought in his own people. His mason, a M. Sourri, was young, about twenty-five but, as the French say in their highest compliment, serious. With M. Sourri working for me, Rene assured me, my septic tank would be perfect in less than two weeks.

Other problems I hadn't noticed were instantly exposed to Rene's expert eye, a stone wall that had been bellying dangerously was slated for immediate replacement, and when that was finished, the driveway would be completely resurfaced.

None of this was inexpensive work, fifteen thousand francs for the septic tank and forty thousand for the wall, seventy percent by check and the other thirty in *espèces* (cash); still, both the septic tank and the wall would be done in time for my party, and I could count on Rene's people to do it correctly. His standards of work were the most exacting I had ever encountered. He watched every stone and every corner. If it wasn't perfect, he made them redo it.

And he had other marvelous ideas for building a pool and a poolhouse below the villa. I was not to worry, he would draw the plans himself. He would get the workmen, the supplies, everything.

Rene was changing France for me. And I told him so: "I owe you so much. You've taken so much time for me. How can I repay you?"

"Friendship. That's the coin between us. If you'll have it, Anna."

Oh, I would.

After that we became inseparable, out to dinner every night, on the phone five times a day when he wasn't at the villa putting his wonderful, knowing nose into everything. An intrusion that didn't sit that well with *l'équipe,* who were no doubt a little jealous. After all, here was someone who knew it all, and he was on my side.

And then there were those wonderful, long evenings together at restaurants with lots of wine and talk. I hadn't felt this good in a long time. Nick had trained me that freedom was good. Conversely, whenever I felt good, I felt free. But because I'd been through such a bruising in the last year, I winced a bit and backed off feeling too good. Scared to be too free without Nick.

Scared enough to start finding all the negative things about Rene, things that belittled and demeaned him in my mind. While his head was lost in the landscapes of ideals of friendship and honor, I was busy looking at his hands and thinking they were like bear paws and that he was too short to hold such a powerful frame. And that his clothes were like a peasant's with his too tight jackets and polyester pants. And his social graces too primitive. And his laugh too loud. And his jokes not funny enough for Nick.

For Nick, who wasn't even there.

I recognized that these were my defenses. I was that cowardly ingrate again, who would betray the purity of a friendship by insisting on old shibboleths, the very ones that Nick had freed me from.

But now with Nick gone, I was in danger of retrogressing.

Unless somehow I could force myself to remember again how he had unlocked my life. To think again of the upheaval of those early days so long ago. Of Nick's boldness, which had changed everything for me, even my work.

I was not a trained poet and certainly wouldn't have had the courage to try such a radically different discipline. But Nick convinced me he saw talent, and I trusted him and he took me by the hand and word by word led me along. Strange how he could teach me something he himself had never done. But when it came to writing, he could do it all.

And he was right. It had given me a new life.

Now what would Nick think if he could see me inventing reasons for slamming closed those doors again? For curling up in corners and being scared? Had he wasted his time on me?

❋

In the next eleven days both the septic tank and the wall were completed. I gave M. Sourri a check for 38,500 francs and 9,000 in cash and arranged to get the other part of the thirty percent *espèce,* 7,500, from the bank the following week.

I called M. Sourri and left word on his machine that he could stop by on Monday to pick up the cash. He never returned my call. And he never came by on Monday. I called again on Tuesday. No answer. Somewhat unusual, a worker not picking up his money. Additionally, he was supposed to have the *devis* for the new work.

That night I told Rene I was a little annoyed, Sourri had promised that *devis* days ago. Rene said not to worry, he would call him and get everything organized. It was important to set the date for the driveway as soon as possible before the August hiatus, when all of France goes on vacation. I asked if possibly M. Sourri didn't want to do the other work. But Rene said, Sure he did, but they're all the same.

"Sourri is better than most," he said, "but they all have to be pushed."

🌟

This morning, Wednesday, Mme. Bareau asks if she can talk to me. Of course, I say, yes. She, who always seems so sure of herself, appears extremely uncomfortable today. I figure she's had it and hates me enough to finally quit.

But I'm wrong. She is there only to further torture me. She is even more jealous of Rene than I thought. She has this wild story about M. Sourri, the mason, and how he complained to her that he was losing money on the job.

"Nonsense," I say. "If he's losing money, how come he didn't come to pick up the cash I owe him?"

"Because," she tells me, "it wasn't for him."

Since this is important and in French, I go over it all again. What does she mean the money is not for him?

"It is for M. Hillaire," she says.

I don't know what the word for liar is, but I find a way to tell her that M. Sourri is dishonest and she's wrong for believing him and I can tell my friends from my enemies.

"M. Sourri is here now, in my house," she says. Will I talk to him?

I despise being taken for a fool, being manipulated. I wish she had really come to tell me she was quitting. As soon as this is over I fully intend to fire her. The whole lot of them.

"Yes," I tell her, "I will see M. Sourri. But perhaps we should have M. Hillaire here, too."

"But first, please see M. Sourri alone."

"Why?"

"Because he is afraid."

You can't beat these people, they're always one step ahead of you. I agree to see the mason right now.

We're back to the translating mode. M. Sourri tells Mme. Bareau in French, who then tells me in French, also, but this time simplified for a slightly deaf eight-year-old child. I understand every word.

The nasty little M. Sourri is claiming that Rene is skimming thirty percent off the top of his price, the same thirty percent I pay in cash. The way I figure it, Sourri is trying to gouge me out of additional cash. He must be dumb to think I won't tell Rene.

"I think I'd better call M. Hillaire now."

"No," says the mason.

I thought so.

"No," he repeats, and turns to Mme. Bareau and in rapid French, too fast and heavily accented for me to understand, tells her a long, complicated story.

I think he's sorry he started the whole thing. And he has a right to be afraid. Rene will be furious. And terribly hurt.

Mme. Bareau listens to everything and then turns to explain to me.

M. Sourri wants to call M. Hillaire himself.

I can't figure this out. Mme. Bareau goes on. According to the mason, he has been turning over all the cash he got to Rene. Once he did it in the gas station at the foot of the hill, another time at a bar in Cannes.

Why is M. Sourri telling me all this? What is his motive? Big, deep honesty? I don't believe it.

Yet there is a sincerity about him and an earnest look on his face that is beginning to make me slightly queasy.

In the movies when the Mafia comes to collect extortion money, there is always one holdout. One guy who just says, No, I won't be bullied by you bastards, and he goes to the police. Could M. Sourri be that holdout? He says he is.

I'm aware of sweat gathering on the top of my lip, and I have to raise my hair in the back to cool my neck.

I don't care what it looks like, it can't be true.

Mme. Bareau explains that M. Sourri will call M. Hillaire and that I should listen on the extension and record the conversation on my answering machine.

I'm more than sick to my stomach now.

But there's no stopping this.

We go upstairs to my office to use the speaker phone and the recorder. I keep my head down and eyes away from them as I set the tape.

Of course, I know his number by heart, so I'm the one who dials. Besides I am, after all, the patron.

Rene answers on the third ring.

I hand the receiver to M. Sourri. Immediately Rene admonishes him for not returning my telephone calls.

The mason apologizes, and Rene goes on to tell him that is not professional behavior.

That sounds fair and just like Rene. For the first time I feel comfortable enough to look up at Mme. Bareau and M. Sourri. Perhaps they don't think my French will be good enough to know what's going on. They're wrong; total concentration has made it one of my understanding days. Besides, I've become fluent in money and septic tanks.

Rene talks to him about the plans for resurfacing the driveway, and I am horrified to be overhearing even this innocent conversation, to be betraying my friend's trust and raping his privacy. How disappointed he would be in me. I must end this now.

I whisper to M. Sourri, "No more," and put out my hand to take the receiver.

"Call her today," Rene says, "and make sure you deliver the *devis* and pick up the seventy-five hundred francs."

"Can't you pick it up?" asks the mason. "It's for you anyway."

I drop my hand. And hold my breath.

"No, you must bring the new *devis* at the same time."

"I don't have it."

"Then get it."

"I can't this week, I have to go to Menton for my brother-in-law's —"

"Forget the *devis,* then. Just get my seventy-five hundred and tell her you'll bring the *devis* when you get back. And do it today."

I'm not just breathing again. I'm gasping and my heart is pounding against my ribs.

"I can't," M. Sourri says. "Why don't you pick it up? Tell her it's for me."

"I don't want to take the risk. There's too much other work at stake."

It's almost not like Rene's voice. Did I never notice the stammer? The gasping, almost grunting, that makes him sound so much like a pig?

"Hang up," I say to M. Sourri.

He tells Rene he'll get the money and give it to him when he gets back, then hangs up without waiting for a reply.

I turn to stop the tape and, with my back to my employees, say, Thank-you, and that I'll take care of the rest.

I hear them leave the room. They walk down the steps quietly, hushed, the way you do for a sleeping baby or a death.

I've turned my phone off and locked the door to my bedroom.

"Friendship. The coin between us. If you'll have it, Anna."

In my heart I knew it had a little too much flourish when he said it, but I was so hungry. . . .

Turns out it was all a scam. And I was the fool who swallowed it whole. Just like those people who give con men their life's savings. And I always thought, How could anyone be so dumb?

Is it true that no one does anything for nothing? Is friendship not a fair return? Would I have been as easily fooled in my own country?

I play the tape again and again.

And I want to cry. Or kill him.

I want revenge.

Of course, Nick wouldn't have fallen for such a trick, but if he knew I had, nothing would have stopped him from taking off after Rene. Nick's mind had a wide-angle lens that saw the whole picture faster than anyone, and he trusted his responses and moved on them.

He subscribed to the "leap into action" school and could be quite bold. And terribly courageous.

I saw it once when we were driving up Broadway in heavy but fast-moving traffic. As we neared Seventy-second Street there was a drunk weaving his way across the street. Cars were whipping past him on both sides, missing him by inches. I said, "Oh, my God!"

Instantly Nick swerved the car over to the curb, screeched to a stop, and jumped out. I watched in horror as he darted in and out of the whizzing cars to get to the trapped man. And then, grabbing him by the arm, he ran with him to the safety of the sidewalk.

I wouldn't have done it. I would have said, as I did, "Oh, my God!" Gasped. Covered my eyes as we passed and then looked back and said, "He's going to get run down. Isn't that terrible!"

Probably a lot like I'm going to do now. Cover my eyes till it passes.

But if I didn't . . . if I were like Nick, how could I act on this situation? Suppose I stayed silent and had the dinner party. I could invite the woman from the bank and instead of Sinatra, during cocktails, I could play the tape.

Or I could confront Rene and tell him what a fraud, piece of shit, he was and throw the tape in his face.

Or I could shut the door and stay in my room, locked in forever. Safe, where no one could hurt me again.

It's only when I voice such thoughts in my mind that I realize how far I've fallen from Nick. I'm orthopedic shoes and he's dead and he's still silver taps. Heavy furniture, that's what he would have called me.

And rightly so. I lost all my humor and in the process betrayed Nick. Laugh, he said, or you dry up and die. And in the process bore other people a whole lot.

He kept his credo right to the end. He lived it, talked it, and wrote it. Late in the short run of his life, when the chemicals of the cancer treatment had robbed him of most of his hair, he wrote about it.

I still remember parts of it. "Strand by strand," he wrote, "the thatch on my head has fallen like the snow upon the landscapes of my days: on the breakfast eggs, on my clothes, on the furniture. In an improbable twist to the natural order of things, I have been getting hair all over my dog."

And then later, in a moment of unaccustomed vanity, he insisted on getting a wig. I offered to go with him, but he preferred to do it himself. They must have been waiting for him, waiting to unload some little mud brown three-hundred-dollar item that had nothing in common with reality.

That night he went into the bathroom and emerged with what appeared to be a well-behaved little animal sleeping on his head. He looked at us, Lily and I. We looked back at him, our faces frozen with self-control. He smiled. We didn't move a muscle. "That bad?" he asked.

And went over to the mirror.

That's when he started to laugh.

That was it. We screamed and fell down on the floor in hysterics. For an encore he did a vaudeville dancing exit, waving his hair in the air like a flag.

He wore it faithfully for almost five months. But we never laughed at it again. And when they gave up on the useless medicine and his own hair began to grow back, he wore it until his chestnut strands began to creep out all around the edges, and then he threw it in the closet.

I found it later.

And I picked out the piece of memory I wanted, the wonderful dancing exit, and I smiled.

It's going to be harder with you, Rene, because you're not smart enough to be funny. Still, thanks to you, with your bear paws and assorted inadequacies, I will be enjoying my first French discount. Seven thousand five hundred francs off the top.

The hard way.

❈

I must not look crushed, especially in front of *l'équipe*. Days pass, and though I smile more often, I speak less. And I never step outside the door without arranging a happy, without-a-care look on my face. Perhaps I'm not fooling them. Still, I don't know what else to do. Not that they appear to be enjoying my embarrassment, but surely, among themselves, it must be a hoot.

The only way I can think of to show them that I have not been defeated is by going back into the worst of it and taking on another construction job. This time, of course, handling it myself.

There are a number of things I can improve inside the villa, but I decide instead to have work done outside, where everyone can see. I choose the driveway as my theater. It desperately needs widening. As it stands now, the turn into the carport is nearly impossible.

Unfortunately this will mean taking out M. Carson's monument, the gazebo, a decorative but completely useless, never-sat-in sitting area that ornaments my turning space. As a result of the tight squeeze, I have green car marks on the gazebo and white gazebo marks on the car.

It must go.

Of course, I will incur the wrath of the entire *équipe* by suggesting its removal, as it was only recently completed by M. Freney, the thieving mason, at great cost.

Except for the joy of self-torture (M. Carson must have suffered the same difficulty with his car), I can't see its purpose. However, the more I know about my Rebecca — and you do pick up personal information when you're living in someone's home — he was a man who liked challenge.

I understand that, but his challenge was artificially contrived, as if life weren't difficult enough, he arranged for a gazebo to be built in the middle of his driveway and, according to Mme. Bareau, opened every shutter in the house the minute he got up in the morning. Even if he had to close them all ten minutes later when he went out.

He dried the inside of the shower doors every morning because he feared the calc, a deposit from the high calcium content in the water, might leave a residue. And indeed, after a year or so, it well might. In this land of rainless summers, he moved the cushions in every night and out in the morning. He had a number of other small, annoying, unnecessary daily tasks that, much to Mme. Bareau's displeasure, I don't do.

And each one I ignore is a statement of my independence. A way to build my self-respect. Something I need desperately right now.

The change in the driveway is a necessary statement.

My announcement is met with a response akin to a new salt tax levy by Louis IV.

I will not be deterred.

NEW YORK CITY

It was dinnertime at the Buchwald's large Central Park West apartment. Daniel Buchwald, Steven's father, was celebrating his fifty-eighth birthday. His wife and his twelve-year-old daughter, Eve, sat on one side of the large, overly ornate dining room table. Unfortunately, his older daughter, Linda, couldn't be there with them. She was in the middle of exams at Boston College.

On the other side of the table sat his only son, Steven, heir to his investment business. And next to him was the traitor, the betrayer, the whore, the liar — Anna, the fiancée. But of course, no one knew that.

They certainly didn't know about what happened last Thursday night at the hotel or about the plans for San Francisco tomorrow morning. Thursday night was history, and there was no way to take that back, but San Francisco was another story. A story that didn't have to happen. Anna still had time to change her mind.

Helen, Steven's mother, did notice that her daughter-in-law manqué didn't look her radiant best that night. In fact, she had asked Anna if she was feeling well. Helen was concerned; she genuinely liked Anna.

She was a nice woman, Mrs. Buchwald, calm and undemanding, albeit pale next to her vibrant, successful husband and strong, handsome son. Anna thought she was the most unimportant wife and mother she had ever met. She simply didn't count. A gray and light brown backdrop to the center stage life around her.

No one was unkind about it, they just didn't pay any attention to her — unlike Anna's mother, who was also second to her husband, but at least had the day-to-day power over the children and the kitchen; Mrs. Buchwald had neither.

But Helen was no trouble to anyone. She seemed to ask for little. Though she was not noticed, she was not forgotten. Special occasions brought her the expected rewards of her station — the jewelry, the furs, and the new cars.

And she could always be counted on. You could count on seeing her at Georgette Klinger on Monday mornings, her art lessons on Tuesday afternoon, a charity luncheon at least once a week at either the Plaza or the Pierre, and the rest of the time divided between D'Agostino's, the Beverly Bridge Club, and Bloomingdale's. Mostly Bloomingdale's. She didn't look unhappy.

An enormous masculine energy coursed through the Buchwald house at all times, nearly obliterating any trace of this uninspired woman and making the home severely male-dominated even though they were in the minority. Eve, with her adolescent pep and spirit, still had some promise, but Linda, the older daughter, was deadly ordinary, like her mother.

From the beginning, when she'd first met the family, Anna had decided that all the strong genes had been swallowed up by the males. Along with that, most of the looks, too.

She also saw quickly that it was normal not to pay any attention to Mrs. Buchwald. At first she tried to buck the tide, but Mrs. Buchwald herself deflected all attention toward her husband and son. So Anna gave up and like the rest of the family benevolently ignored her.

But she worried. Men were supposed to find women like their mothers. Did Steven in some way see her as a young Helen Buchwald? His mother's features were pretty enough, she had dark hair like Anna's and a good figure, but like everything else about Helen, it all went unnoticed.

Would marriage to Steven sap Anna of color and turn her into a Helen Buchwald? Never. For starters, Steven's mother would never be fucking someone else two and a half weeks before her wedding. Suddenly the betrayal was beginning to look like a credit. And then reality with its attendant wash of guilt flooded Anna's throat, nearly choking off her ability to swallow. And she was quieter than usual. Normally she felt the responsibility of marching the flag of her sex right down the center of the dining room, defending women the world over. At least the beleaguered ones in this house. Today she felt maybe they all deserved to be trod upon. Starting with herself. How could she continue this travesty?

The conversation moved to the wedding. Anna could feel the heat on her forehead and the sweat forming on her upper lip. She dabbed her face with her napkin.

"We're going to have to add two more people to the list," Mr. Buchwald told her.

The Buchwalds had already exceeded their estimate of guests by at least twenty percent. Her father was going to explode at the new additions.

"Maybe you'd better tell my parents. They have to deal with the seating arrangements. . . ."

"Don't worry," Steven told his father, "I'll handle it." And then to Anna, "Do you want to show my parents the pin?"

There was no way to avoid showing it, since it was fastened to the front of Anna's sweater. The pin in question was an aquamarine fantasy piece outlined with tiny diamonds. Steven had given it to her a week earlier, Friday, the night after the first time she had slept with Nick.

She had accepted the gift with a deluge of uncustomary enthusiasm, wildly overcompensating in her praise for the modest, if not ordinary, piece. Holding it up to the light, she had marveled at its design, its originality, and its perfect little diamonds, not that with her limited interest in jewelry she could have known the difference between the real thing and glass.

But she couldn't stop herself. She had carried on about the little points of light caught in the prisms, the way their reflections danced on the wall, and on and on, until out of the corner of her eye she began to see that Steven was watching her with a certain confusion. She skidded to a stop with a sweet thank-you and a warm, sisterly hug.

Steven was delighted, if somewhat overwhelmed, at her

response and more than a little surprised. His mother had loved the piece, which made him think perhaps Anna's taste was more like his mother's than he had suspected. If Anna had known of the comparison, she'd have lost the damn thing down the toilet. As it was, on guilt alone she could barely look at it for a week. But Steven had insisted she wear it tonight to show his family.

And now here she was at the table, showing off her gift exactly the way she had seen Steven's mother do so often in the past. That seemed to be the only time they paid attention to Mrs. Buchwald. And now they were all paying attention to her.

A young Helen Buchwald. . . .

The older Helen Buchwald said, "I told Steven it was one of the prettiest pieces I've seen. It's something I would have worn at your age. Right, Daniel?"

Anna didn't even hear if Daniel agreed. Or even answered. It didn't matter; she would never wear the pin again.

"Did they get back to you on that property in Oyster Bay?" Mr. Buchwald asked Steven.

"I think we're more interested in the apartment in the Village right now," Anna answered for Steven.

Again he spoke to his son: "Don't let that slip by, Steve, it sounded like a good deal to me."

"I'm not, Dad. I put in a call to the agent."

"Don't you think it's a little premature, Steven?" Anna felt herself getting a touch annoyed. "After all, we're not going to be considering a house for—"

"I've got it under control, Anna," Steven cut her off. But gently. "What do you think, Eve, you like Anna's new pin?"

"It's almost the same color as your eyes, Anna," said Eve.

Anna smiled at Eve, but she spoke to Steven. "I think it's a waste of time to consider the land now. Besides, I don't have any time to go out there to look at it. We're so busy with the back to school advertising. We could have up to forty pages this week."

Steven ruffled the front of Anna's hair. "Brenda Starr, girl reporter. You get to handle all the good stuff, and I get stuck looking at real estate." In other words, he would look at the property

himself. And then to his family he said, "Anna's got a story coming out next week about the roller-skating craze. It's right up your
alley, Eve."

Damn, Anna thought, why couldn't it have been the piece on
the Supreme Court, the one she'd done the week before?

"You write really good," Eve said. "I love your stories, Anna."

At least Mrs. Buchwald didn't say she used to love to write
when she was young.

Everything about Steven and his family was driving Anna
crazy that night. Especially Steven. Though he wasn't behaving
any differently than usual, she found herself annoyed with him.
And instead of staying quiet and safe, she began poking and irri-
tating the conversation at every turn.

"I don't know whether we'll ever get to move to Long Island.
Well, certainly not if I get a job on one of the New York papers,"
she said.

"We'll see," said Steven, sounding just like her mother used to
when Anna was little and wanted permission to do something
special. "We'll see," her mother used to say; and Anna knew it
meant no.

"I have no intention of making a four-hour commute every
day." Now there was no stopping her. The family watched with
fascination as she dragged the dead horse into the dining room
and beat it again and again. "No way. Actually, I hate the suburbs
anyway."

"Well," said Steven, "you don't want to bring up kids in the
city, do you?"

"Why not? I grew up here."

"Well," he said, "we got time."

To Anna that was cousin to "We'll see." She mumbled something about hating birds, and when Mrs. Buchwald asked her
what she'd said, she answered, "Nothing."

Steven got involved in a conversation with his father about
something called a "sale lease-back," effectively excluding the
women.

Eve excused herself from the table to watch "The Brady

Bunch," her favorite television show. And for the rest of the dinner Anna said little, slipping silently into the background with her future mother-in-law. Neither Steven nor his father seemed to notice.

When dinner was over, the Buchwalds retired to the den to watch "Let's Make a Deal," and Anna made an excuse for leaving early. She said she would grab a cab, but Steven insisted on giving her a lift.

Once they were out of his parents' apartment Steven suggested they go to his apartment.

"Not tonight," Anna said. "I really have a full day tomorrow. I may go to Baltimore with Barbara. . . ."

"What for?"

"An old friend from school —"

"I thought we'd go out to the Hamptons this weekend. The Bernsteins are having a party on Sunday. I said we'd come."

"You never mentioned it."

"I forgot. I didn't think there would be a problem. You like them, right?"

"Still, I like to be asked."

Steven took Anna by the shoulders in mock outrage and said, "Well, now, Miss Green . . ."

"Ms. Green."

"Miss Green. You're never going to talk me into Ms. It sounds like something off the plantation." He found the perfect spot between a smile and serious concern. "Come on, Anna, what's bugging you tonight?"

"Nothing. I just have a lot on my mind."

"I have something that'll take your mind off all your troubles. Come on, baby," he said, taking her in his arms.

"Please, Steven, I really want to get home. . . ."

Now he was annoyed. Steven didn't take well to being refused. "You've been weird all night. What happened? Did my father make some unforgivable error?"

In the past Anna had objected to Daniel Buchwald's macho opinions.

"What about your mother?" Anna asked.

"Are you kidding?"

"Yes, I'm kidding. Nobody said anything wrong." Now she wanted it all to go away and went for the easy, vague excuse. "It's just that between the work and the wedding . . ."

"So drop the work. Barbara can handle your stuff. After all, it's her uncle's paper."

"What's that got to do with it? Besides, Barbara can't do my work. And even if she could, what about her own work?"

"Big deal. She's your best friend, let her do you a favor. How long can it take her to write a couple of extra stories? My guess is she's probably got a lot of free time at night."

"What does that mean?"

"I mean they're not breaking down her door for dates."

"I have to get home."

He was no dummy. He saw his error and tried to lighten it by saying that he was really crazy about Barbara. She was a "great gal."

But Anna had turned off. And when they arrived at her apartment building, she told him not to bother walking her up.

But he insisted. No way he was going to let his—with the emphasis on *his*—fiancée walk up alone.

Outside her door he asked if she was going to Baltimore for the weekend, and she said, yes, absolutely.

Nick was at the airport by eight A.M. Two hours early. He had on the freshly pressed pants to his gray suit, a new white shirt, and his crew-necked burgundy sweater. It was August and he was hot, but he had been told that San Francisco was always sweater weather and the plane would be cool.

No question wearing the sweater was a mistake, but he had been confused about what to take and consequently had taken too much, and now there wasn't room in his carry-on suitcase to pack the sweater. He'd never been to San Francisco. But that wasn't the problem. The problem was that he had never been away for a weekend with a woman. He'd spent time with women, slept with many of them, even stayed with them for days on end, but he had never gone away with one. Certainly not one he was in love with.

He didn't want to make any mistakes with Anna. He knew there were things about him that didn't suit her. Like the way he dressed. She didn't think he knew, but he did. Only thing he didn't know was how to fix it.

He never took chances with his clothes. Gray suit, crew-necked sweater, white shirt. What could be wrong? But something was. And it was in the territory of their differences.

Nick bought the *Times* and tried to read it, but he was too busy bobbing his head up every few seconds searching for Anna to know what he was reading.

She'd said she was coming. She wouldn't just not show. Would she? How did he know she wouldn't? He'd known her for exactly twenty-four days, on thirteen of which they hadn't exchanged more than ten words.

But love can make such enormous leaps. In a moment it can spring the locks on those deep recesses of your hidden life, lift you up out of yourself, and drop you deep inside the core of someone else, someone you barely know. And like magnets, you clamp together, so solid that one strong, unbroken steel beam is forged between you.

At last, in this world of billions, you have found the doppelgänger of your soul.

That was how he knew Anna was coming.

And she did. Just moments later she came through the electric doors at the far end of the terminal. The *whoosh* of air that always shot through his body at the first sight of her did this time, too, but was cut off abruptly when he saw that she wasn't carrying any luggage.

She had come to tell him face to face that she wasn't going. Nothing to do but meet it. He folded the paper, got up, and forced himself toward her.

Anna scanned the large waiting room but didn't see Nick at

first; then she found him. But before the actual recognition, in that instant when he was still part of the undefined mass, another stranger, she saw him with great clarity and no kindness, no familiar lines to cut the fierce objectivity.

He looked young, almost a teenager, raw and grim. Physically, no one she would notice. An unimportant part of the background: an extra. She was used to Steven. Steven would stand out in any crowd. He was bigger and better looking, but that wasn't the difference. The difference was the way he fit into the space he occupied. He was solid in it; it was his. He always looked as though he knew where he was going. Nothing tentative about Steven. Wherever he was, he belonged.

Whereas there was a tentativeness about Nick: half there, half not, the invisibility of the observer. She watched Nick walk through the crowd, making way for other people, keeping his own direction but bending and changing his path. If Steven the man, were there, the others would bend and change for him. Nick would, too.

Maybe there was too much boy about Nick. But hadn't Samuel Johnson once said that in all great love stories, the women are women, but the men are boys. Look at Pelleas, Lancelot, Tristan, and of course Romeo, the boy of them all. Would any (grown) man ever take such mad risks or the terrible sacrifices that had to be made for love?

Perhaps that was part of it for Anna. A longing for her own great love story.

Now Nick was nearly upon her, too close for the luxury of observations, and moving fast. There was no joy in his face; it was tight and pained. Why?

"Anna," he said, trying to force his face into a smile, but all that he managed was a grimace.

"Am I so late?" she asked. "I'm sorry, there was traffic. . . ."

"You're coming?"

"Of course, that's why I'm here."

She was going with him. Still not believing his good fortune: "Your luggage?" he asked.

She swung out her large shoulder bag to show him. "Finally something to fill it."

And he saw that it was indeed stuffed. Certainly enough for two days, but something about it struck him as slightly strange, just a touch off. He wouldn't have wanted to put his clothes in a bag like that. Just jam them in; certainly they were going to get wrinkled. Yet, he rationalized, not wanting anything to threaten his relief, her clothes were always sort of silky anyway. Maybe they were the kind that didn't wrinkle. All this flashed by in the time it took to reach out and grab her into his arms. And hug with all his might.

He would remember those thoughts later and wonder how it was that you always seem to sense when something is amiss, no matter how insignificant, and unconsciously record it on some mental notepad.

He was dying to ask her what happened when she told Steven. But that same sense that told him something was a touch odd warned him not to ask now. He could see that she was excited in a nervous way, and the combination of the heat and her lateness only exacerbated that state of mind. She was there. Wasn't that enough?

It was for Nick. The feel of the joy was in his chest, as if all the breath in his whole body were held in there, pressing his rib cage to nearly bursting. It was more than enough. Two nights and three days. And he hadn't even used an hour of it yet. He had it all in front of him.

And it would all be perfect. It was always perfect when they were together. Well, they did have that argument in the hotel, but as long as she was close enough for him to touch, he wasn't worried.

"Relax," he said, "we have more than twenty minutes. Do you want to sit down? I'll get you a soda."

"No thanks. Why don't we get on the plane. We can sit there."

It wasn't excitement, it was nervousness; Nick could see that.

"Something's wrong?" he asked, risking the devastating answer he feared was waiting for him.

She seemed shocked at the question and fumbled for a second, then answered, "No, not at all. It's just that I'm not the greatest flyer in the world."

That would have been a good enough answer if she hadn't looked around when she said it. As if she were worried about being seen. Another unconscious note went on his mental pad.

Anna felt as if she were ruining the weekend already. Five minutes into it and her craziness had gotten the upper hand. How was she ever going to get through it? And poor Nick, he was in for such a lousy awakening. The woman he loved was a destroyer, a killer of beautiful things. A coward.

She knew all too well the question he didn't ask — Steven. But as long as he didn't ask, she could prolong her choice — to lie or tell him the truth. To tell him that she hadn't told Steven where she was going. Just some quick story about her and Barbara going to visit a friend from school in Baltimore. She was ready to elaborate, but Steven hadn't pressed her because he knew she was annoyed at him and it would be wiser not to lean on her.

But Nick wouldn't be so easy. Eventually he would want to know. But she didn't have to make up her mind until he asked. In the meantime, she had to relax and get rid of the grim face. It was a tip-off.

Stop right now, she warned herself. Stop. Turn. Touch him. Smile. And so she did, and the smile warmed her lovely face and calmed him. And her touch had the softness of love, and the worried look in his eyes quieted.

Anna tucked her arm in his and led him toward the gate. Everything behind them faded away like a scene in a movie, and everything that mattered was ahead of them.

It was partly true; she was nervous about flying. She had heard Shelley Berman at the Village Vanguard a few weeks earlier describe flying as hours of boredom broken only by moments of sheer terror. But Shelley Berman obviously hadn't flown with someone he'd just fallen in love with. If he had, he would have barely noticed that he was off the ground.

They talked the whole five and a half hours to San Francisco, their words cleverly couched in ordinary language so that the eavesdropper would be fooled into thinking he wasn't listening to magic and therefore pay no attention to the miracle right before his eyes. They talked over the green of the eastern mountains and into the flat plains of the middle states: How they first met. How they almost didn't meet. What if they hadn't met? What if they'd met five months earlier? What if they didn't meet until the end of August? Till after the marriage?

And on and on, across the whole country, over the barren stone mountains of the West, past Colorado and other empty expanses where it seems to the easterner no one is ever home.

And when the pilot announced the landing, they were both surprised. Could all those hours have already passed?

At the airport there were choices of mass transportation into town, but neither of them could bear the thought of sharing any moment of their magical time with other people. They took a taxi to be alone.

They were in San Francisco, but they might as well have been driving through Queens for all the sight-seeing they did on the way to the hotel. They didn't even ask the driver the normal questions that showed they knew where they were going and he better not try to scam them and take the long way round.

The driver made an effort to point out some sights, but since they paid no attention, he couldn't resist taking advantage.

It made no difference to them. And even when Nick noticed what was happening, all he did was smile and whisper in her ear that they had probably just gone over the Triborough Bridge.

That surprised her, and she sat up to look out the window. "You mean they have one here?" she asked.

"They have one everywhere. No matter what city, what country, it's axiomatic: if you don't know the way, they take you over the Triborough Bridge."

Twice the fare later, they arrived at the hotel having loved every minute of the trip, even the unnecessary ones.

That first day, Nick signed in at the convention registry, picked up his name card and a visitor's pass for Anna, and that was the last anyone saw of them until the next morning.

Despite the fact that they had made love for hours and only fallen asleep at four A.M., Nick was up before seven. He had barely slept for waking every half hour just to check that she was still there. And then her proximity would keep him awake another half hour.

He couldn't have had more than an hour's sleep all night, but he was alive with energy that next morning. And words. Words waiting to be spilled, words to tell her how much he loved her, how superbly happy he was, and then a million more to tell her what they should do for the rest of their lives — together.

He watched her sleep, willing her awake until the strength of his need broke through into her unconsciousness and her eyelids flicked open. Where am I? read the shocked, sharp blue eyes. And then the mind told them and they warmed, and her lips spread into a smile.

Her arms raised, inviting him. Gently he lowered himself into the heavy sweetness of her sleep-warmed body. With barely a movement he slid himself between her thighs and into that wet, waiting place, its lips thickened by her desire and warm against the length of him. He pressed deeper into her, invading tightly closed depths that sucked at the billion live nerves that was his penis. Depths coated with his own juices, juices that he had filled her with the night before.

The thought that she had held his semen inside her, those seeds of his life, through all these sleeping hours, the thought tingled in his loins until he could no longer stay gentle and plunged himself deep and hard into her. She returned his fierceness by sending her hips ramming up against his body, moving up and down with the force and speed of his own rhythm.

He had been halfway to climax just watching her sleep, and she herself had been awakened from the deep sexual wildness of her own dreams. It took bare moments before they both exploded into ecstasy.

Instead of being wiped out from passion, Nick was energized and overflowing with words. Words he had to tell her. Thoughts that had been shooting through his brain all night long.

Their life. That's what he had to tell her.

"I'm going to give Resnick notice. A month, that's enough. There's always another sucker with dreams of New York newspapers. He'll have no trouble replacing me."

"Why?" He had taken her by surprise.

"Because we're getting out of here. Europe."

"Bucharest?" she said in a tiny voice weighted with fear.

"Of course not. Paris. Rome. Unless you want to go to Bucharest?"

"No, no . . . absolutely not." Now she was smiling. At herself. He thought it was for him, and he was delighted and encouraged and rambled on.

"I love Italy, but France would be better because at least I have some fluency there. Okay, so we can't work. Americans can't there, except for other Americans or off the books. I have this friend, this guy I knew at Columbia, who works as a guardian at some villa near Menton. He's off the books and they pass him off as a guest. He's been there two years and he's ready to move on."

"Menton?"

"It's perfect, right on the coast, just over the border from Italy. Anyway, they're going to have to replace him. He said they have two or three kids, maybe they could use an au pair, too. You could do that. I could write to him today. From here."

"Wait. You're talking about doing this for a while, huh? Not just a couple of months."

"Three years, that's what I'm thinking of, but maybe more. You could learn the language and I could get more fluent. Maybe I could even get a job with the *Trib* in Paris. And you could write. You said you wanted to write fiction. Where could you find a better place than the south of France? Look at Fitzgerald, Hemingway, MacLeish, all of them. It's a literary tradition."

"I don't know if I would want to start a family so far from home."

That stopped him. He looked at her with surprise, not sure if she was joking or not. Then he saw she wasn't.

"We've got time for that. Lots of time. I want to write novels first. Don't you?"

She ignored his question and moved to the pragmatic approach. "I don't even really have the money to buy my ticket. I think it's about a thousand or so round trip." She had checked because Steven had mentioned it as a possibility for a honeymoon. Two weeks in Paris. At the George V. No au pair stuff there.

Nick wasn't to be stopped. He'd thought it all out a dozen times. "I have about two thousand in the bank, and then maybe I could borrow a few hundred from my father. What about your family? Do you think they'd lend you something? Or if not, I have enough for us to get there. And then—"

"Actually, I do have some money that my dad put away for me, but I don't think he'd . . . well, I just don't think he'd go for this."

"But it's your money. Your decision, isn't it?"

Yes, the money was in her name. It was her money. But she'd never thought of it that way. If she wanted to buy something for her new apartment, the one with Steven, then the money was hers. No questions. But for something as unacceptable as this— running away to Europe with some stranger—they'd go crazy, her parents.

Those were the kinds of things other unfortunate parents had had to endure when their well-brought-up children went wild overnight and turned their backs on a lifetime of normal expectations. "Normal" being all the things that resembled their parents' own very orderly lives.

There was the daughter of friends who had joined a Hare Krishna group and another who had married a Greek tour guide. In Greece, no less.

Anna had heard about these aberrations and how such deep ingratitude had left in its wake only embarrassment and shame. But these were other people's children, certainly not the offsprings of careful, loving, generous, third-generation, successful American families like the Greens. No sensible child would consider abandoning such a comfortable, rewarding life-style as theirs promised.

She could just see herself trying to explain to her father— always her father, her mother just went along with his decisions—

how she was in love with this writer and they were going to France, and no, she wasn't going to marry him, not yet, anyway, and maybe his friend could get them a job with this family . . .

Impossible! She could never tell them that. Even in her own head it sounded stupid, childish, the nonsense kids plan when their world is still safely sheltered in childhood, and suddenly it all seemed very unappealing.

A picture of that life raced through Anna's head. Living in some garret, some drafty room above the garage or whatever they had in France to approximate servants' quarters, all alone there with only Nick—who the hell was Nick?—not speaking the language, not knowing anyone, taking care of some snobby French children who would probably make fun of her terrible accent. Lonely. A million miles away from family and friends.

No, she was not going to let him force her to do things she knew she would hate. He had no right to make such demands.

There was no way she was going to agree to these plans. They simply were not her style. Maybe they were Nick's. Maybe that's what she saw that first time in the office. That he wasn't her style. Maybe that was what was so different about them.

She felt almost panic. She had to stop him right now.

There was suddenly no reason to tell this stranger the truth. If the coward's way would free her, she would take it.

"Please, you have to slow down," she said. "This is crazy. You put so much pressure on me all the time. Can't we just enjoy this weekend without all these huge life decisions?"

"I'm sorry," he said, embarrassed. He knew he looked foolish. Somehow he'd shown her that wrong side of himself. The one so different from hers.

And he'd gone too far. He always forgot that she wasn't up to where he was. He was a million miles into his love, and she was just starting. Besides, she was the one who had to do all the hard work. She'd had to make a total change in her life and in other people's, too. She'd had to call off a marriage. A marriage that had taken months to plan, a fact that existed in reality, not just future plans; it was on paper, in money; it was a pronouncement.

And certainly Steven must have suffered terribly when she'd told him, and that had to have been difficult for her. But she'd done it, and Nick had just taken it for granted. Like she owed it to him. And now he was demanding that she do even more. And instantly.

It was so easy for him. His family didn't give a shit if he went to Europe or China. They might miss the weekly few bucks he threw into the pot, and they'd like him there for Christmas, but beyond that they didn't seem to care much.

That was not to say they didn't love him, but holding on to him just wasn't their way to show it. Besides, boys, young men, were supposed to be on their own instantly. Even middle-class kids like Nick; the minute that last college payment was made, that was it. Out! It was expected. It was almost demanded.

But not for a girl, not one like Anna, not even in the early seventies. The normal break to freedom, if it could be called that, was marriage; other breaks could be made, young women did, more and more of them, but it took strength and a lot of determination, because that was a true cultural rupture. And the parents felt impelled to fight it.

What was the matter with him? His love for her was making him tyrannical. He would lose her just as surely this way as he would have by continuing to be so timid. If only he could find the right place to put his feet. If only he didn't screw it all up. It was within his reach. Maybe even his grasp, but he had to do it right. Bullying wasn't the way.

Anna considered herself a new woman; she certainly had all the markings: the education, the job, the look, the smart mouth. She thought she had it all until something scratched below the surface. Nick had dug beneath the veneer, and she was coming up all wrong.

She was coming up like her mother. That's who she really was. That shiny outside was one coat deep. She was a phony. And had been — maybe without knowing it; at least that was in her favor, or was it?

All this time someone else had been making the decisions in her life. Sure, it looked as though they were her decisions until one of them disagreed with the expected. That showed her where she really was, and it was right back on that same old track as her mother. A little more streamlined, modernized, with the illusion of moving faster, but generally every bit as powerless. And worse. Because her mother really didn't have the power. But Anna could have it if she had the strength and courage to reach out and grab it.

There it was again, her old bête noire, courage.

And then there was the writing. Having to write, really write, not doing it as a delightful adventure. All the running off at the mouth, all the years of denying the life-style she was leading, of talking about being a writer. Now she would have to come across. Nick took her writing seriously, as seriously as he took his own. That was scary, because for the life of her she couldn't think of a thing she wanted to say.

She was glad Barbara didn't know the truth about her. Gentle, little Barbara, who always admired her so for all the phony reasons she was able to put over on her, little Barbara would have the strength to wrench her life off that old track and run it somewhere all new. All on her own.

She wished she'd never met Nick. Never saw the choice. Never saw herself.

Nick watched Anna hiding herself under the covers, pretending to go back to sleep. He played along. That's what he would do — play along — until he found the handle. Just like in writing. Nothing works unless you find the handle.

Keep it festive. Keep it light. At least you can't go wrong that way. Minimize the risk. The best way to do that was to open the chilled champagne split from the little refrigerator. This was a dream holiday; what better way to start it off than with champagne?

Nick got the bottle out of the refrigerator and popped the cork. And like Nick, he spilled some because he wasn't prepared with the glasses. But there was still more than enough to fill two glasses.

He bent down next to Anna's side of the bed and kissed the

tiny part of her forehead that she had allowed to peek out from the covers. There was no way she could ignore his kiss; light as it was, it moved through her whole body with a sweetness that coated all the anger and forced back the misery.

Anna pulled herself up against the back of the bed, easing the pillow behind her head. The sheet slipped down, uncovering her breasts. She felt the coolness against her skin but made no move to cover them. She reached for her champagne glass.

Everything was new again. Fresh and untainted. For the moment. She had to understand, nothing this strong could be easy, and she was here, that had to mean something.

Something about this Nick made her want to be here. Was the fascination his promise of freedom or her fear of it?

Or was it her love story?

Nick had always encouraged me to be less disciplined; he claimed that left to my own devices I'd make hospital corners on everything I touched. Don't even tuck it in, he'd say, just toss it up in the air and see where it lands. The whole idea is to surprise yourself. That's how you know you've found something new.

He held my hand, and I did it. I tossed it all in the air, and when it landed it was like nothing I'd ever done before. And I loved it.

But, reeling from my debacle with Rene, and without Nick at my side, I'm back to the safety of folding corners. And following lists. It says, "Make friends." I close my eyes and do it.

Who would have thought making one lousy friend I don't even want would be so difficult? Still, I persist, and five days ago I found a promising one.

At least until last night. Last night, at my suggestion we, my new friend and I, went to a local restaurant. The menu was satisfying, and we had just finished the cheese course when the waiter arrived to take our dessert order.

That's when I killed it. In a voice rich with confidence and pride, pride in being savvy enough to recognize what was surely the house specialty since it was written in large letters at the bottom of the dessert *carte,* I ordered the chef. Literally.

Since I adore poire Hélène, I reasoned that Hélène Leger could only be a wonderful, light, new variation of my old favorite. True, the name was preceded by a few words I didn't quite understand, but in my haste to show off my fluency, I just assumed it meant "recommended by the chef." The word *chef* was there. In big letters. Turns out it was right next to her name, Hélène Leger. It still sounds delicious.

My disastrous request aimed at the waiter was instead missiled into the heart of one of those rare silences — that strange instant when everyone in the room stops to take a breath at the same moment. It probably happens no more than four times a decade, and I was lucky enough to fall into an early one for the nineties.

My faux pas could be heard at tables reaching as far north as the front door.

Ah, how they woke up, my fellow diners. Couples eating together who hadn't uttered one word to each other for three courses now were joined together in delight with a million witty comments to make.

First they repeated my order to each other, chuckled, laughed, clucked, and then turned to their neighbors. Normally the French would choke rather than say a word to the people at the adjoining tables unless perhaps they were on fire, but now they couldn't stop themselves from behaving like Americans.

Just repeating my gaffe was not enough; now they had to embellish the moment with descriptions of the chef being served with whipped cream encircling her head, cloaked in a sauce anglaise, strawberries for eyes, and a hat of Île Flottante.

It reached such heights that someone was sent to retrieve the chef from the kitchen to enjoy the merriment. Hélène Leger turned out to be a strapping young woman whose cheeks splotched red at being taken from the safety of her kitchen and who was almost as embarrassed as I was.

Almost. No one could possibly be in my condition.

Though the diners were enjoying themselves shamelessly, there seemed no cruelty to the merriment. I, on the other hand, had never felt so cruel about a group. If only I could have erased them from the earth.

How could I have done this to myself! Especially tonight, when I was so close to my first accomplishment. I almost had a friend. Not like Rene, this time a true friend, but now it was over.

Had she been a Frenchwoman, obviously she would have been as delighted and charmed as the rest of the restaurant. But my guest was Swedish, though like most of the Scandinavians totally fluent in English, she suffered from the same lingual inadequacies in French as I. Like all foreigners, we had been outdoing each other trying to show how perfectly we understood everything. But in truth she was only on my level, which meant the shame was even greater. Now she, too, would be tainted by my failure. They would treat her like the foreign fool I was.

The friendship was now impossible; she had seen me at my most naked. Actually worse than naked: in torn underwear. I could never regain the lost ground.

We would forgo the dessert and coffee and flee. There was almost no heart left in me to ask for the check. I wouldn't have spoken another word of French in that place for my life. She, the other leper, whispered, *"L'addition, s'il vous plaît,"* while I searched deep in my purse for the eject button that would catapult me out the back door.

Why couldn't we laugh about it? Because it's too serious. Learning a new life is not a game. Not for her, my almost friend, either. She was escaping from a kind of death, too. Hers was the death of a marriage to a man she still adored. He had left her for a neighbor's wife.

Every other word out of her mouth was Hans. Every story was about Hans. And even now it was Hans who was in charge of the arrangements for the divorce. His lawyer was acting for her, too. And royally screwing her, since Hans was a man of some heavy money.

After my husband died some peripheral friend whose husband had also run off with another woman said to me that I was lucky: at least I knew he wasn't with someone else. I swore I would never see that friend again, but to see the agony of Hans's ex-wife made me understand how she could think that.

Her name, the ex–Mrs. Hans, was Gena, and her need for this new life was just as crucial as mine. She couldn't afford to be involved with a loser. It was too depressing and difficult enough as it was.

I had met Gena waiting on line in the post office. I was buying stamps and picking up a package. I had never picked up a package before, and as with all new things, even ones as trivial as this, I was a little nervous. She was just behind me and seemed even more nervous. I could hear her making little achy noises, shifting her position constantly, taking deep breaths and holding them until they forced their way out as terrible sighs.

I could feel her leaning closer to me as if she were about to speak and then backing away as her courage diminished. Having done the same thing many times, I recognized the syndrome. Finally desperation gained the upper hand and she spoke to me in French: "Excuse me, is this the right line to buy a *carte grise* for my car?"

"Oui, madame," I said, boldly capturing the perfect French lilt, knowing instantly she wasn't French and that I wasn't taking any real chances and could fool her if I didn't say much. "Yes, madam," was perfect since the French rarely say just "oui" alone, they generally include titles.

The poor thing struggled through another question, and though I was enjoying her mistake, it was becoming too cruel. Besides, I didn't really understand her next question.

"May I help you?" I asked her, and for an instant I was bilingual, in her head, at least, and brilliantly so because my English was accentless.

"Can I also buy the stamp for parking tickets here?" she asked. Despite the imperfect features, she was very pretty, with aqua eyes and silky yellow hair that shimmered and slid lightly around her face when she moved her head. She had that spectacular kind of complexion that seems without pores. Early forties, no more. We were a perfect match. I was nearly in love.

I admitted I didn't know anything about parking tickets, and then she asked if I would be so kind as to ask the man in front of me since her French really wasn't good enough.

Bye-bye bilingual. The man in front turned out to be Dutch with even less French than we had. We finally found an elderly Frenchman who was only too happy to help Gena with anything. For the rest of her life.

And so was I. At last I knew I had found a friend.

My turn was next, and I prayed it would go well and she would be impressed.

The stamps were easy. Ten four-franc stamps. And the package seemed also to be an ordinary procedure. Besides, I had had fifteen minutes to study the instruction for packages on the glass partition. How different could a French pickup be?

I gave the woman in the cage my delivery receipt (I had been out when it was brought to the house) and proper identification. I had studied some of this in advance with Mme. Bareau. The part about the ID, at any rate. Amazingly enough, I don't need lessons for breathing yet.

All was going well enough for me to loosen the normal grim set of my face when approached by a new chore, well enough even to allow a small smile to relax the muscles. A smile I directed at my new friend.

She returned the smile, and we were both enjoying it all when quick as a roach the woman behind the glass popped my package into a larger box that seemed to be attached to the other side of the cage gates.

And then it was gone. Not a trace of my package. I felt an instant of panic until I realized that she was slipping it to me through the box on the other side of the bars. Indeed, there was a door and handle right directly to the side of me.

With a great relief I grabbed the handle and started to pull. But it was stuck shut. I pulled harder.

Meanwhile in rapid provençal-accented French that came out as one long attached excited word, the woman behind the cage began making all sorts of motions, waving her hand back and forth and vehemently shaking her head, no, no.

I wasn't turning it right. I wasn't pulling it hard enough. I turned. I pulled. Her gestures grew wilder.

Nightmare at three in the afternoon.

By now I didn't even want the fucking package and would have fled, but for Gena.

God knows what would have happened if it hadn't been for the intervention of the kindly old gentleman who had helped Gena before. Excusing himself, he reached over and removed my hand from the door handle and held it still for a moment while the terribly distressed postal clerk closed the door on her side.

Gently he opened the door on my side.

Of course. Security reasons. She had to close her door before mine would open.

Such a simple thing. Of a million such simple things is life made. And each one is just a hair different from what I have known all my life. Just enough difference to terrorize.

But my meeting with Gena more than made up for the little horror in the post office. As for Gena's parking ticket, and my perfectly spoken "Oui, madame," I was wrong there, too. She would have to pick up the stamps at a *tabac*.

But we would do it together.

Together. The very thought brought a little catch to my throat. And behind that, a welling of tears I managed to swallow. God, could it be that bad?

And now after the restaurant fiasco, that beautiful, new, unbloomed bud has been ripped from its stem. The friendship will never flower. My fault. My failure.

My good sense, my judgment, all that experience should have taught me, has abandoned me. I can't seem to have one success. Why am I here?

Perhaps I should go home.

☀

The phone is ringing! Please God, don't let them speak French.

"Hello," I say, making enough of a windstorm of the *H* to discourage a French response.

"Hello . . . hello . . . Anna, it's me!"

"Barbara?" I can hardly think of anyone I would rather talk to than my old, dear friend, Barbara Fowler, née Glassman. "Where are you?"

"In New York, of course, silly!"

Goddamn connection is so good, it makes her sound as though she's down the street. Still, even if it is only the phone, it's Barbara. Just when I need her most.

"God, it's good to hear from you." I can feel the tears welling.

"I'll bet." She laughs. "Just what you want, a boring old friend from New York to tear you away from your gorgeous Côte d'Azur. Oh, you lucky girl. It's steaming hot here and reeks of garbage. They ought to be giving us hardship pay to stay in town for the summer."

All I can safely manage without breaking down is to say her name. "Oh, Barbara . . ."

"I don't know if I can bear to listen to how fabulous it is there," she barrels right along, strangely insensitive to my misery.

Barbara has always had too many illusions about me, though once, a long time ago, in a brief insight, she'd cut through those exterior disguises she'd always so foolishly coveted and found the truth. And my life was rerouted forever. No matter what, she'll always have my friendship for that.

Once before she'd saved me. Will she do it again?

"But tell me anyway. Have you gone to a million fantastic parties and met lots of dukes and counts and whatevers? I have to hear everything no matter how much it hurts me."

No. She won't. Years have passed, and illusion has become the friend she prefers. It suits her life.

And mine now, too. In a flash I know that in this case, the opposite of admiration will be pity. I can't have that.

"Actually, it's unbelievably marvelous." I'm prepared to spin the wildest lies, but she interrupts me.

"Don't spare me. I want it down to the last yacht. I can just picture the villas, the galas, midnights at the casino . . ."

She's going to do it for me.

Shamelessly I let her. And then she tells me how much they all miss me.

"But you were so right," she tells me. "And so strong. God, we envied your courage."

Suddenly I feel perhaps I can tell her the truth. This person who really cares about me. Who knows the taste of sadness. Her daughter had died of leukemia two days before her third birthday. Barbara understands loss. But before I can start, she interrupts me again.

"And now you're reaping the rewards. What an adventure! Everything brand-new. What excitement. Do you know I go to sleep every night fantasizing about your new life?"

And then it's all so clear to me. Barbara's not being insensitive. That wouldn't be possible. It's just that this is what she needs. She wants finally to be able to stop worrying about me. To stop feeling miserable every time she thinks of me or Nick. And to stop feeling guilty for having a husband and loving him.

And I'll let it happen because I love her and she doesn't need another burden.

"As new lives go, it's not too shabby," I tell her.

"You must be almost fluent by now."

Not only do I not have any new friends, but now I've given up my old ones.

Despite my decision to release her, it becomes almost unbearable listening to her chat on about how she pictures me sitting on my terrace overlooking the sea surrounded by brilliant, vaguely left wing, literary types, all of us gabbing away in French.

"Tell me about the parties. The villas, the châteaus . . . I just love France."

I'm not going to be the one to disabuse her of the notion that I'm courageous and wise. I might as well get some pleasure out of the pretense.

I love France, too. So far it just doesn't love me. And if Barbara knew how undesirable I was, maybe she wouldn't love me, either. So I lie.

Not from whole cloth, just by omission. Truth with some tiny holes in it.

I tell her about living with the Mediterranean outside my window. A sea is a much more serious body of water than a lake or a sound, more impressive, like an ocean but without the fierceness, particularly a sea that has the good fortune to lap against the Côte d'Azur; that sea would be a kind of tamed French ocean.

And I describe Cap d'Antibes and how I can see it stretching out into the rich, blue water like a slithering caterpillar with humps of green that roll over and over itself, a piece of literary history that feeds my private daydreams.

F. Scott Fitzgerald wrote *Tender Is the Night* there. In fact, the whole group of them, the Fitzgeralds, the Murphys, and the Hemingways, were all there. Until they came in the twenties, Nice was the place. Cannes was a backwater.

There's magic in the words — the south of France. The light that Renoir captured, those soft blues with thick streaks of pinks and yellows, are still out there. I see them at sunset almost every day. The flowers can't be stopped. And though we're well into July, when I drove east last week on the Board de Mer I could still see snowcaps on the Alps in the distance. And on a day the mistral blows — that's a strong, good weather wind from the northwest of France — those days are dry and clear, and the dark mountains are crisp against the cloudless sky. In the winter season, from my terrace, I can see the faint outline of Corsica far out to sea. And on all clear days, to the east, the mountains of Italy seem to go on without end.

Always, the air is perfumed with some scent, heavy mimosa in February, light orange blossoms in November. But in spring and summer, when the jasmine and pittosporum bloom and the air is still and thick with their aroma, just breathing is seduction enough.

And they still burn leaves here. I know it's wrong, but oh, the smell of eucalyptus, rich enough almost to color the air itself. And more ordinary leaves, and the memories they carry.

From my terrace I can see other villas in the distance. All in the pinkish orange or pumpkin hues of the land. There's a group of hilltop houses huddled together in the distance toward Cannes that are whitewashed the color of the mountain walls along the Board de Mer on the route to Monte Carlo, the white dazzling in the sunshine, fresh and unsoiled by the grime of northern cities.

And everywhere are stone walls either blue gray or beige intermingled with slabs of slate. The best walls are built dry without cement, just stones piled one on another, but the pattern that emerges always looks as if worked from a detailed plan, so perfectly are they arranged according to shape and size. Rounded corners nestled against scooped-out, rounded places in other rocks and flat edges that fit perfectly against other flat edges.

It's not possible that they were constructed from prearranged patterns, it would take far too much time, but when I watched some workers building a wall against the neighbor's property I understood that it wasn't exactly accidental, either. They, *les ouvriers,* seem to have had an innate sense of the pattern and could pick and choose the right shapes quickly, just from feel and because they were good at what they did. They had a sense of beauty.

All France seems to have that sense of beauty. The things they build, the gardens they tend, the markets, the shops, the wonderful colors in the clothes they wear. And they wear them well. What the average Frenchwoman wears to the morning market I would be happy in for a cocktail party.

Not for them my American casualness; no, everything has to look its best, its closest to perfection, at all times. They arrange themselves and everything else to add to the excellence of their landscape, their music, their language, their wine, and their food. Oh, God, I've become a Francophile ad nauseam.

With all this perfection it's no wonder they are mistrustful of change unless it's French originated, but that, of course, is rare.

They have a jewel and they mean to protect it. Because someone always wants it. Thieves. Whole countries of them hanging over their borders, ready to grab it with guns or summer bathers. But, incredibly, without using any muscle, because they are not a muscle people, and depending solely on a unique French weapon, that special Gallic arrogance, a hard-to-love combination of self-ishness and blind self-confidence, they guard the gates, intimidating all comers.

And for Barbara, I pretend to be part of all this.

It's very quiet when I hang up the phone. At least with Barbara I had my pretense. Now all I have is the honesty of silence.

❋

I'm like the fish that suffocates and dies if it doesn't keep moving forward. But to do that I need a plan, a way to get out of my head and back into the world. How big can the distance be? I was there once, and it was natural and easy. Just like making love.

I must keep telling myself that it can happen again, that beggars do ride. Except, even in the most encouraging of circumstances, it can't be done without a horse.

So, the first thing to do is find that damn horse.

Or at least an approximation of one. Which leads me to consider Glu Gla, my Slavic prince. Perhaps he could fill in for a real person. And with the severe language barrier between us, we would never have to talk about it again. He seems ideal. And all I have to do is invite him home to study. The rest will take care of itself.

Since I have very little real communication with my deus ex machina, I have no idea where he lives or if indeed he does even exist outside of school. I will find out first thing tomorrow morning.

I can practically taste him. Well, perhaps that's a little strong.

The important thing is that a decision has been taken. And I have taken it; it hasn't taken me.

My first step back.

SAN FRANCISCO

They took a cable car down to the pier, where they sat on the wooden dock in the bright, sunny noontime eating sweet, warm Dungeness crab and dangling their feet off the side. Nary a thought of the convention passed their minds. Later they wandered around downtown, admiring the clean perfection of the little city.

When more than five hours had passed and they could bear it no longer, they raced back to the hotel and into each other's arms. And stayed there the rest of the afternoon and well past dinnertime, not recognizing for the longest time that the rapacious hunger they felt might actually be for food. When they did, suddenly they were starving.

While Nick went in for a quick shower, Anna called Barbara to check that there wasn't any problem with Steven. Not that she expected there to be one, but lying was unnatural for her, and like all inexperienced liars, she worried excessively.

This time, it turned out, with good reason. The unexpected, that monster of reasonable certainty, had happened; Barbara had accidentally run into Steven on the street.

"Oh, my God!" Anna was horrified. "What happened! What did he say!"

Nick could hear her "Oh my God!" from the shower. He turned it off in almost panic, ready to rush into the room and save her. But when he swung open the bathroom door, he saw that she was okay, just was sitting on the bed, her back to him, on the phone. Safe, in one piece. And so involved in her conversation, she hadn't even heard him. He was too curious to close the door all the way. Softly he pulled it almost shut.

"I think it was all right," Barbara told her, trying to sound more certain than she really was. In truth, Barbara was every bit as unaccustomed to lying as Anna and had stammered pretty badly when she saw Steven. Actually, she hadn't seen him, he'd seen her first, which made it worse. She was totally unprepared.

But he was surprised, too. What was she doing here? Was Anna home, too?

She felt as if it took her forever to grab hold of a reasonable story. In truth, her reaction had been quick, and at first she thought he might have believed her.

"I told him that at the last minute I couldn't go, so you went alone. I kept it simple."

"Well, what do you think? Did he believe it?"

"He was surprised, but then I went on about how it was me who was dying to go and how I talked you into it. And then how bad I felt to back out at the last minute. And on and on with that nonsense. I thought if I put the emphasis on how badly I felt and all that, it would sound more natural."

"Barbara, I have to know. Did Steven believe you?"

The nanosecond Barbara took was too long. And then when she said, "I don't know," Anna's heart dropped.

"Oh, how horrible!"

Although Nick could hear only Anna's side of the conversation, it was no trick to know what was happening. She had lied to him. She hadn't ended it with Steven, she'd told him some kind of story, and now he had found out the truth. Indeed, now they both had — Nick and Steven.

He slammed the bathroom door shut.

The sound jolted Anna out of her horror about Steven long enough to realize that Nick must have overheard her.

"I can't talk now," she said to Barbara, "I'll call you when I get home."

Anna sat there staring at the closed bathroom door, knowing she'd have to face Nick. But her mind was on Steven.

The door swung open to reveal Nick, a towel wrapped around his waist, his hair dripping wet and his face steaming with anger.

"You lied to both of us. And damn it, you got caught."

"I did. Oh, what a stupid mistake."

The way she said it sounded to Nick as if she expected his sympathy. She read him all wrong. If she was bothering to read him at all. "How could you do that?" he said. "A goddamn lie. This whole weekend . . . everything. It's all a fraud."

"No, it isn't." Now she snapped back to the current situation. And with clarity.

"What is it, then? Just fucking. Why did you do this to us?"

She answered his question in the simplest truth she could find. "I lied to you because I knew you wouldn't understand, and I lied to him to be with you."

But Nick was too angry to deal with the truth.

"That makes it my fault," he said. "You did it all for me, right?"

"No, I didn't say that." She tried again: "I wanted to be here, but I just wasn't ready to give everything else up."

"But I forced you, didn't I?" His voice was hard. He couldn't stop himself.

"I said you wouldn't understand. All you see is that you love me. And want me." Anna's voice hardened to match his. "After that, it's a million miles of clear road. Nothing else counts. Finally, not even me. But you have to get it through your head that I don't just end with your love. There's a whole life to me, and it goes on beyond your feelings."

"A life called Steven."

"That's part of it." She buried her face in her hands, she was near tears. "Oh, what have I done to him?"

"Maybe he'll take you back," he said as unkindly as his love would allow.

That drew the battle lines for Anna. My God, what was she doing! She had known Nick for less than four weeks. Steven had loved her for more than three years. And Steven was someone she had always known, he was one of hers. But Nick, Nick was a stranger. And might always be one.

What was she doing with this person, this stranger? Up until now they had never said anything but wonderful things to each other. Never criticized each other. Or fought. Or even chosen a movie or a restaurant together. Until now they were in perfect agreement, all they ever wanted to do was to make love.

Because of that indulgence, she had caused pain to someone who was a serious part of her life. What a selfish fool she had been.

Anna's introspection suddenly turned to panic: the only thing that mattered was to get home to Steven.

She flew into action, throwing on her clothes, grabbing her things, scooping up all her jewelry, and stuffing everything into her enormous bag.

Nick stood there, still dressed in the towel, and watched in horror.

She never stopped moving until she got to the door; then she turned to look at him, and there was a wildness in her eyes. And a blindness. It lasted only a second, and then she was out the door.

Suddenly he was alone in the room. In his life. There was no Anna. Ever again.

"No!" he shouted. "No!" And holding the towel tight against his waist, he raced out into the hallway.

He couldn't see the elevator from his room and sped around the convoluted corridors calling her name: "Anna!"

And then around the last, and there she was. The elevator hadn't come.

"Anna, forgive me. I'm sorry for being so dense, so unsympathetic, so narrow-minded, so goddamn stupid." And with his arms extended in a final plea, he said simply, "I love you."

And the towel dropped to the floor, leaving him as naked and vulnerable as his words.

Now, indeed, the elevator arrived. The doors opened and a small but astounded group of conventioneers watched as the naked young man embraced the fully clothed young woman.

Anna and Nick never even knew the elevator had come. Not until they heard the applause.

Except for their eyes, they didn't make a move. Not until the door safely *whooshed* shut behind them. And then they laughed and were terribly embarrassed. But no performance could ever feel as good as that embrace.

And with arms still around each other, Nick holding the towel discreetly in front of his by now shameful exuberance, they went back to the room.

"You were right," Nick started immediately, "tunnel vision, that's my problem. That and the brilliant teenage certainty that love is the solution to everything. I'm not going to say I'm sorry again. Instead, this time I'll try the adult move: What can I do to help you? I love you so much."

"I don't know," she said, back to being miserable, "you tell me."

"I could run off with Steven."

"Then I could catch up with you later. And you could both be in my life. And then when I wanted to be with you, I could lie to Steven."

"And when you wanted to be with Steven? . . ."

"I don't think I'd ever want to be with Steven if you were any-place within reach. Which brings me back to the same question: Is what I feel for you a sexual infatuation that will pass, or am I so deeply in love with you, so marked by you, that my life will be crippled without you? I don't know anymore. I only know that you touch something at the core of my life, something I never knew existed, and you release it and a new dimension flies out into the air. Nick, you free me. But you scare me, too. And still I keep asking myself, do I want to live the rest of my life without you?"

"Why does your decision have to be based on loss? It's such a negative approach."

"It's the only way I can gauge your power and my need."

"I'm in love with you and I trust what I feel. Why shouldn't you? Our souls have touched. Why are you doubting it? Rejoice! So few people ever even know they have one."

"How do you know all that?"

"Only from my own experience."

"All, what is it, twenty-seven years of it."

"That's right. That's really a lot of experience, those first twenty-eight years. If you consider everything you learn by the age of four, imagine how much more you can pick up in those other twenty-three years.

"Look," he said, "it might not turn out the way we want. There's no guarantee, except that this particular moment, this choice, is never going to come again. And what if I was right? Don't answer. I know I am. And I'm ready to risk everything for it. It's the only way to love."

She knew he was right. There were no degrees of love. And only one way to do it. For the first time Anna felt she had tapped into Nick's strength and there might be enough steel in it to hold her up, too. If she believed in his love, there was only one question left.

"Tell me how I should do it."

He almost exploded with joy. But beyond the uncontrollable light in his face, he contained himself. He said, "Tell Steven the truth. As soon as we get home, arrange to see him. And then just say everything as kindly as you can."

"Suppose I call him now?"

"And tell him over the phone?" Nick was shocked. It seemed to enhance its unavoidable cruelty. Rejection was wounding, no matter how kind it tried to be. And telling him on the phone . . .

"It's cowardly, isn't it?" She was ashamed and waited for him to condemn her, but when he didn't she took courage and went on, "I could do it right now, or think about it and change my mind a thousand times before I get back to New York. Tell me, what should I do?"

"How can you ask me? I'm his enemy."

"You're right, I can't ask you. You said seize the moment? I'm seizing it."

Anna took the phone off the night table, put it on the bed, and dialed it. Almost instantly, it seemed, Steven answered. His first question must have been, "Where are you?"

"I'm here. In San Francisco," she said, and looked at Nick, "and I'm not alone."

It was too terrible for Nick to witness. He went into the bathroom, closing the door tightly behind him.

Still, he could hear the muffled sounds of Anna, first strong, determined, then tearful, and then almost silent. That's when he got scared and opened the door.

"Yes," he heard her say, "I'll be home by tomorrow night."

Steven talked for a long time. And then she answered, "All right, I'll be out there Monday afternoon. I'll make the three-thirty jitney."

Nick was beside her when she hung up the phone. Her body was shaking. He held her in his arms.

"You were right," she said. "That was a bad way to do it. He wants to see me, and talk. He has a right to hear it face to face. I'm going out to the Hamptons on Monday afternoon."

So much for his fucking good advice, Nick thought, and his stomach sank at the picture of Anna alone with Steven in his beach house. Nick's strength would be seriously diminished by his absence and by the power of the other presence in her life.

But it was the right way. He had to let her do it. He couldn't keep her his prisoner forever.

FRANCE

It is deep into the summer, and I have accomplished two important forward moves. The first is the gazebo. I have found a new mason; everyone should have a fair chance at the American pigeon. Despite the continuing terrorist rebellion in *l'équipe* camp, I have plunged ahead. M. Tonguy, a Breton (I see this as a slight advantage; he, too, is something of a foreigner down here in the south), is starting a week from next Tuesday.

The second move is even more astounding: Glu Gla has agreed to come to my house to study.

At least I think he did. I gave him my address and the best instructions I could. Actually, I drew the entire coastline to Italy. Now that I've made up my mind, I can't bear to have it go stupidly wrong with bad directions.

It is almost four in the afternoon, and he's coming any moment now. I have planned some short — say, ten- or fifteen-minute — study time, and then I offer him a glass of champagne. Glu Gla is more the red wine or beer type, I think, but I have to get this thing moving and I'll need more instant fortification than either of those can bring.

From my bedroom window I can see his little gray Deux Cheveux parking on the road way down at the bottom of my property. As expected, he rings the bell at the downstairs gate. I press to allow him entrance.

I can see him looking up toward the house. He seems to hesitate and then, with a certain resignation I can read even from this distance, puts his head down and starts the grand climb — seventy-seven unrelentingly steep steps — to the house.

Meanwhile, up at the castle, Rapunzel puts the last touches on her face and races down to greet her prince. Hoping to beat Mme. Bareau so that she doesn't have to make any explanation. Or, God forbid, introduction.

"This is Glu Gla, Mme. Bareau, he's here to fuck me."

I beat her to the door, and when she sees me she retreats back to her part of the house.

I watch for Glu Gla's head to emerge from the staircase. First the top of his thinning brown hair peeps up, followed slowly — it's a hard, long, push uphill — by the rest of his by now weary head. Then comes the slumped shoulders and chunky body, all clad in a brownish polyester kind of Eastern European suit and tie. He's dressed for the occasion. Maybe he knows. He's not carrying any books. I hope he does know, it will make it easier for me.

Drunk may not be enough.

"Ili, so nice of you to come." I smile and invite him inside. For some reason he wants to go into the kitchen, but I gently lead him into the living room, chatting all the time half in French and half in not French.

He smiles but doesn't utter a word.

Though he heads for a tiny, solitary, wooden chair against the wall in the entrance of the room, I redirect him to the couch. Once installed, his pants' crease corrected, he seems to relax a bit.

"Some champagne?" I shove a glass at him. We'll drink and study at the same time.

He smiles and nods his head in some Russian type, *da,* and accepts the glass.

I down mine. And another. He's neck and neck with me.

I get right to the books. And for the next ten minutes and the rest of the champagne, we study.

Studying with Glu Gla has given me new hope for my lingual ability. He seems not to have the least understanding that he has to try to sound different from his original language (whatever that may be).

I open another bottle. My French has become brilliant. He's given up completely and gone back to his own language. And in that he has a lot to say. Actually, he seems much nicer and smarter in his own language, even though I can't understand a word of it. It has given him confidence and made him sit straighter and surer.

And become a real person. The one thing I can't handle in my plan.

Another half hour passes and a second bottle of champagne, and I sense he's responding to me. Pleasure relaxes his face as the cruelty of my mission begins to bite at mine. How could I have been so deeply self-involved as to belittle this man for my own selfish ends? To use him and never even bother to find out his real name.

As gently as possible, I thank him for his visit, pry the glass out of his hand, and show him to the door.

He seems surprised that we're not going upstairs; I guess he did know after all. Maybe I wasn't taking as much advantage as I thought. Still, he's a nice man and thanks me and leaves pleasantly.

I watch him start down the steps. I run upstairs to my bedroom, where, from the terrace, I can see right down to the road.

From there I watch my reentry into the world disappear down the stairs.

Stop! I could shout. Helllllo there! Come back. Come back and fuck me!

But I don't.

Now I lose sight of him as he turns down into another level of staircase. There's still time. He would come back. Happily, I think.

We could do it. And then I will have done it. I will have started. I could have my first check on the list.

He appears again, farther away and smaller now, but he could still hear me if I called to him. And at that size it would be easier.

But of course, nothing this important could ever be easy. It has become a test for survival. And though this afternoon shows I'm still failing somewhat, I have recognized the enemy and I mean to overcome him.

Just not with Glu Gla.

BROOKLYN

Nick arrived home in Brooklyn after twelve Sunday night, to find his parents still awake. This was an unusual contradiction to their normal habit of going in to bed after the eleven o'clock news. Tonight, not only were they still dressed, they seemed to be waiting for him.

Just the night he needed the comfort of silence, they grabbed him at the front door, wanting to hear all about his trip. He didn't even realize they knew what he was doing. They never showed an involvement, not until tonight.

Could some extra sense, some unsmelled whiff, some stiffening of the hairs along their spines, have alerted the primordial parent genes deep in their DNA to the danger their offspring was in?

"How was San Francisco?" his father wanted to know, and with real interest.

"Do they really have all those steep hills?" was his mother's question.

"You know, San Francisco has more stop signs than any city in this country." It would be one of his father's extraneous facts garnered from some magazine article with little pertinence to the main story. Those were the things he gathered.

As a small child Nick was fascinated and thought his father was brilliant to know all those things. Later, he saw it for what it was: unincorporated, unnecessary facts with no purpose, like a parlor trick.

At eleven-years-old, his brilliant father was replaced by this very common man whom he could see too clearly. It took a while to get accustomed to the loss.

"And," his father continued, "they have more Dungeness crabs in the bay just off San Francisco than any other waters in the world."

They tripped over each other's questions in their enthusiasm to unearth every piece of knowledge their son had acquired in two days.

Could he have inadvertently discovered a true interest of his parents? Traveling? San Francisco? Something they wanted to hear from him, not tell him?

Or was it a trap to insinuate themselves into his life? Were they suddenly going to start getting involved now?

Well, it was too late for that. But then it had always been so. The distance between their differences was too great. They were truly, he and his parents, as out of touch as antipodes can be.

Even as a small child Nick's thinking made them uncomfortable. His creativity argued against their processed information, and they felt slippery on it. How could you be sure of anything if you didn't read it or hear it said by someone else? All the what ifs children ask were classed as either foolish or immature. Original thinking was a dangerous, uncharted jungle where responsible people mustn't venture.

For Nick it was home.

Long ago he'd stopped asking them anything. It was okay, though. It kept them away.

Now he gave them travel book answers, but it wasn't easy because he hadn't seen much of the great city outside their hotel room. But his parents loved every description, even the piped ones.

Though Nick's mind was still captive to thoughts far away, to his terrible worries, there was something comforting about the simplicity of the scene. Their interest, though uninvited, was touching.

There they were, his family, late at night, together, in the house he knew so well. The house that had always been his home, from far back as he could remember, from the time his feet had stuck straight out when he sat on the kitchen chairs, all through the years as they came closer to the floor, until at last the triumph when his toes could finally sweep the worn gray linoleum when he swung his legs. Up until now, this very moment, when the chairs seemed almost too small for his long legs. And the life hopelessly narrow and out of step with his future.

He studied the floor, that same linoleum that was always going to be changed to something called Kentile, but it was still there. The danger of replacement was long past. Now they talked only about moving on. Retirement.

It made Nick uncomfortable to think of people so anxious to get into the limbo of life — the waiting room of death. And to be so enthusiastic about it.

Still they questioned him about his trip.

They seemed more interested in him than they had been in years. Certainly since he'd come back to live with them. And ingrate that he was, Nick hated every minute of this new dependency: a grown man stuffed back into the box of an outgrown childhood that had never been a comfortable fit.

It was almost a month now since Nick had come to live with his parents. Only because of a fluke: an old school friend had promised him a sublet, but the current tenant was in the hospital and couldn't move for another three weeks. Maybe he should have gone to the Y. Anywhere.

They interrupted his misery. What did he hear about the surrounding areas? They wanted to know everything. It was well past midnight. God knows the last time they had seen such an hour outside of their pajamas.

When were they going to ask the direct questions? Whom did you go with? What does it mean? Are you going to marry her?

What would he say? What would he tell them? He couldn't tell them about Anna now. Impossible. They could never understand.

He began to get jittery as the conversation continued with no sign of easing off. He tried a couple of times to claim exhaustion, but they didn't seem to notice, or if they did, they didn't seem to care.

They kept at him. California, was it as fabulous as it looked in the movies? What about the weather?

"Bet it was expensive," his mother said with an accusatory tone to her voice, as if the high prices were his fault.

"They paid for everything," Nick told her.

"Who?" she wanted to know.

"The paper."

They both looked at him and shook their heads in a vague, "Oh, yeah, that's right" way.

That's when Nick realized they didn't give a shit. As always, they were interested only in their own minuscule, undeveloped, shriveled world.

Of course, he understood at last, he was in no danger; all these questions had nothing to do with him. It was all about their retirement.

Should they go to California?

He threw them a bone.

"The weather is fantastic, and if you live outside a big city like San Francisco, it's half the price of New York."

It was a gorgeous bone, and they would chew it for months. They would get books on it, ask questions, write away to state organizations, use every possible means to discover why California was absolutely wrong for their retirement. They were happiest when they had reduced life to it smallest, its closest to their skin, their own needs and desires. And its most negative.

But they were always right out front. They never hid their selfishness. Once, when someone had asked his father about the Vietnam War, he'd said he thought we should go in there with everything we had, right through China if necessary. He could judge objectively, he claimed, after all, he had no one in it. Well, Nick thought, following along with their selfishness gene, at least they would be off his back.

At last, when they saw they couldn't get anything more out of his limited knowledge of California, they became caring parents and insisted he looked tired and should get to bed.

He fled the room.

To his bedroom, with the old three-quarter bed, a size he had never come across again since leaving home, covered with its still sharp white chenille bedspread, in perfect condition except for the few little bumps missing here and there, bumps he'd picked off over the years, in anger or boredom.

The framed poem still hung above it. Kipling: "If." "If you can keep your head when all about you are losing theirs . . ."

He'd spent years dreaming of the time knowing that poem would save his life: All those who can recite "If" step to the side. The others — shoot 'em! Or for a million dollars, who in this audience . . .

He was still waiting.

He looked around his room at his childhood, at his World War II books, the old dog-eared Mickey Mantle poster peeling from the wall, his writing trophies, and his collection of cheap, badly assembled balsa wood planes. But for the writing curse, he could have been the all-American boy.

He studied the plainness, the bareness, the emptiness of it all; the almost aggressive lack of originality, of taste and sophistication. Just like the rest of his house. His home. His background. His family.

Anna wouldn't like any of it.

And his parents would be intimidated by her. Overwhelmed by her beauty and the sweep of her world. It wouldn't fit in to their pea-size life.

Suddenly he felt sick and ashamed. How quickly he had betrayed them, his people. There wasn't anything worse than ordinary about them. Of course, as their son he could find cavernous flaws in them, but there was probably plenty in Anna's life that was ordinary, too.

Besides, they were so peripheral in his life, their choice as well as his, and if he came from ordinary, he had never felt that way.

He had a talent. That was his specialness.

Something Steven didn't have. Not that Steven didn't have talent, he couldn't say, but it wasn't in Anna's world.

Like Nick, writing was her fascination. They had that together, and that was the advantage he was counting on. But now, tonight, he was like the man falling from the top of the Empire State

Building — happy, as he passes each floor: So far, so good.

So far, so good.

And with that thought he slept peacefully for the first time in two days.

FRANCE
Early August

In the dream — and even as it's happening I'm aware that it is a dream — Nick and I are playing a duet on one of those enormous baby grands. Strange choice, since neither of us played. Nonetheless, we're in a loft somewhere downtown, and the sunlight is shining into our eyes, blinding us. Our hands cross and our fingers become entangled. The feel of his skin hits my brain, and I'm startled awake.

And everything disappears, leaving only the sunlight streaming into the emptiness.

It happens often, these dreams of Nick. And then the loneliness of waking up without him. A forever kind of without him.

There are the other kinds of dreams, too, uncomfortable ones with a hint of shame and a taste of betrayal. But they happen, too, and they leave me aching in all those hidden places that want touching, caressing, rubbing, entering. . . .

Lately, even the memories of such feelings arouse me, concentrating my sensations and bringing instant interest rushing in from my extremities.

No question but that my plan with Glu Gla was a disaster. Perhaps I had been looking in the wrong place. Or not taking the word *approximation* literally enough.

An approximation — something much like, resembling, coming near, but not exact. A fairly close estimate. But absolutely not human.

And then it hits me. Just by taking that one extra step I arrive at the perfect solution; a facsimile.

The sublime embarrassment of the plan that comes to my mind

is guaranteed to bring out my defensive craziness, never far below the surface and always ready to pop up to creatively disguise anything that, when viewed too sanely, might bring out discomfort. Actually, shame.

But this would be my secret. The beauty of it is that since there would be no other human being involved, no one need ever know.

I am perfectly aware that there are actual manufactured facsimiles for sale — such as vibrators — but aware also that it would take me, at a minimum, two to four years to gain the courage even to enter one of those shops, and then how do you say "vibrator" in French?

And whom do you ask?

No, this has to be completely secret. And safe. No other living person can even suspect. I barely allow myself to think of it in the privacy of my own head. But when it comes to me, I know it is perfect. Right up there with the wheel. And I even know the word for it in French.

Courgette.

The deed would be done first thing in the morning at the Marche Moutan, a busy, colorful, open-air market in Antibes.

I have already achieved a certain market fluency and comfort that allows me to select and buy with almost normal ease. Like real people going to buy dinner.

Well, not quite that fluid; I can still be broken by an unexpected question that departs from the context. Or a friendly joke, the dreaded friendly joke, from one of the jolly vendors.

Market work is hard, though, relentlessly demanding; the stall owners open before seven every morning whatever the weather and, despite some small cover against the rain, have little protection against the penetrating cold and dampness. Or the discouraging winter emptiness.

And not only do they work the market, putting together the inventory for an entire outdoor store every day; promptly at one-thirty, they dismantle the entire show to make room for the parking lot that starts a half hour later.

Once the market is over, the transformation is so complete and careful that there is not a single sprig of leftover parsley ever to be found on the ground.

Despite all this hard work, the vendors always seem in good form, with a happy attitude, the air of a market party, one and all, every day.

This joyful place is to be the theater for the great event. The purchase of the zucchini, aka *la courgette.*

Courgette, cousin to the word *courage,* courage.

Am I at last moving forward?

NEW YORK CITY

They did a strange thing, Anna's parents, they didn't ask her anything beyond Are you okay? They knew something had happened because Steven had told her he spoke to them. He didn't say what had been said, but even if they didn't know the circumstances, they knew enough.

They handled it well, not pretending, just keeping quiet. She knew it had to be her father's decision because it had a subtlety and was at the same time wise. He did know how to handle her.

Or, she considered, was he manipulating her? Did he trust that in a struggle she would choose the less bold way? And by allowing her what appeared to be the space to make her own decision, not fighting her, he was exerting his greatest influence. In the family of "give them enough rope . . ."

Well, she might surprise them all.

Though she had been nervous for the rest of their time in San Francisco, she'd loved being with Nick. They never seemed to run out of things to tell each other. And the sexual magnetism between them was so strong, it was almost tangible. They had tested it. They had drawn apart far enough to leave an empty channel between their bodies, and that space was warm with the heat that rose from their flesh.

Occasionally the differences between them showed. Generally he appeared more conservative than she. Not just politically, but in his life-style. The most apparent was his clothes and his taste in popular music: Julie London, Sinatra, Ella. She liked them, too, but was drawn more to the Beatles and Simon and Garfunkel.

Artists were a pet peeve of his. He loved good art, especially the Impressionists, but, he insisted, there was no correlation between being a good artist and having an intelligent mind. And too much credence was given to what artists had to say. Like children of old, they should be seen and not heard. It made him crazy when they talked in their artist gobbledygook and people listened and said how brilliant, and nobody understood a foolish word they said. According to one well-known artist he had interviewed, the most crucial ingredient in life was color. Shut up and paint! That's what he wanted to tell him.

But any conservatism Nick had stopped when it came to his writing. His style was graceful, bold as was necessary to convey his thoughts, with an obvious respect for the craft, and, most important to Anna, an originality.

She loved to creep into his mind and hear all the unexpected thoughts. Even the most ordinary of them seemed to have a unique spin that turned them slightly askew. Just different enough to open up whole new areas of consideration. Often the spin was a humorous turn, wit rather than joke.

And it was all there in his writing, there with a surprising freedom and no apparent inhibitions. He was much more cautious in his words to her, but perhaps that had to do with their relationship. She could feel how carefully he trod. As if always on the edge of the one mistake that would destroy everything.

As the adored one, the sought-after one, Anna had none of those fears. She had the marvelous freedom of the well loved. She could take any piece of hidden madness in her brain and give it words. And she did, because she found, for the first time in her life, a desire to spill it all out. Empty her soul to someone.

Her fears were in her surrounding life. That's where her conservatism lay: maintaining the status quo. Status quo: the enemy of originality, of progress.

It was a subject Anna had thought a lot about lately. The status quo of her father, the life around her, the one she had always known. Was it that that kept her from breaking free?

On the other hand, there was much to be said for things as they were. She had chosen freely. Up till now nothing had been forced upon her. Unless you considered that her entire life had been a preparation for Steven, and in that way the accumulation itself had forced her choice. But there's an accumulation in everyone's life. That's the sum of the person.

Yet she couldn't help thinking that if status quo was a character in her life's play, it would be Steven.

No way to go forward without dealing with him. And the sooner the better, while she still had the feel of Nick's touch on her skin. Before she cooled off and got scared.

Tomorrow afternoon. East Hampton.

The rest of her life.

J ust as I'm leaving the villa, Jake calls. He's in Paris and will
be down at the beginning of the week. That's four days from
now, and I have nothing for him. If I were in my right mind,
that would make me crazy, but all I can think of now is my market caper.

Not fifteen minutes later I am stealthily slipping into the market, my large straw shopping bag in hand, looking to the casual
eye like any other Cannoise (I hope. Perhaps a little less elegantly
dressed). I spend the first forty-five minutes loading up on gro-
ceries for an imaginary family of five.

Everything but the vegetables.

I had carefully selected the stall for my special purchase well
in advance. It was to be one of the smaller ones close to the exit
(for obvious reasons), though not the very small, makeshift ones
that displayed all their backyard farm wares on low tables. No,
though those were right adjacent to the exit, they were too popular
with their obviously just picked fruit and vegetables. No, this
would be one of the slightly larger ones just behind them. The
particular one I had chosen was run by two older women.

Somehow that mattered, that the vendors be women. The men,
like Frenchmen everywhere, tended to notice their women customers too much, and today I must not be noticed.

Every day a different stall gets the crowds. I suppose it's about
price. I'm not much at comparison shopping even in the United
States, and certainly that would be sophisticated beyond my interest and ability here. My luck, today, my selected stall is rife with
activity. They're jamming in, grabbing their metal *plateaux* and
buying up everything in sight.

I'm certainly not in a terrible rush, I prefer to wait for the action to quiet down a bit.

In order to keep a sharp eye on my designated stall, I take up a position across the aisle at the chicken stand. From there I can keep watch out of the corner of my eye.

The chickens look wonderful (in the Vallauris market, they're alive; here they don't go quite so far in the quest for freshness), plump with clean white skin and all their natural appointments still attached.

Fifteen minutes later, with two cut-up chickens, a demikilo of livers, and a dozen eggs stuffed into my straw basket (all for God knows whom), business at the stand across the aisle has at last slowed down. I must jump in right away because with their popularity today, they could be out of my item shortly.

I start small. I fill my *plateau* with a bunch of silvery green grapes, a couple of apples, three gorgeous white peaches, and a box of *framboise*. I slide along the front away from the fruit, easing myself toward the vegetables.

I can see the *courgettes* clearly, but they are in the second rung, a little bit of a reach. Not a far reach, but noticeable. Your hand is going to be out there in the middle away from body cover. At least my hand is.

There's a bountiful crop of the little guys today. And they don't seem to be selling. Can I be the only person interested in *courgettes*? God knows, in my special way, undoubtedly.

The important thing is to keep the humorous feel to this caper. But somehow, the closer I get, the more covert and uncomfortable I feel.

Now the crowds have come back and I have to edge my way over until I'm directly below the offending vegetable.

Courgettes come in all sizes, as they say about their approximations. At first I look at the mini-things. Then I say, What the hell, it's certainly not the money. That allows me the courage to move on to the larger ones.

A close perusal informs me that there are at least three different kinds of *courgettes*. Immediately I discount the ones with the flowers attached. After all, I'm not a pervert.

That leaves the other two, both deep green, but one is smooth and shiny, and the other is rough. The shiny ones are slightly slippery, as if they had been oiled. It's a consideration.

But the roughness of the other is not unpleasant and has an interesting feel to its imperfection: almost like a touch of reality. Its shape is brilliantly mocking. And when you take one in your hand, and close your eyes, and run the fingers of your other hand lightly over the length of it, the deception is exquisite. Or, hold one in each hand, or even an armful of them pressed tightly against your—

"Qu'est-ce que tu fais, ma chérie?" a familiar French voice sings out right alongside me, startling me so that in my guilty desperation for cover, my hands shoot up to my face, the speed and power of the movement sending a fountain of *courgettes* cascading into the air.

Horrified, I watch as the green missiles come crashing down in all directions, some crushing nearby peaches and nectarines, others hitting targets halfway up the display case, squashing grapes and devastating box after box of fragile cherry tomatoes.

Those with still enough spit behind them barrel on, forcing a landslide of other vegetables in their path, and, reaching the counter edge, thump down to the ground, where they roll and bump against legs and shoes, causing a jumping and skipping commotion of the nearby patrons.

I've been caught!

Nightmare of nightmares, how can I possibly explain this?

I force myself to face my accuser. It's the little rat shit who lied to me about the movies, the one who took me sailing and nearly broke my back in two, and now he's caught me. Red-handed.

Everyone freezes. The entire market has stopped to watch. There's no way I can lie my way out of this one. Tears of embarrassment crowd my eyes.

"I'm so sorry," he says, and seems almost apologetic, the beast, "I didn't mean to startle you. You seemed so engrossed. . . ."

Before I can catch it, a terrible "aaahhh!" sound escapes my lips.

I must look in excruciating pain, because now I see he's

sincerely concerned. He knows he's gone too far. He takes me by the arm and gently leads me out of the crowd.

"You're not well, I can see that. Come and have a coffee with me. Here, let me take this," he says as he pries my frozen fingers from my overstuffed basket.

I follow blindly, all will drained from my body. We're almost out of the market when he stops and turns to me.

"Les courgettes? Tu as oblie?"

I study his face for the creases of a smile, a bellhop's wink, some trace of the cruelty I know is there, but all I see is concern.

Still, I'm not fooled.

In my coldest voice, with as much dignity as can be mustered after being caught in flagrante delicto right there in the open market, I thank him for his offer.

And then, in the only possible triumph left to me, I reject it, snap my basket from his hand, and stalk off.

Somewhat mollified in the wasp of my triumph: my first given rejection.

NEW YORK CITY

Nick kept staring at Anna's empty desk that Monday morning, the same scene obsessing his mind for hours. He could see her as she stepped off the bus in East Hampton: Steven, the wounded behemoth, waiting for her, appealing to her sense of loyalty, the love that they had had together, the perfect life they had planned.

Nick knew this would be the heart of Steven's plea: the plans they had made, starting with the beautiful house in the best part of the north shore of Long Island. That's what he thought counted. His Anna liked possessions. After all, she had so many.

But that's where he was wrong. He wanted to make her a prisoner of Bloomingdale's because he didn't know the true Anna; only Nick did.

That scenario gave Nick at least fifteen minutes of relief, until he began to question the power of Anna's resistance against Steven's strength. And make no mistake about that, Steven was strong. He'd won her in the first place. He had something that appealed to her. Could he call on that allure to win her back?

Agony set in for Nick as he thought about the other possibility, the one where Steven convinces Anna she's being foolish and immature, running off with a nobody who's been in her life for less than four weeks. Giving up all the brilliance of their future for some ordinary-looking guy with bad clothes and no money; add to that a crappy job on some throwaway rag and you've got the perfect loser. Nick could go on and on, finding a million reasons why he was a bad shot for Anna.

Finally Steven would appeal to her sense of pride, the embarrassment of calling the wedding off, the pain for her parents. How it would turn her very private life into everyone's gossip fodder. And, obviously, she would be admitting a very serious error in judgment.

And then, of course, those boxes, those shiny white boxes she would have to find to return all those gifts.

Suddenly Nick understood that he had to get to East Hampton, and fast, to fight his case in person, or he would lose. He didn't know exactly what he had going for him, but he sensed the power of it lay in his proximity to her.

From the few times he and Anna had spoken together on the phone, with just that ordinary distance between them, the strength of his contact seemed diminished.

One time in particular, not more than a week earlier, on the phone, he'd sensed with the beginnings of panic that she was slipping out of his reach, but later that same day, when their fingers touched, the time apart was blown away, and if anything, their passion had grown.

The being apart, that was the danger, the enemy's advantage, and too big a risk for Nick to chance. He had to get out there to East Hampton, make his presence felt, fight for her.

Unnoticed by Nick, Barbara had been studying him from across the room. Though he sat at his desk not ten feet from hers, she could see he wasn't there. He was instead caught up in some private, silent, raging battle of the mind.

She watched him. First he shook his head yes, then no, then yes again. For a moment his face seemed to relax; perhaps a small victory. But it was short-lived, and immediately the war resumed.

This went on, the backing and forthing, for five or ten minutes, and then the odds seem to turn against him; his eyebrows creased and his jaw locked into a downward thrust as the inner enemy massed more troops and defeat loomed.

Barbara sat fascinated, watching the transformation as he forged his desperation into determination. If she couldn't see it rippling through his body and crashing into his mind, she could certainly read it in the fierce stare of his eyes as they blindly pierced the middle distance.

With anger as his fuel Nick suddenly shot up, whipped his jacket off the back of the chair, and without a word to anyone stormed off to meet the enemy.

❦

As soon as the jitney pulled up in front of the old five-and-dime that served as the East Hampton stop, Anna saw Steven's Jaguar. He was standing alongside, his elbow leaning on the low hood, waiting for her. With his seamless tan accentuating the sun-streaked white of his yellow hair, he looked like a fantasy ad for life's dream — full bloom of youth, beauty and obviously, money.

Anna had to admit Steven could be very good to look at. And together they were noticeable, their beauty made even more exceptional by their contrasting tones, hers dark and glistening, his light and clear. People stared at them. She'd felt them looking, felt their admiration, and though she knew it was the essence of the superficial and felt guilty enjoying such an unearned advantage, still the pleasure from it was satisfying. Was it irresistible?

There would be other unearned advantages with Steven. Could she give those up, too?

She would.

It was a terrible task, this telling Steven, but she felt better about doing it the right way, face to face. She was nervous about his anger; he had a temper. She knew he would use his skills to intimidate, to dissuade her. He was, after all, the injured party, and as such he had every right to his justified outrage. He would go on the attack and like his father perhaps even try to bully her, but she was fortified by the power of her love. Safe from any attack he could mount.

Certain of that, she wanted only to get this unhappiness over with quickly and get on with her life: her life with Nick.

She was prepared for the chill of Steven's silence. She could anticipate the tight, sharp nod with which he would greet her, followed by the drive to his house, certain to be frigid with the icy bite of his anger.

But she was wrong. Very wrong.

It was warmth and love that greeted her.

A very nervous Steven walked to meet her and took her in his arms, pressing her gently but tightly against his chest, against his pounding heart. She could feel his deep affection.

Immediately Anna was unnerved, thrown out into unfamiliar territory, empty of plan or expected response.

"Don't leave me," Steven said, still holding her close, his voice almost cracking.

Gently she moved back away from him. "Oh, Steven, I'm so sorry," she said, and found that tears were already streaming down her cheeks.

"We'll talk," he said, taking her by the hand and leading her to the car. "There are things I have to tell you. Mistakes I've made. . . ."

When he opened the door for her, she got in, saying nothing. She was too touched to speak.

The black Jaguar drove away down the main street and turned at the corner toward Dune Road.

*

They had been talking for hours, Anna and Steven, when the rented blue Civic pulled up in front of the house.

Anna's heart dropped as she watched Nick get out of the car, take his jacket from the backseat, and slam the door, then open it again to release the trapped sleeve. She hoped Steven didn't see.

Nick was angry, that was apparent from the way he strode toward the house.

Anna jumped up and hurried to the front door, too late to stop him, but at least she could calm him before he got to Steven.

Meanwhile, Steven remained in the living room, waiting patiently through the anguished whispers from the front hall.

Suddenly Nick burst into the room with Anna behind him, her hand on his arm trying to hold him back.

"I think this is a conversation I should be part of," Nick said in a voice too loud and too heavy with the pent-up antagonism and determination of his two-hour car drive.

Nick's first sight of the competition was unnerving. He'd expected him to be good-looking but had convinced himself that despite that small advantage, Steven Buchwald would be essentially ordinary. But this tall, golden-haired man standing in front of him could never be dismissed as ordinary; in fact, he was uncomfortably arresting. And with a good three inches in height on Nick, strong and broader in all the correct ways, Steven was man to Nick's boy.

Undaunted, knowing that whatever physical advantages Steven had, he had the brains to match him—indeed, to better him— Nick planted himself directly in front of his adversary as solidly as his 145 pounds would allow. His stare unwavering, his stance challenging, as he waited for the return blow from his demand.

But none came.

Steven just looked at him. Not in hostility, just sort of sizing him up, and then finally said that he agreed, Nick did belong there.

"Come in," he said, pointing to a low, oversize armchair opposite the couch. "Sit down."

Without thinking Nick followed Steven's instructions and found himself swallowed up in a mass of thick, soft down cushions. The seat was so low to the floor that when he tried to move forward to find a stronger position for himself, he found his knees drawn up in front of his face. If he slid back, that meant he had to push his legs straight out in front of him. Aerobically sensible, the position was exquisitely uncomfortable. The only other alternative was to pull both legs up alongside his body, a position far too feminine for the circumstances, so he went for agony and stuck both legs straight out.

He also found that no matter how erect he tried to hold his back, he still had to contend with the disadvantage of being a good six inches lower than Steven and Anna, who sat towering over him on the couch opposite.

So much for easily outsmarting the dumb Steven.

Anna watched as Nick struggled in the chair, as he wiggled around searching for some position that would afford him a little dignity, a little of the importance he had come to claim. But it was impossible in that ridiculous piece of furniture made only for reclining in front of the TV.

A memory came back of the time she and Steven had made love there. She couldn't help juxtaposing it with the ridiculous sight of Nick with his legs stuck straight out, fighting the billowing corduroy cushions that complained with whining sounds every time he moved.

The thought crossed her mind that Steven had purposely put Nick in that chair. But she dismissed it when she checked Steven's face for some sign of amusement and found none. In fact, she read his demeanor exactly as he meant her to, serious and sincere. And though, she knew, sometimes he could be condescending, this time he'd kept it so well hidden that she couldn't find a trace of it. He seemed to be behaving admirably in the face of the terrible blow she had dealt him.

But Nick knew absolutely that the son of a bitch had tricked him into the fucking chair, but he had no choice but to work from it, since the only other alternatives were standing or sitting on an even lower hassock. It was as if Steven had decorated the room with this confrontation in mind.

To make up for his handicap, Nick took the offensive. He set down the proposition they would work from:

"Look, I know this has been tough on you, and I'm sorry. I don't know you, but I know how much Anna cares for you, and she's been suffering a lot about telling you. But there was no avoiding it," he said, and then added the triumphant line: "We're in love."

"Yes, I know," Steven said, allowing just enough pain to seep into his voice to reduce Nick's triumph to nothing but rude braggadocio, "Anna and I have been talking about it. About that and other things for the last three hours." Now he looked toward Anna, because this was only between them. "Some tough stuff, but we're going to handle it."

With those few words, Steven deftly lifted the ball from Nick's hands. He had taken over. And his deep understanding and humility weren't lost on Anna.

Alarms went off in Nick's head. This guy was a professional, smart, tough, cunning, with a million disguises, and fighting in his own arena. One on one like this, Nick felt he was sure to lose. The smartest move he could make was to grab Anna and run.

"There isn't much more to say, is there, Anna?" Nick said, trying to work himself into position to get up from the chair. If he ever could.

"Well," said Steven, "we think there is."

"We?" said Nick, the shock of the word propelling him out of the hated chair, too stunned to be grateful for that small favor.

He turned immediately to Anna for a response, for some denial.

Anna—who hadn't said a word since her whispered warnings at the front door, where she'd begged him not to interfere, not to become antagonistic—seemed not to have noticed the strategic turn and simply went on with Steven's thought.

"It's not the kind of thing you can do in two words," she explained to Nick, somehow taking the position of impartial observer. And then, further clarifying: "There's a lot that has to be said."

Her voice seemed younger, more tentative, with a softer quality and a sound to it Nick hardly recognized. Though Nick had asked the question, it was to Steven that she directed her reply.

Nick felt the ground slipping under him. Who was this other Anna? It came to him that he had never seen her in any other circumstance than at the office or with him alone. Now he was seeing a part of her that had been hidden before. The way she related to the man she was going to marry. This very traditional man he, Nick, could never have imagined for her.

And he knew instantly what was different about her; her confidence, that easy sense of equality she radiated, that was what was missing. That's when Nick realized there would be no quick escape; he would have to stand and fight. And on enemy territory.

He knew he looked like a kid next to Steven, but that could turn out to be in his favor. Steven would underestimate him. Think everything was as easy as trapping him in the chair. He'd find out soon enough how tough Nick could be when it came to Anna.

She was the only thing in the world he cared about. His need to win her would cut through any Buchwald defense.

But there was one possibility that could defeat him.

Anna.

If she didn't love him enough. But he couldn't believe she didn't.

Still, he had to know. "Anna, I'll do anything for you. Forever. But if you love me, you have to leave with me now. It's yes or no."

"Hey, what are you doing?" Steven stepped in front of Anna as if to protect her from Nick. "You don't shove someone around like that. We're not deciding what restaurant to eat in. This kind of decision takes time."

"I'm talking to Anna. Please stay out of it."

"I'm part of this, remember? I'm the fiancé."

"Nick," Anna said, sensing the rise in tempers, "it's a bad mistake to do it this way."

Some awful intransigence came over Nick. "Do you love me?" he demanded.

"My God! Why do you think all this is happening?" she said, and there was anger in her voice. But it was strong again, it was her voice, the voice he knew. If she was breaking out of his control, she was also breaking out of Steven's.

Still, Nick couldn't move off the track. On the surface it might have seemed irrational, this insistence on her saying she loved him, but he was convinced that those words alone would free her. He had to make her say them in front of Steven.

And he demanded again, did she love him?

Steven saw it, too. Nick had found the soft spot. If Anna said those words, he lost. He had to stop her.

The strategy that flashed through Steven's head and his attack were almost simultaneous. He rammed himself up against Nick, overpowering him with his size and force. If he had to, he'd beat the shit out of this little prick.

With his broad, muscular body blocking Nick's view, Anna and the crucial question were literally shoved into the background, while Steven, the powerful one, threatened to make the foreground a killing ground.

The two of them stood rooted like two stags with antlers locked ready to commence battle, and Anna was no more effective in her efforts to stop them than a tiny *mouche* buzzing around their heads.

This was a bad turn for Nick. He knew there was no way he could hold his own physically against this solid wall of a man. And Steven was strong enough and secure enough to make him look lousy trying. He'd give Nick the chair treatment again, only this time standing up.

No, Nick couldn't take that chance in front of Anna. It would destroy his credibility. There would be no way to take him seriously after such an embarrassing defeat. He had to do it his father's way. A rare occurrence. And one of the few stories his father had told him that stuck.

Seems when his dad was a kid of about eighteen, he had gotten into some trouble in a bar outside his own neighborhood. He didn't have a friend in the place, so it was just him against this other guy, and two of his gonzos: all three big and well into their twenties.

For no reason the tough guy was provoking him, just looking for a fight.

Now if you know anything about street fights and growing up in Hell's Kitchen, a very tough area on the West Side of New York, as his dad did, you'll know that all fights have a kind of form and pacing. And they move to a rhythm.

Each fighter feels the beats of a fight and knows when he's reached the point where he can throw the first punch. If there are fifteen beats to get there, after the tenth it can happen anytime. But it doesn't usually happen on the third or fourth beat, there's something unsportive about that, and even a deadly fight has some vestigial sport about it.

But his dad was badly outweighed and outnumbered. So he hit the guy on the fourth beat and knocked him down. And then he fled while the other two, too stunned to move, looked on in amazement.

"Look, kid," Steven said, hissing the words into Nick's face, "you're not telling anyone what to do. I'm telling you. You're getting out of here. And alone."

The countdown had begun, Nick could feel it, and just like his father, on the fourth beat he let go with the biggest punch of his lifetime, and Steven, all six feet two, 190 pounds of him, crashed down.

Anna dropped to her knees next to a very dazed Steven. "What are you doing?" she shouted up at Nick. "Are you nuts or something? That was brutal! Disgusting!"

"What do you think he was going to do to me?"

"Certainly not hit you. Good God, where do you come from that you just go off and attack someone like that?"

There it was. Where do you come from? You're not like me. Nick knew he'd played it wrong and lost his chance. If there ever was one.

"Look, Anna, maybe it was a mistake, but unless we get out of here quick, it's only going to get worse. Come with me. We'll straighten everything out tomorrow. It'll be calmer then. Okay? You coming?"

"Of course I'm not coming. I'm not going to leave Steven like this. You go. I'll talk to you tomorrow."

"No, you won't," Nick said, a sick feeling swimming over him, turning his stomach.

Steven could see the loss on Nick's face, so he took his time getting up. It would be politic to let him get away. Winner's charity.

Nick looked once more at Anna, but she turned her eyes away and gently touched Steven's bruised jaw. There was nothing left for him to do but leave.

And when he did, Anna sat on the floor and wept. Steven put his arm around her and comforted her.

More winner's charity.

FRANCE

I haven't fully recovered from my fiasco at the market, but at least now, in a sane state, I have the clarity of distance: of course, he can't possibly have known my true purpose. It was only a momentary confusion that allowed the line between my psyche and reality to blur. But only for me.

Nonetheless, I'm never going back. Besides, if I'm hungry, I have my wonderful new project, the dismantling of the gazebo, where I'm guaranteed plates heaping with gall to dine off, compliments of *mon équipe*.

But I can't even afford the luxury of that misery since my new one is arriving just two days from now. Jake is coming down from Paris Monday afternoon to pick up his new songs.

And I don't have them. I dread seeing him, not just because I've let him down, but because he is the first piece of my old life to reappear. I'm not sure I'm ready.

Meanwhile, just so today is not a total loss misery wise, I plan to deal with the gazebo.

It has taken me into August, almost seven months, but it is at last coming down. The dismantling was started two days ago, and I can feel them, *l'équipe*, watching and grinding their teeth as each piece of the structure is taken apart and thrown into a huge pile in the corner of the driveway. The twisted metal mountain itself is a testament to my betrayal of no less than France: the country, the concept, and certainly the venerable M. Carson, who deserved better than to have his final monument destroyed within eight months of his demise; additionally, my egregious lack of respect for history (but then what would Americans know of history anyway? Their country is ten minutes old, and already there isn't a building left over two minutes) and, of course, the brutal denial of them, the heart and soul of the villa, the true patrons — the long-suffering *équipe*.

If only the mason, M. Tonguy, in his little blue smock (a must uniform for middle professionals such as plumbers, electricians, and the like), would cart away the pile of metal bodies, perhaps the tension would ease. But he purposely leaves them there, day after day, his poison message to me.

Though he was greedy enough to take work he obviously disapproves of, he manages to absolve himself of any guilt by pretending to be a captive slave forced to labor for some cruel but stupid Philistine. As soon as I appear he lowers his eyes and dives into his work as if I've just laid on the whip. Truth is, I wish I could.

The fact that I take off half my front fender and a good chunk of plaster from the opposite wall each time I make the turn to avoid the gazebo, coupled with the knowledge that I've paid for both, wall and car, and in a fashion, since I did buy the house, I own the fucking gazebo, leaves him untouched. Besides, he's canny enough to side with the power, his own people: *l'équipe*.

I spy on them unseen from the corner of my kitchen window and watch as they stand around on my property joking together, convulsed in laughter, exchanging a mile-a-minute French garble of gossip, undoubtedly all about me since Mme. Bareau is the star and can supply them with endless tidbits of inside information about what goes on in my drawers and closets and other personal places she's surely poked her nose into.

When I've had enough, I fling open the kitchen door and appear — the dreaded patron. A knife of silence cuts through their laughter, and they scurry in all directions. But I can feel their hostility; it seems to me lately they've gotten bolder.

Why do they stay if they hate me?

Perhaps they mean to drive me out.

Never!

I will not accept another loss in my life.

NEW YORK CITY

It wasn't even a Dear John letter, it was worse than that: it was a resignation letter that didn't even mention that she didn't love him any longer. Or for that matter that she had ever loved him. It was business note, so distant that it might have been written for Resnick, except it was addressed to Nick.

The letter had come in with Barbara. It said she was planning her wedding and didn't feel she could discharge her responsibilities both to the paper and to her personal requirements at the same time. There was more on the bottom, but he didn't even bother to read it.

"Nice, huh?" Nick said to Barbara, who tried to mumble something about being sorry.

But he wouldn't let her. He flipped the letter into the garbage pail and walked out.

He'd failed. That's all. He wasn't up to it. Nothing could be done. Nothing that involved Anna. All the rest was bullshit now.

But there was one thing he could do, and he'd do it alone, and fast. He could get the hell out of here. Out of the whole goddamn country.

Nick grabbed a cab and told the driver to take him to Rockefeller Center. Fifty-first and Fifth. The passport office.

FRANCE

At least I have my favorite day to enjoy before Jake arrives. I've come to love Sundays. Everyone's day off. The villa is empty of my enemies. It is at last mine.

It's quite warm today, a soft scent of pittosporum mixed with gardenia riding on the quiet air and above me a clear, sharp, rich blue sky. I stand on the terrace outside my bedroom, admiring the miles and miles of perfection.

But now, way in the distance, far over the water, I begin to make out what looks like a small blemish on the otherwise impeccable horizon. As it moves in my direction I see it's a single gray cloud the color of wetness. Its shape is strange, not full with a belly of rain, but unusually long and relatively narrow.

I watch this curious formation as it moves at a steady pace and with surprising speed, sliding easily through the empty blue. It moves fast for a cloud. More like the brush of a big broom being pushed by some unseen force.

On the ground no signs of life or sounds break the stillness. But I can smell lunchtime approaching. The hardy aromas of the big Sunday feast are beginning to overwhelm the sweet floral scents.

The whole family is coming. Not mine, of course. And not to my house. My house is empty. Not even memories fill these rooms, and even if there were any, I couldn't retrieve them because they're not mine. I have not yet put any memories I would enjoy recalling into this house.

In my home in New York, my real home, I can dig memories out from every corner, layer upon layers of them. Always with him. Because Nick was always there.

He was a writer, too, nonfiction books, mostly history based: wonderful tomes that won awards and great reviews from the *Times* but, being somewhat esoteric in subject matter, had limited audiences and could never command the big advances. So in lean times, and there were many, he would play the free-lance game. The word itself, "free-lance," was a pseudonym for one of the world's most exquisite man-made tortures.

The game is played with a magazine and a gerbil wheel. All the writer does is sell an article, step up on the wheel, and start pedaling. From there the rules are simple: you stop for water, you starve to death.

And for Nick it was a greater sacrifice than could be imagined. He had what could only be described as a pathological relationship with deadlines. And magazines have serious deadlines.

It would always start with the same picture. In the far corner you see all of us romping in the sunlit fields of a new assignment. Money is coming in. We're saved. Our daughter won't be barred from the schoolroom. There's not a worry line to be seen.

And there's endless time: at least four weeks per story. The first week he spends luxuriating, the second he plans the attack. By the third week, if you look closely, tiny mosquitoes of concern can be seen nibbling at his ankles. It's probably a little uncomfortable, but he's still smiling. He's smiling because he knows that by staying home for the weekend he has plenty of time to get started.

Somehow the weekend speeds by, dragging Monday and Tuesday in its wake. Now it's just five days to the deadline. But there's still no serious worry because he can write four pages an hour, which means he won't have to start until late Thursday night.

At this point the doorbell rings and Hieronymus Bosch steps in to put the final touches on the painting.

I watch this all in silence, powerless to stop the agony, the sweating, the bleeding, and the cries of "Never again!" And I collaborate. Not in the writing, just in the suffering.

It is I who answers the phone when the editor calls. I who tells that nice man who is holding up an entire magazine how Nick has long since finished and is on his way downtown this very minute to deliver the manuscript. He's taking the subway, I tell him, but there might be some delay because I'd just heard that the E train was held up. A suicide on the tracks, a mugging, a murder, people caught in the doors, children pinned between cars, anything to help my love, whom I now deeply detest for having made me lie and cheat and listen to that relentless phone ringing unanswered day after day.

The worst was the time he was so late that the editor called to say he was coming himself to pick up the manuscript. On a Sunday. And he wasn't taking the subway.

Nick leapt to the typewriter, only eighteen pages to go.

My heart went out to him. He was truly a condemned man. He was awake in a nightmare, and desperation had finally rendered him impotent. A terrible silence hung over the typewriter.

All hope had fled. This time there could be no reprieve, when suddenly I smelled smoke. With nothing cooking in the kitchen, I ran to the hall door, and sure enough, black smoke was billowing from the fourth floor.

I ran to tell Nick that the building was on fire.

"Thank God!" he cried, and together we raced out of the apartment, to the comforting screams of fire engines growing in the background. We laughed all the way to the movies.

My life with Nick is so filled with memories that I could have my choice of hundreds. And if I were to choose one, it would be with us, at home. We both worked there, and though we never formally collaborated on anything, we always worked together, helping each other out with new ideas, unblocking word jams, or just throwing out pithy suggestions here and there.

Occasionally these exquisite hours of uninterrupted closeness turned normal.

"I would cut that paragraph. It's repetitious," one of us might say.

"What are you talking about? It is not," the other would respond.

"Okay, then it's cliché."

"No more of a cliché than that stuff you did about the what-ever."

Whoever. Whenever.

From there on it could escalate into your ordinary, everyday variety argument involving big noises like slamming books, slap-ping typewriters, shoving chairs, and ripping papers. Like Tol-stoy's happy families, all arguments are alike. And foolishly, impetuously, one time a gold pen was thrown out the third-floor window of our Greenwich Village apartment into the garden below.

Since I had originally given Nick the pen and it had obviously not been a favorite because he hardly ever used it, it was a sore spot even before I flung it out the window. Since it was Cartier, gold and worth about three hundred and forty-three dollars with tax, we couldn't just leave it there.

He went down to look for it, but it was summer and the garden was hopelessly overgrown. Besides, neither of us had watched it fall, so we didn't know where to look.

The nosy twelve-year-old boy next door was fascinated by the little family drama. Five dollars if you find the pen, we offered. Instantly he leapt into the search and threw himself to the task, burrowing around in the deep weeds and assorted backyard garbage. But he, too, didn't know where to look, and it was a fairly large garden.

A brilliant strategy emerged (it was for many years a bone of contention as to whose brilliance it was. It was mine. Survivor's advantage): I would stand at the window and with another pen try to re-create the arc I had used to throw out the original one. Ide-ally this should take the new pen to the same area as the gold one.

When the annoying kid from next door, who had been under the assumption that I had accidentally dropped the pen, found out that I had instead thrown it, he was wildly curious to know why I would do such a dumb thing with an expensive gold pen. Obvi-ously it could never be explained to an unmarried twelve-year-old, so Nick cut him short.

"You want the five dollars?" he asked him.

"Yeah," the brat said, greed overcoming curiosity. When he thought about it later, maybe in about ten years, he'd know the answer.

So there I stood, at the window, flipping pen after pen out into the garden. Compensation had to be made for the extra weight of the gold, but we were narrowing down the area. In a few minutes I was out of pens and they were ducking pencils and eyeliners.

Within fifteen minutes the kid had his five dollars and Nick had his gold pen. And together we had a *bon souvenir* we laughed about for years.

Not two weeks later, in an attempt to please me by using the pen more often, he took it to a restaurant and accidentally left it there. Gold pens don't wait long to be claimed. It was gone when he called an hour later.

Nick could lose things.

But he had little to lose in the way of things because he had so few possessions. That was by design; he rejected emotional ties to material acquisitions. With the exception of the perennial pack of cigarettes, he traveled light.

When he left his home that night twenty years ago, when we ran away together, he packed all of his belongings, his clothes, his collected history, every detail of his life that wasn't part of his body, and we put it all in the backseat of my Peugeot. With room to spare.

It amused me then, the difference between us — me with all my collected accoutrements of every phase of my life, and him, unencumbered, moving spare and fast.

Now, thinking back on that exciting, happy night, I can feel myself smiling, a facial formation that has become something of a rarity for me lately. The awareness of the pull on my mouth takes me out of my ruminations.

And brings me back to my quiet Sunday and the strange cloud. Incredibly, in the few minutes I had spent meandering around in my past, the long, gray formation had gained miles of sky and is almost at the water's edge below me down the hillside.

I can see the dark blue shadow it casts on the water beneath, though on each side, free of the cloud, the sea remains clear Mediterranean aqua. Now I can see that it isn't as narrow as I thought. In fact, there is surprising depth in the long tail of dark sky that follows behind.

As the grayness approaches me, it begins to seem less curious and more ominous. I look around to see if other people are watching, but the neighbors are all inside at the table.

The cloud creeps off the water, dragging its dark shadow beneath. As it moves over the first few houses at the bottom of the hill, I can see that what I thought was shadow on the water is more like fog on the land. And the houses below me are being swallowed in its mist. One by one, they disappear.

Suddenly it seems serious. Is it some nuclear residue from Chernobyl that has been circling the water for the last six years and is now going to contaminate the earth? Maybe the people aren't inside eating their lunch, maybe they're dead!

And I am next.

Or . . .

Maybe it is some gentle mist from Shangri-la that will carry me back to any fantasy moment I choose. Why not? A cloud as strange as this one could be anything.

But given the choice, where would I go?

I would go deep inside the safe time.

It would be one o'clock in the morning in the apartment on Waverly Place in the Village. We're in the kitchen. One empty bottle of Beaujolais is sticking out of the garbage, and the second, half-full, is on the counter.

I am standing on the kitchen table, shrieking softly so as not to wake our daughter. Nick is lying on his stomach across the stove, hanging over the edge, holding a wet towel spread open in his hands. Poised and ready for the drop.

We are waiting for the mouse who is trapped under the stove to make another attempt to escape. The idea is that when the mouse comes out, Nick will drop the heavy, wet towel, which will land on the little creature, covering it and holding it captive with its weight. Disposal has not yet been planned.

What actually happens is closer in concept to a toy machine that replays the same scene over and over again. The mouse sticks its tiny head out from under the stove and with shoulders thrown forward dives into its run.

At that instant Nick lets go the towel, I scream, and the mouse — now safely past the danger but stunned by the action and noise — stops, turns, and rushes back to its prison under the stove.

Put another coin into the machine and it replays the same scene.

Fifteen coins later we are wondering if the mouse really wants its freedom or is just relieving a boring life of endless mouse runs.

For Nick it's a challenge — man against beast. It's also his idea. For me the game is life or death. There's no way I am going to sleep in a house with a free-running mouse.

I'm not even coming down off the table.

Look at our faces. We are two people who are secure in the knowledge that we will outsmart the mouse and live forever.

That was only eight months before the cancer that had been comfortably luxuriating in thick clouds of cigarette smoke, silently growing and mutating in Nick's lungs, would clog his windpipe, causing a minor winter cold to degenerate into an infection resistant to all antibiotics.

We were concerned about the infection but never thought of the possibility of cancer. After all, you don't run a fever with cancer.

Well, you can.

And then you have to have major surgery to remove the lung. That's if you're lucky, and it's operable. Otherwise you just have chemotherapy until you die, bald and skinny and crippled. And in awful pain.

And all the while, the people who love you are stuck on the other side of the sickness, offering inadequate palliatives, begging and screaming at uncaring doctors and nurses to increase the dosage of your painkillers.

One time, near the end, Nick had briefly come home from the hospital because there wasn't anything they could do for him there that couldn't be done as ineffectually at home.

"Why are you bothering to get dressed?" I asked him. Some friends had stopped by. "It's only Sarah and Don. Be comfortable. Don't try to put on jeans, it'll be too tight for the catheter."

"Don't tell me what I can't do. Only tell me what I can do."

Since then I've never told anyone what they can't do — sick or healthy.

The days moved slowly with agony and indignity. But time passed quickly. And the sixteen months were being eaten up. Sixteen months, that's the length of life after discovery of lung cancer. But the catch is you never know at what point in the sixteen months you came in.

Much of those last months I spent staring at him. Devouring him with my eyes. Nick brushing his teeth. Nick sitting at the computer. Nick dialing the phone. Nick anything, just as long as I could see him, see him holding the newspaper, cutting a sandwich, combing his hair.

I couldn't stop looking at him, looking at his live fingers, smooth, gentle hands, crinkly eyes, smiling mouth, serious mouth, wrinkles, freckles, all of it frozen forever into my mind. I would be prepared. I would have him locked in there never, never to be let go.

The last of the days passed with me always asking him the same stupid, pointless questions: what can I do for you, get for you . . .

Get me death.

But it's not possible if the mind stays sane. Right? I know the body is wasted and paralyzed, but maybe we can still save the head. After all, the head is really him.

Besides, it's not possible to die if you're still thinking so clearly. You see it coming. Death needs complicity. How will death overtake him when his mind is still so alert?

Sleep.

At the low time in the body's clock — four o'clock in the

morning — alone and unprotected in a hospital room, it slips in. On a weekday. A Tuesday. No one is ever watching on a Tuesday.

The sound of my scream when they told me he died is still trapped in my mind and the image of myself stamped on my brain as I ran to his closet, pulled out his old leather jacket, and buried my face in its lining. And then, with all the power in my lungs, inhaled, pulling for the last time the live scent of his body into my mind.

❋

I weep with tears rolling down my cheeks and my breath coming in small, fast, swallowed gasps. Very quietly. When people are watching.

But alone, I sob. I keen. My heart breaks with great wrenching sounds, deep, hard, crying moans that retch up from my stomach and lungs and tear at my throat, like laughs gone wild, and at a pace that uses every breath and keeps me gasping for more.

I sound to myself like a child but louder and stronger because I can build on that freedom that a child has to cry. I can make my whole body sob, though for that you need room to jump and leap and pound. To tear at your hair, at your clothes, at anything.

I find the middle of a double bed the perfect place.

I scream my heart out. And still there is no relief.

❋

I started this memory deep in the safe time, but as you can see, the safe time was already on the lip of the nightmare.

Maybe the safe time was only an illusion, like this mist that has erased the road below me and is already licking at the first level of grass at the beginning of my property. If it's going to wipe me out as it has the road and everything below it, it's not going to find me here, in this alien land.

I'll be back there, back on those walks together, the ones that started at our apartment in the Village and went all the way up to the Fifties along Eleventh Avenue. Few people ever take that walk, understandable since at first glance there seems little to see. Certainly none of the important landscapes of New York are on Eleventh Avenue. But there are lots of nice traces of the ordinary history of the city. Remains of an aborted railroad line weave in and around the old buildings between Thirtieth and Fortieth streets.

Nick always seemed to know the history of everything, and each time we passed he'd add on another bit. He said the railroad had been part of the Erie-Lackawanna from New Jersey. The freight cars were ferried across the Hudson and then loaded with goods from the ships that docked on the Manhattan side. Or sometimes those same trains were used for local deliveries to the factories around the area, and the tracks actually wove in and out of the streets and around the buildings.

At places the line was elevated to make it easier to deliver coal. I always meant to ask why they would want to deliver the coal to the roofs when it went in the cellars. Or did it? Or maybe I misunderstood, but it was such a nice story, I didn't really care. All I cared about was that I was with someone I loved and he was telling me stories.

Tell me a story. Once upon a time . . .

Nick had all kinds of obscure but fascinating information about the architecture of the old factory buildings along Eleventh and the intricacies of the metalwork on their facades, and often he could even tell me the histories of their grandeur.

My tastes ran to the more pedestrian; I especially loved an old factory building on Twelfth Avenue with a huge truck as advertisement poised on the roof. Such a wonderful, innocent, foolish idea.

Around Fortieth Street we'd swing over to the abandoned piers on Twelfth Avenue. Sometimes, on an early spring day, we'd take a picnic lunch and a blanket and go out on the old wooden pier at Forty-fourth Street to sunbathe. With just a little imagination you could easily be on an ocean liner just pulling into New York Harbor.

The best part was that all this was happening while the rest of the world was locked in their offices. The only time we were aware of the world was at lunchtime when a few office workers would stroll out to the pier to digest the hot dogs or heros they bought from the carts near the Circle Line.

After lunch we'd walk leisurely over to Central Park, to our strip of grass near Central Park West and Sixty-fifth Street. There was a special bench there that we'd sit on. It was our bench. A part of our history.

Seven weeks after Nick died, I came back to spread his ashes on the ground behind that bench.

I had borrowed my sister's car to drive uptown. It was an unusually warm March day, the air was fragrant with a hint of early spring.

Weeks before, after the memorial service, a friend had put the cardboard box of his ashes into my closet. I hadn't touched it or even looked at it since then. But when I lifted it that day to take it to the car, I was surprised at its weight, but then I had never felt a box with the ashes of a whole person in it.

Were these really his ashes or just a shovel full of someone's, anyone's, remains? It was important to me that it be Nick's. But I had no way of knowing.

I put the box in the car and parked as close to Sixty-fifth and Central Park West as possible. I kept the box in the trunk, out of sight, while I unpacked the outer cardboard around it. Inside was a round metal can about fifteen inches tall; the top was sealed closed. There was a lip all around the top, but you needed a bottle opener to lift it. Of course, I didn't have one in the car.

Luckily there was a Sabrett cart across the street. Surely they would have a bottle opener I could borrow.

I didn't want to bring the canister over to the cart, so I would have to take the opener across the street to the car. Realistically, there's no way you can tell a recent immigrant who has been working his ass off all day long in all kinds of weather, pushing a heavy cart through this dirty, hostile city, that you want to borrow his bottle opener for any reason, no matter how exotic.

In fact, he wouldn't want to lend you any of his hard-won possessions under any conditions. This isn't a small village in Latvia. In New York he knows he'll never see them again. And every penny counts. Buying the opener was the simplest solution. If I gave him three dollars, he would ask me questions; for five he'd just take the money.

With the canister inside the trunk, I still couldn't get the proper leverage to pry up the sides. I had to take it out and put it on the ground next to the car. It turned out that the only receptacle more poorly designed for opening than an ash container is a caviar tin.

I twisted it and bent it up all around but still couldn't release the top. In order to get the right grip, I needed someone to hold the canister on the ground.

Even an ordinary, nonthreatening, fortyish-looking woman is suspect in New York, and the first two people didn't even look at me. The third person was a well-dressed man in his late fifties; he wanted to help me in any way possible, any time, any day.

Normally I would have waited for someone else, but I was desperate to get the can opened. The realistic difficulties were beginning to rob the experience of its sentiment.

"If you'll just hold the bottom here, I'll work on the top," I told him.

"I love to hold bottoms," he said.

He bent down too close to me, his face inches above mine. I didn't look up. I could feel the stiff hairs from his beard brushing against my hair. And the heat of his breath was on my forehead. And his Paco Rabanne was everywhere else.

I attacked the rim furiously, prying up every inch of the edge. By now I was in a sweat, overdressed for the expenditure of such energy, my scarf dripping in my way, cramped, with my legs bent in a squatting position and my backside just inches off the sidewalk.

"I like the way you smell," he said, not referring to my Chanel. Obviously this guy was on a fifteen-minute break between obscene phone calls and I was lucky enough to find him.

But I had to open the top, and besides, I could always use the tool as a weapon.

I wedged the point of the opener under the lip and jammed it down hard; the top flipped up and white ashes flew out, burying the tips of his shoes and spraying his pants. He jumped back, brushing himself furiously. From the look of horror that whipped across his face, I knew he had suddenly realized what was in the can.

I didn't have to convince him to leave; he fled.

I walked into the park. Fortunately no one was sitting on our bench. I had planned to spread his ashes all around it, but that was before I understood the logistics of the situation.

You're not just talking about a handful of cigarette ashes that would take off unseen into the wind. This was at least two pounds of a heavy gray-white matter.

I'd always thought of burial and an open casket as barbaric. Now that seemed calm and civilized compared to the horror of immolation. Burning a human being to death, albeit a dead human being, and then dealing with the remains was true barbarism. And the terrible fact was that this was someone I had loved. I suddenly thought, Maybe I can't do it.

I sat down on the bench to decide. To try to feel something of him, something that might guide me. But besides my own emptiness and loneliness — lonely as a child, that always seemed the loneliest you could get — there was no message from him. What message could there be? Nick was dead. And dead is gone. Wiped off the earth.

Think of it any other way and you're fooling yourself. When they say youth is lost, and you know it's not redeemable, that's only practice for the big loss.

History may hold your little traces for a moment, but to the people around you, the live ones who made up the pieces of your life, the ones who loved you so deeply, it's bullshit, for them it's all gone.

All they have left is the grief.

And a can of ashes.

Nonetheless, I was here to do a job, that's what it was now. And I would do it.

My plans had to be restructured: this was no longer a question of sprinkling, now it was more like littering. The romantic and graceful moment I had pictured would have to be reduced to simple efficacy, I would have to empty the entire contents quickly and discreetly behind the bench when no one was watching.

It no longer had any meaning to me. I'd stopped talking to the ashes.

For at least ten minutes, every time I got into emptying position, someone would come along and I would retreat back to the bench.

Finally a clear moment came, I grabbed the canister and ducked behind the bench. I turned the entire thing over, like a child emptying a sand pail.

I stared at the small ashen pile that I knew was no more than that, but tears began to stream down my cheeks. And all the sadness and hopelessness overcame me, and I wept for my loss. And for his.

From out of nowhere, a gust of wind swooped down and swept into the little pile of ashes, lifting them up into the air and swirling them around like a miniature tornado.

Almost instantly the wind abated, and tiny particles drifted down over me and the bench, covering us both with a fine layer of white dust.

I had to believe it was Nick.

The mist is upon me. I am inside the cloud, and everything is blurred and damp. I'm not afraid. Losing, truly losing, makes life so much less valuable, you become fearless when it comes to more loss.

I wait inside the grayness. I cannot see beyond the edge of my terrace, so thick is the air. Still, I won't be driven inside.

Minutes pass, and then a pinpoint of light pricks the darkness, and I know the world is still there. And I waited it out.

Not quite a triumph, but a good feeling nonetheless.
One of the first.

✻

The dreaded Monday at last is here. Jake is due in this afternoon
at four. I have no new songs for him. Not even a bad attempt. I
feel very uncomfortable about letting him down, but I will free
him to find someone else. There's still time.

But more than the undone work, I dread facing things I'm not
ready to face. The reason I left America was to put distance
between myself and the gaping hole in my life so that I could
have the peace to heal. And then I would come back fortified.
And when I did that I would walk through Central Park, go past
the corner building on Fifth and Sixty-third, sleep alone in my old
bed, and meet once again our old life and the people who were in
it. I'd do all that and not be devastated. When I was fully healed.

Though my life hasn't yet had the forward thrust I want it to, I
feel a certain initial healing has taken place. A light protective
coat has formed over the wound, and I won't bleed at the sight of
Jake. Jake from my old life. My Jake, Nick's Jake.

But is it enough?

Waiting for him at the Nice airport, I realize it may not be.
I'm more nervous than I expected. Additionally, I've never
missed a deadline before; it's an irresponsibility I have very little
patience with. Even when it's my own.

The plane is on time, and in less than ten minutes I see him
coming into the arrivals area. He makes it halfway down the corridor before some kid spots him and the word flies through the
crowd.

The impact of that first sight of my old life hits me with such a
force that I back away, slipping deep into the safety of the knots
of waiting people. I see Jake searching for me, but I stay hidden.
Fans begin to come up to him for autographs. He's starting to
look anxious; where am I to save him?

But I'm not there. I see him spot the safety of a telephone

booth, break away from what is now a small crowd, and head toward it. They follow him.

I watch, surprised at my thumping heart, the heat in my face, my fear and my panic.

At last compassion finds its way into my head, and I step forward and save him. The sight of his gratitude pains me. But I lie and apologize for being late. He hugs me hard, and I feel the warmth of his affection, but my discomfort so numbs me that all I can manage to return is pretended pleasure. Thanks to his annoying fans I don't have to do anything more than smile in his direction as we wait for the luggage.

In the car driving home, I do the tour guide. Since he hasn't been in the south of France for at least ten years, he is interested in all the sights. Either that or just kindness keeps him from asking me any personal questions.

I am able to waste another hour after that showing him around the villa and getting him installed in the guest room. It is nearly six by the time I run out of diversions and have to face him.

I lead him into the living room and sit down on the far corner of the couch. He sits down next to me. It's just like with Glu Gla. I open a bottle of champagne and hand him a glass. Déjà-vu Glu Gla.

Jake takes my hand. "You've been away a long time. We've all missed you. Are you okay?"

"Pretty good. It was a great idea, going away. Really great. Rejuvenating." I sneak my hand back. It's hard to lie and touch at the same time.

"Yeah?"

"Yeah," I say.

Now if he would only go home. But of course he's not going to, and worse than that is the way he looks at me, his head just inches from mine. Waiting for me to get back to being Anna again. But that's not going to happen. Maybe it'll never happen.

"I didn't get the work finished," I say, anxious to change his pity into anger. I can handle anger.

"Well, is there enough for at least one song?"

I shake my head no.

"How much more time do you need?" he asks me. I can see there's no hope for anger.

I tell him that I can't do it. He's going to have to get someone else.

"I can wait," he says.

"No," I tell him.

"Or maybe we can work on it together. I have a sweet melody that's been running through my head. . . ."

"No."

"We'll give it a try tomorrow."

I don't even answer him.

"Anna . . ."

"Leave me alone, Jake," I say, getting up and walking to the window. "Don't be nice, don't be anything. Just leave me alone. I can't do it."

And I begin to cry. Floods of tears course down my cheeks. I'm stunned to be so out of control. I hear my gasping sobs, feel my shoulders shaking, my knees weakening so that I must sit down. I collapse onto the armchair and, burying my face in my hands, weep. And weep.

Through my sobs I hear Jake calling my name. "Anna, Anna, please . . ."

But I can't stop.

I don't want to stop!

That's the revelation. I want to cry. Cry it all out of my body. Wring myself dry of tears and wash out the pain.

But no relief comes, and then the fright of not being able to stop takes over. "Oh, Jake, help me, please!"

Jake bends down in front of my chair and puts his arms around me and hugs me, pulling me in against his chest. "It's okay to cry, Anna," he says. "It's okay."

I feel his warmth and the safety of his arms around me. But still I can't stop. I'm too far outside myself for control.

I've got a right to cry, to cry for all that hideous dying time that tore at my heart and all the dead time since. For all the anger that has distilled into hate for the injustice of it, for Nick and for me. And for Lily.

"I want Nick!" I plead. And then I hear myself say the classic words of childhood: "It isn't fair."

Jake moves me onto the couch and holds me tighter. I feel his own tears dropping on my forehead.

And that's the way we sit, holding each other, until at last the tears stop and the only sound in the silence is the air of our breath moving hypnotically in and out of our bodies. With my head still on his chest, I feel his heartbeat thumping against my cheek. It seems to beat too fast for the slow pace of his breathing. He's warmer than I am, and the odor of the morning soap of his shower is reconstituted to full strength by the sweat of his body. I could stay in his arms until I forget whose arms I'm in.

Neither of us moves, then I feel him kiss me lightly on the top of my head. I hug him in answer, and he draws back to look at my face.

"I'm sorry," I say.

"If only I could help you," he says. "Tell me, what can I do?"

I shrug my shoulders. It's the unanswerable question: What can be done?

"How about coming with me?" he says. "Come on the tour. It's going to be fabulous. We go all over the place. First to England, then Ireland, and then shoot over to Munich and Moscow and a week in Tokyo. Have you ever been to Tokyo?"

"No, but—"

"And then we end up in China. Mainland China. After that we could go off on our own to Thailand and Ankor Wat. Anyplace you want. It's just what you need, Anna. Get you out of this sludge. Can't you see it's no better here than it was at home? You're still drowning. You gotta come with me."

"I can't. I love you for asking me, but I can't leave here. I can't run away again. I'm like General Grant, I'm going to fight it out along these lines if it takes all summer."

"Even he didn't do it alone. Come with me, Anna. I can help you."

"You're the best, Jake. I could put myself in your hands and just forget everything."

"So what's wrong with that? Everybody wants someone to take care of them."

"I can't afford that luxury yet. I still can't face my own life. And I have to do it by myself. No cutting corners."

"You always make things so hard for yourself. What for? What are you proving?"

"I'm proving that I own my own life. Turns out I guess I didn't. Nick did. And now with him gone . . ."

"That's not true. Your work has always been your own."

"Yeah? Then why can't I do it now?"

"You can. You're just giving up too easily."

"Look, Doctor. You weren't there last week. You didn't see me sweat all those hours and nothing came. Nothing. Not even bad stuff."

"Take it easy, Anna. Maybe you're expecting too much, maybe it's too early to be cured."

"It has to be now, because I can't stand the pain anymore."

I see a rush of pity and concern flooding his face, and I know I can't take either one of them. I have to stop him. Before he can speak, I tell him straight out that I'm not going to talk about it anymore.

"Let's go eat," I suggest, and without waiting for a reply tell him about a nice restaurant I found close by, just outside of Cannes. "Want to go there?"

"Sure, if you want," he answers. He knows how to play the game, too. "Do we have to change?"

"No, jeans are fine. We'll go disguised as Americans."

I've turned down his offer of help, and the mood of friendship has been shattered. Dinner is almost awkward.

I am the great destroyer. No one, not even nice Jake, can survive around me.

I know from the size of his suitcase that Jake had been planning to stay a few days, but the next morning I pretend he has to get back to Paris. He doesn't dispute me. He knows I want him to go. I wonder if he knows why.

It's too dangerous to have him here.

I drive him to the airport. We don't talk about business because that would bring up the songs I didn't write. We don't talk about ourselves because that's too uncomfortable. We don't talk about our friends because he doesn't want to tell me good things that might make me feel I'm missing out or bad things that might depress me. That leaves little else. So I give him the tour guide going back to the airport. Same story, only in a different direction.

I pull up in front of the departure entrance.

"The offer's still open," he says. "The tour. . . ."

"Would you like the scenario for that?"

"Sure."

"It's almost four days into the tour and we haven't fucked yet. And that's all we're thinking about. That and Nick."

"Come on, Anna. Why are you doing this to us? It's unfair."

"What, you think we wouldn't fuck?"

"So what if we did? What's wrong with that? Neither of us is dead. Only Nick. Is that too cruel for you to hear?"

"Is this the slap-in-the-face cure?"

"The truth cure."

"I would hate you if I slept with you."

"I wouldn't hate you," he answers softly into my anger, and then shakes his head ever so slightly. "No, I don't think that would be my problem."

Without turning away from me, Jake reaches into the backseat for his suitcase. With his hand on the handle, he waits, still looking at me.

I turn my face from him, and then I hear him get out of the car and close the door.

"Anna," he says, leaning in to the open window, "I can't wait much past the end of the middle of August for the lyrics."

"Get someone else."

"Maybe as late as the twenty-fifth."

"I told you. I can't do it!"

And I just step on the gas and pull away. In my rearview mirror I can see him watching me from the curb. I swing around to the other side of the parking lot and head in the direction of the *autoroute*. In the distance I can still see him still standing there.

Leave me alone. Let me drown.

NEW YORK CITY

It took Nick almost two weeks to make all the arrangements to leave. Despite his misery, as far as the trip went, things kept working out for him. A friend of his father had a son living in France. Normally he would steer clear of that kind of connection, but the young man, Ken was his name, had married a French girl and they were living in a large house in a great location on the Left Bank. And they were willing to rent him a room on the top floor. Who could resist an attic in Paris? God knew it suited his mood. Nick accepted.

He got his ticket at a bargain rate by agreeing to go as a courier for a Wall Street company. Only trouble with that was that he couldn't be absolutely certain what day and what time he would be leaving. He knew it would be around the time of the wedding, which was a Sunday, the thirteenth of September. Unlikely that they would need a courier on a weekend, so the chances were that he would leave before that Friday, the eleventh.

That was good; he didn't want to be here, in the same city, when the wedding happened. He didn't want to be tempted in any way.

For the first few days he leapt to the phone every time it rang. They had to know, his parents, that something was wrong. Of course, they had never known when it was right, so he figured they didn't have any idea of the truth.

Any fool, and they were not fools, could see that he was very disturbed. What disturbed a twenty-seven-year-old man? A woman, of course. Anyone would know that. He always thought of them as insensitive, but this time they proved him wrong; they never asked one question. In fact, they seem to go far out of their way not to ask him anything. That in itself was so peculiar and unusual that he decided it was almost as bad as their prying.

There was nothing he cared about or wanted to do. He went into the newspaper office—he had given Resnick notice—and did his job. By the end of the first week a new editor was hired, and it was just a matter of a few days before Nick would be able to leave. He had to get out of there; it was agony being in the office with the ghost of Anna in every corner and everyone knowing what happened and feeling sorry for him.

The last Thursday night he took the paper to the print shop, Walter found Nick so uncommunicative that he didn't even try to make contact.

After that one night with Anna and Nick, his moment of foolishness had left him depressed. He'd felt so ridiculous, old man playing at newspaperman, that he was thinking of quitting, too.

Nick's last day at the office was the thirtieth of August. After that he had nothing to do but wait for the phone call from the courier company. He could start nothing. Not a magazine or a book. He just sat and waited. Or spent the days walking around the neighborhood, his childhood neighborhood, a place normally filled with memories, now as empty as his heart.

Friday, the eleventh, passed and no word from the company. It looked as though he would be here for the wedding. His misery was complete; and then on Saturday, the twelfth, word came. He would be leaving on the morning of the thirteenth. He had to be at the airport by eight-thirty in the morning, a safe four hours before the wedding.

An eight-thirty flight meant leaving his house by six-thirty. His parents were up to say good-bye. He couldn't stop his mother from making bacon and eggs and fried potatoes. Actually, he had eaten so poorly in the last weeks that there was an accumulated hunger and he devoured everything on the plate. His mother was pleased and ready to make more. But he declined. Then his father, awkward and uncomfortable at the emotion, tried to give him some going-away advice but ended up just giving him a hundred-dollar bill and an address book he had gotten from some insurance company.

That morning, his suitcase jammed with mostly winter clothes, carrying his portable typewriter and wearing his old school back-pack, Nick kissed them good-bye, his father, too. And left the house.

It was a brilliant, sunny September morning, still dewy and early morning fresh, with only a hint of the heavy heat that would descend later to suffocate the day.

He took the subway to the bus terminal and the bus to the air-port. He felt unhappy, rejected, and nervous. He could have been going to Columbus, Ohio, for all the excitement that he felt about leaving the country, going to Europe for the first time. An aching sadness overwhelmed all possible pleasure.

When he presented his ticket at the airport, they told him that his flight had been postponed; at the moment it was rescheduled for one-thirty that afternoon.

"Shall I reschedule you?" the man behind the desk asked, his hands poised on the computer, ready to enter the new flight.

When he looked up, Nick was gone.

Gottawin!

It was a sign. It had to be. Like the last time, with the horse.

Go get her! Stop that wedding!

Nick ran through the terminal, his luggage bumping along with him. Outside, he grabbed the first cab he saw, threw his gear into the backseat, and jumped in.

"The Pierre Hotel," he said, and then realized that it was only eight-thirty in the morning and the wedding wasn't until noon. No problem, he'd wait across the street in the park. That would give him time to make his plans.

All the way into the city he tried to think of some reason why she should run off with him.

Love. It had to be.

Jesus, that sounded trite.

Love.

Was it enough for him to say he loved her? He'd already done that, and she'd still gone off with Steven. No, he would have to show her. Make her feel his love and hers. How?

He would have to see her alone. Count on the heightened

drama of the eleventh hour. It was all he had to give her, this one last chance. But it could be the right moment.

✻

His taxi pulled up at the hotel and he realized he had another problem—his luggage. He couldn't leave it in the park, and he would be too noticeable lugging it around with him. Maybe if he told them he was with the wedding, they would hold it for him at the reception.

He was lucky, there was only one young man, a bellboy, at the reception desk.

"Excuse me, sir," Nick said, all charm and manners, almost tipping the hat that wasn't there, "I'd like to leave this here during the ceremony for the Green wedding."

Before the bellboy could answer, another man, an assistant manager by his name tag, appeared. "You're a guest?" he asked.

One look at his face and Nick knew he had to abandon the guest story. "Oh, no"—Nick smiled—"no, I'm just the hairdresser."

"Very well," he said, "bring it over to the bellman's counter and they'll hold it for you."

First hurdle passed. Now Nick decided to forget the park and wait in the lobby, but discreetly out of sight. Though Anna's family had never seen him, Barbara, of course, knew him, and she was the maid of honor.

That was how he would get in to see Anna. Barbara would help him. She would certainly be arriving early since she was part of the wedding party. The trick was to grab her when she came in.

He waited the hour from ten to eleven on a seat behind a pillar, out of sight, but with a good view of the revolving doors. Finally, at about twenty minutes before eleven, he saw Anna and what had to be her mother and Barbara alighting from the limousine. His heart did what all lovers' hearts did when seeing their beloved. It jumped up into the top of his chest, pulling with it a draft of cold air that tingled through his body, raising fields of goose bumps along its path.

Nick watched as the three waited for the elevator. But just as it arrived, a woman came up to Anna's mother. From the enthusiasm of the greeting, it was someone she hadn't seen in a long time. There were introductions all around and lots of pulling back to get a better look at each other, and then delighted oohing and ahhing about Anna from the other woman.

The girls, Anna and Barbara, went up in the elevator, and Mrs. Green and her long-lost friend walked over toward Nick. They sat down on the love seat just the other side of his chair. He couldn't help but listen.

"It's so good to see you, Laura. I think of you so often. Anita said you were in Morocco," Mrs. Green said.

The other woman took her hands affectionately. "I was. For almost twenty years. My God, Netta, is it that long since we've seen each other? You look beautiful. And Anna looks just like you did at that age."

"The last time you saw her, she was, what, four years old? Remember those wonderful years? All of us together. How did we let the distance separate us?" From the looks in their eyes, they were indeed wonderful years, filled with true affection.

"And now Anna's getting married. You must be so happy." There was a wistful sound to her voice.

"Relieved. Up until last week we didn't think she was going to go through with it."

"Well, if she's that unsure, why is it happening?"

"Because now she's certain this is what she wants. It took her a while, though, but Steven, that's the groom, was magnificent through the whole awful business. A marvelous boy. But that's the difference — he's not a boy, he's a man. But enough about my problems, tell me, what's been happening with you?"

"It's all history, done and gone. And there'll be plenty of time to tell you. Unfortunately, I'm here to stay."

Netta pressed her friend, but Laura only wanted to hear about Anna.

"Well," Netta said, actually happy to get it off her chest, to tell her old, dear friend, even at this late date, only hours before the wedding, how difficult it had been.

"There was someone else."

"Oh, my. Somehow you don't think of that happening to your children, do you?"

Though Nick could hear every word, he moved still closer, possessed by both fear and an uncontrollable curiosity.

Mrs. Green continued. "Of course, she didn't think we knew. Don't you love how they think we're so blind and stupid? And we go along with the fraud and watch it all silently. I wanted to say something, but David convinced me that would just drive her into his arms — the other man, I mean."

"Who was he?"

"A nobody."

Had a sledgehammer crashed onto his head, splitting his brain, Nick could not have been more devastated. But he listened, paralyzed, unable to move, though he knew by staying there, he might be witnessing his own destruction.

"I'm not talking about money, though I'm sure he has none," Mrs. Green went on, "but this kid was a nothing. Someone she worked with."

"You met him?"

"Are you kidding? She was smart enough to keep him well hidden. No, a friend told us."

Barbara! But he always thought Barbara liked him. Maybe even more than that. And she was smart; that first day, she had come to his aid. If Barbara, who liked him, said those things, they had to be true.

Mrs. Green continued, "He said —"

At least it wasn't Barbara. Maybe it was some friend of Steven's, someone who would be prejudiced. That would be more acceptable. It was a question of loyalty. It didn't have to be true. Certainly this wasn't.

"— he was this skinny kid, sweet, but a sort of pathetic young man. Nothing to look at. Not that that's so important, but he was quite ordinary and unsophisticated. No comparison to Steven."

"Then what was the attraction?"

"I don't know. Maybe a little forbidden fruit, or maybe she just felt sorry for him. Anna was always like that. You know, sweet with misfits, cripples, lost puppies, that sort of thing."

Whoever had told her had nailed him. That's exactly what he was—a misfit—he'd always known it. Anna had never loved him, she'd only pitied him.

What was the point of his trying to talk to her now?

Nick had heard enough.

He picked up his suitcase at the desk, strapped on the backpack, and walked out of the hotel.

Defeated.

A nothing.

In the sumptuous mauve-colored suite reserved for the bride, Anna sat on the edge of a chair, still in her jeans. Yards and yards of her bouffant, white satin-and-lace gown covered the king-size bed.

"Maybe you should start getting ready," Barbara said, gently trying to prod her dear friend out of her daze.

"What do you think?" Anna asked her.

Barbara knew exactly what Anna was asking. Still, she felt as a friend, as a maid of honor, she shouldn't encourage this last minute vacillation. "Forget it," she said.

"No, tell me, do you think he'll show up?"

"Here? And what, run down the aisle and swoop you off your feet? Hey, I think I saw that movie." There was an edge to Barbara's voice, an impatience not normally there. Certainly not when it came to her best friend, her idol, Anna. All at once, Barbara, the deprived, was tired of Anna's ingratitude. Here she was, spoiled, beautiful Anna, with a husband-to-be in two hours and a lover to save her from him.

She didn't deserve Nick.

"Don't be angry with me, please," Anna said, and there was so much sadness in her voice that Barbara melted. And loved her again.

"Just answer me this: Why are you here, marrying Steven, if you still have doubts? I don't understand."

"It was my decision. And I have to trust it."

"Okay, then that's it."

"Right."

"Should we start getting dressed?"

"But. . . ."

"Okay, Anna, just suppose Nick was down in the lobby."

"Impossible. Adam told me he stopped by the paper Saturday. He said he was leaving for France today."

"But what if he didn't? What if he changed his mind? . . ."

"And he came here and asked me to run off with him?"

"Yeah."

Anna got up and walked over to the bed. She ran her fingers lightly across the satin gown. It was a beautiful dress, made especially for her. She loved wearing it, loved the way the silky tightness caught the lines of her body when the dozens of little white pearl buttons were fastened down her back. It made her waist look as if she could reach her fingers around it.

And then there was the veil, with its endless clouds of white voile bursting from a pearl-and-rhinestone crown. It all held a magic, a transformation waiting to happen, waiting from early little girlhood. A transformation that was pure and good. And sewn together with irresistible fantasy.

"If Nick came here and asked me to go with him to Europe today . . ."

Yards and yards of fantasy.

". . . I would go with him."

"Is this a joke?" Barbara was truly horrified. "Because it stinks. It's not funny. You have to stop this, now. Or pack your things and go. Just get out of here."

"I can't do it alone."

"I'll help you. You tell Steven and I'll explain to your parents."

"I need Nick here. I'm afraid."

Barbara looked at Anna and for the first time was aware of an unpleasant weakness in this woman she'd adored for so many years. Anna looked more than vulnerable, she looked like a broken doll, small, with her thin arms jutting from the white T-shirt, her pale face drawn and lifeless. And for the first time, quite unappealing.

"What are you so afraid of?" Barbara asked.

"My lack of courage—the heart of every hero, the most exquisite human trait anyone can have. The only one you can't fake. I've yearned for it all my life. But I don't have it."

"That's not true. I've seen you brave. That time that guy was hitting the woman in the street."

"I can be strong for someone else, but not for myself. For myself, I'm a coward."

"I never knew that."

"I never let you see. How could I? You admired me too much."

"But all these years, Anna, I would have seen it."

"No, you wouldn't have. No more than I see inside your soul. What is the personal worst of Barbara Glassman? I'll probably never know. Most people can get through their entire lives without ever being tested."

"Come on, Anna, everyone has things about themselves that are disappointing. But you're not condemned to live with them forever."

"Yes, you are. When it's that real shame, the inside kind that turns your stomach when you come up against it. That's the kind you never get rid of. Best thing you can do is wind your way around it, circumlocute. But this time I couldn't. It was a head-on crash."

"So, you're going to go through with this? You're going to marry Steven because you haven't got the courage not to?" There was no way for Barbara not to show her disapproval, her superiority.

But, strangely, Barbara's response didn't touch Anna, who felt suddenly much older than her dear friend, and wiser. "Wait until you find yours."

"My what?" asked Barbara.

"Your shame," Anna answered, and got up, took her under-clothes out of her small suitcase, and went into the adjoining room to dress for her wedding.

Barbara watched her disappear into the other room. She stared at the closed door. She didn't have to take that, didn't have to be a maid of honor for someone she didn't respect. And how could you respect such a coward? Someone who was ready to screw up innocent lives just because she didn't have the courage to do the right thing? Barbara should just walk out.

But if she did, that would be the end of her life with Anna. She would never see her again. She would lose her dearest friend in the world. In truth — and this was the moment for truth — Barbara recognized that what she'd always felt for Anna was embarrassingly close to worship; the very thought made her squirm.

Way deep inside her desires, Barbara would pretend Anna's soul was hers, and even deeper still, in her fantasy of those same desires, she would envision herself in that exquisite outside shell as well.

Was that the shame Anna spoke of?

Perhaps, if it were carried one step farther. If, after her insidious devouring of Anna, she could admit to an appetite for one more morsel — Nick.

Now her stomach turned.

Ever since that first day when Nick came into the office, more like whirled in, Barbara's heart had leapt at the sight of him. Actually, something about his picture, the one she had seen earlier that week in her uncle's office, had touched her. She just liked his face. And when that face came to life in the office that day, her first thought was: He could be mine. Were he a Steven sort, she'd have immediately stepped back for Anna. But if the world were truly divided into classes and types, Nick would have fallen squarely within Barbara's domain. No reason it couldn't have happened.

But it hadn't. And the more she'd yearned for it, the guiltier she felt. Always guilt: the dull ache of deceiving her dearest friend. It made no difference that it was only in her mind. And even as she'd watched with painful longing and envy the passion that had exploded between them, the disgust she'd felt within herself was the queasiness of guilt. The shame of betrayal: loving your best friend's lover.

Until now. Now another feeling was rushing in with a raw force that wiped out everything in its path.

Just at that moment of self-revelation, Anna came back into the room.

"You were right," Barbara told her.

Anna smiled. "Hallelujah. About what?"

"About your soul. The thing inside it that scares you so much."

"You're not a coward," Anna said. "As a professional, I can tell one a mile away." But then she saw that Barbara was truly disturbed. "I'm sorry I've upset you," she said. " I shouldn't have said those things. You're my best friend in the whole world, and if you have any flaws, they're not in my league. I didn't mean that about your shame."

"But you were right. There are things I've kept from you."

"Well, we all have private —"

"But I want to tell you now," Barbara interrupted her.

Anna waited, ready to respond with the understanding and comfort only a friend could give when a wounded soul was about to be bared.

"I don't blame you for Nick," Barbara said.

Anna was taken aback. She had been prepared for an inner revelation, a weakness of the spirit. But Barbara was going in a completely different direction. And instead of the pain she expected to see on her face, Anna saw only anger.

"He was attracted to you immediately." Now the anger was in Barbara's voice as well. "But you weren't interested. You knew I was because I told you. But you paid no attention. You didn't give a damn, dear friend and all. All you cared about was his reaction to you. I could see it in your face when I asked you to say something to him. You were looking right past me. Already tasting your new admirer."

"That's cruel and unfair. I didn't make him fall in love with me."

"Remember I asked you to put in a word for me? Way in the beginning. Did you?"

It was true she hadn't, but how could she explain to Barbara that the moment had come and she'd let it pass because . . .

"Well," Barbara asked, "did you?"

Because . . . Why? Anna remembered that instant and the tiny silence as Nick waited. Obviously he saw she had something more to say. But then she didn't. Was that the beginning? Was it some primordial attraction buried under consciousness that had held her tongue?

"You don't have to tell me," Barbara said. "I know you didn't."

"I'm sorry," said Anna, "I should have —"

"Forget it, it was just something I wanted to know, but it's only part of the reason I'm so goddamn angry at you."

"I don't know if I want to hear this."

But Barbara went on, "Nick is a man I could have loved."

"Hey, look, he didn't love you. That's not my fault." Anna's own anger was beginning to rise.

"Right. Maybe he never would have loved me, and maybe I love him right now. It doesn't matter. What matters is that this minute I find myself loathing you for being so caught up in your own ego that you can't even see what you're doing."

"I don't mean to hurt anyone. . . ."

"But you are. At least take that responsibility. You've got to know you're destroying Nick, and what kind of a chance does Steven have? And as for me, best friend and all that shit, you're making me watch the man I loved being tossed away, too late for me to even have a chance! Why did you have to wait so long?"

"Oh, Barbara, I didn't know. . . ."

"I wanted him!" There was more than demand in her voice, there was an ache of longing. "I did!" she whispered.

Anna was stunned by the power of her friend's anguish. And by the challenge. And then by her own response, which was so instant and so shocking that it seemed to rip from somewhere in the depths of truth.

"No!" she shouted back, her voice ringing with passion. "You can't! I love him!" And the gauntlet was thrown. "He's all I want in the world."

All I want in the world. The words echoed in the silence.

There was nothing more for Barbara to say. And then Anna said softly, "And I'll never, ever, lose him again."

They looked at each other, these two people connected by so much time and so much love, and they each reached out and came into each other's arms and wept.

"Go find him," Barbara said.

"But, the wedding—"

"I'll explain."

But Anna shook her head no. "It's too late. His plane was leaving this morning."

"Maybe he didn't get on it. Or maybe it was delayed. What airline?" Barbara was already grabbing for the phone.

"Air France."

"To where?" Barbara asked, dialing information.

"Paris, I think, or maybe Nice."

Barbara got the number from information and dialed. She smiled at Anna as she waited for them to pick up. When they did she found out that there were two morning planes, one for Nice and one for Paris. The one for Nice left on time, but the one for Paris was actually delayed.

"You won't believe this, but if he was going to Paris, his plane hasn't left yet. It's scheduled to leave in an hour and thirty minutes. That's enough time. You could stop him."

"If he was going to Nice?"

"Then he's left."

Anna's face lit up. He *had* to be going to Paris.

She grabbed her jeans and pulled them on. And then her sneakers, and her purse, and she was ready to race out the door.

"Any money. Have you got any money?" Anna had suddenly realized that she had no more than thirty dollars in her purse. Barbara reached into her jeans and pulled out two twenties and gave them to her.

Anna started for the door, stopped and turned around, and

wrapped her arms tightly around Barbara. "Thank-you for everything in the world. I love you," she said, and opened the door.

And there was Steven.

Anna had only seconds to spare if she was going to catch Nick and save the rest of her life.

"What's up? Where are you going?" he said, putting his arms out to stop her.

She took Steven's hands in hers and said, "I'm sorry, deeply sorry, for all the hurt I'm causing you. But I leave you with the best gift a man could get."

"What are you talking about?"

"You're not going to have to marry the wrong woman."

"Anna!"

But she was already out of his grasp and running down the hall. She called back to him, "Forgive me, Steven. Good luck and all! I really was wrong for you! And for me!"

And she was gone.

Steven turned to Barbara, hardly the most sympathetic friend he could have found. A flash of pain twisted his face for barely an instant before full-out anger took over.

"What the fuck was that all about?" he demanded, striding into the room and slamming the door behind him.

FRANCE

L ily calls from Japan. And we both lie brilliantly to each other. We're fabulous, we say, everything is wonderful; of course, we miss him horribly, but we're managing marvelously. It was a sensational idea going to Japan, a magnificent idea going to France, and then when we both run out of superlatives, we say we love each other, miss each other, and not to worry. Then we hang up and truth comes, and without the courage to face it, we cry. Or at least I do.

I've always had a problem with courage; I'm in love with it, but I don't have it. Once, long ago, I think I came near feeling it. But that was so long ago, and when I look back now, perhaps it wasn't so brave. Perhaps I was just young. Everything is so dramatized, so exaggerated when you're young. It all seems a matter of life and death, until you see what death really looks like.

And in the face of that recognition, I know I have failed.

People do, you know. My husband did. He failed to defeat those ravenous, vicious cells that finally consumed him; he failed to keep his promise to stay with me; he left our daughter; he abandoned his friends, who needed him.

He was washed off the earth. That insignificant little splash in the water that his presence made for not nearly enough time has been flooded over by more water, endless water, and the ocean goes on. Without a trace of him.

All we have left are the ripples of grief that mark our thoughts of him. The pleasure has left with the sea.

I'm ready to give up, to retreat into the core of my misery in a place where every excuse in the world is on my side: I want to go home.

It's time to abandon this mistake, but I'm going to do it my way—with anger and cowardice. I won't tell them, my enemies, a thing. I'll just pack up my meager pile of possessions and slip off.

Cowards are always accused of not confronting their fears. Well, there's no point in being a coward if you don't take advantage of that privilege. However, this time I benefit doubly since my lack of courage will also supply me the perfect weapon—silence.

I won't say a word. They'll be stunned. They'll wonder what I'm doing, what I'm thinking. Will I come back? Are they safe in their jobs? Did I leave in weakness or in strength? Have I a plan of revenge?

Once I'm gone they'll watch for me every day, every minute. The expectation will drain them of their confidence. Make them uneasy. Always looking over their shoulders. They'll ask each other questions about me, but they'll have no answers. In my absence, I will become a grand and powerful presence.

The cost for all this? The promise of a new life, delivery from pain, and salvation.

Put it on my account.

The phone momentarily shakes me out of my fantasy of triumph. It's Gena, the friend I didn't quite make and then lost. Perhaps, though, she's seen it in her heart to forgive my gaucheness, or maybe she's just as lonely as I am.

Whatever the reason, it couldn't have come at a better time. I'm delighted. She's invited me to lunch and swimming at her villa tomorrow.

Her house is on Cap d'Antibes and from the description must be near Plage Garoupe, the beach where Scott Fitzgerald and the Murphys had their villas in the twenties. I should have no trouble finding it since I've toured that area a number of times already.

The next morning I pick up some handmade chocolates at my local *pâtisserie* and start out my usual hour early. Gena's villa is on the same road as the Fitzgerald house, and when I find it, it's lovely.

And far more opulent that I expected. Gena seemed so naive

and dependent that I had naturally assumed her ex-husband would have taken terrible advantage of her. She had put everything, all decisions, in his hands. I guess I hadn't taken into account his sense of guilt. From the look of the villa, it must have been highly developed. Obviously she had made the right move.

It has been more than two weeks since I have seen Gena, and I'm surprised to see how well she looks. The sadness of our last dinner is completely gone, and there stands a contented-looking matron. She is also at least five pounds heavier than when I last saw her. Her arms are browned and slightly plump.

She's dressed less casually than I in a silk flowered dress belted softly at the waist, nipping her lightly between her bosom and hips where the rest of the extra weight seems to have gathered. The roundness is flattering. Her white-yellow hair has the freshly shampooed, not-quite-dried curls of a summer day. An aura of light perfume surrounds her.

And she's smiling. For me. My gaffe of the other week isn't even a memory. I'm delighted, and we kiss in the French manner and I can feel from her grasp of my hands that she is truly happy to see me.

I, of course, am overjoyed. Have I been too hasty in my decision to abandon everything?

On this spectacular summer day, standing here in this warm and welcoming atmosphere on this unique spit of land that I adore from my villa daily, failure seems an impossible concept. How could I have allowed myself to be bullied into leaving all this perfection?

Well, then, maybe I won't.

"I'm so happy that you were free to come today," says my new best friend, Gena, as she takes my hand and leads me through the house and out to the back, where there are masses of impatiens in a mélange of colors ringing a red-tiled patio and, beyond the flowers, the sea.

Gena keeps turning back to smile at me; her pleasure at my company is palpable.

She doesn't seem drunk. Or crazy. Or on drugs. You see how

rejection has conditioned me. I force myself to simple acceptance; after all, I rationalize, in New York people liked me, maybe
my appeal is catching up.

The table is set with great care — for three. Perhaps that's the
answer to her new happiness: she's met someone. And he's coming to lunch. Maybe he's already here, upstairs getting dressed.

I know I'm right; it's too much fussing for just a casual lunch.
Obviously the Rosenthal china with its delicate pink-and-green
floral print is better than just patio plates. Alongside the china
the matching napkins are caught up in rings of ceramic flowers,
and tall green wine and water glasses from Biot, a town close by
where the glass is still blown in the old-fashioned manner, glass
by glass, with the bubbles trapped inside, stand guard over each
setting.

"Are those roses from your garden?" I ask, bending down to
smell the giant yellow blossoms floating in a large round bowl in
the center of the table.

"Yes. I had to clip them short like that to avoid taking the
buds."

"I think it looks beautiful this way. It's different." I tell her
quite sincerely that everything is lovely, and I'm delighted to be
here. And then I ask her who the third person is.

"A new friend," she says, "someone I met about two weeks
ago."

Aha! I knew it. She's met a man. That explains the change.
There she was, crushed, defeated, mangled beyond repair by the
rejection of her husband, and then a new man deigns to come
into her life, and voilà! she's reborn.

An argument that would seem to prove the terrible dependency
we have on men. Perhaps my crippled existence, too, can be
cured only by the arrival of a man. In that case I have been
searching in the wrong corners. Wasting time looking for courage
and spirit and strength, when I should have been looking for a
man, someone whose back I can climb on, whose neck I can wrap
my arms around and cling to, someone who will carry my life.

Beautiful. A century of progress destroyed in one revelation.

And as we speak I hear him coming down the stairs. Exactly as I thought; he was upstairs getting dressed. Gena smiles with pleasure at the sound of his footsteps. We both wait expectantly.

And then . . . she arrives. She? I'm delighted and relieved to be wrong. No less than the entire women's movement was at stake. And my own future, too.

Gena's new friend, Annette, turns out to be German, young, perhaps late twenties, and good-looking in a healthy, sportive way. Her blond hair is cut simply, straight to the shoulders with bangs. She's wearing longish khaki shorts that come to the knees and a T-shirt that says Michigan State. She's very warm and friendly. I like her immediately. And I sense the feeling is reciprocated.

"Is that your school?" I ask.

She laughs and says, "No. You can buy these all over Europe. They've got all the American colleges."

"This is Annette's first trip outside of Germany," Gena says.

"But your English is so good. And it sounds so American," I say.

"I worked for an American family stationed in Munich. I was with them for four years when I was a student."

Gena hands us each a glass of champagne.

One of the first things I learned after arriving in France was how to open champagne. It's something women don't normally do if there is a man around: No, no, let me do that. At forty years old I had never once opened a champagne bottle by myself. But if you live alone, and you like champagne, you'd better learn.

Naturally the first time I tried, I was nervous. I expected the cork to shoot out like a bullet, taking out at least a lamp, a piece of the ceiling, or an eye. I took a strong grip on the bottle, pointed it safely toward the open window, and twisted it slowly until I felt the cork, nudged by the gases trapped inside, begin to move by itself. When it slid to the end of the neck, it burst free. No foam all over the floor, no frantic race to get to the glass, nothing but a nice, solid pop and a little smoke. And the whole masculine champagne mystery was debunked in an instant.

One last thing I did learn about the art. With the cheap stuff the cork will go through the roof.

The afternoon meanders pleasantly with lots of champagne and no movement toward the table. I'm not a bit hungry as long as Gena keeps pouring. Between the wine and the beauty around me, I feel an unexpected pleasure and tranquility. Momentary or not, it's very good.

"Lovely, just lovely," I say.

"Isn't it?" she says, smiling in agreement. "In the beginning I used to come here because it was France. But now I come here because I love it."

I want that to happen to me. If I can only wait it out.

"How did you two meet?" I want to know more about such obvious success.

"At a *vernissage* for Nall, an American painter," Annette says. "I saw Gena as soon as she walked in. I said to myself, That's for me."

"I know what you mean." I tell her how sometimes you meet people with whom you have instant electricity. "That's the way I felt about Gena, too. I just knew we'd be friends."

I don't think that's exactly true, but the champagne has warmed my feelings enough so that I feel maybe it was — a little. Besides, now we are going to be friends, and Annette, too.

It turns out that Annette is not running away from anything. She's just down here looking around a little. She thinks she might like to try photography. Certainly the south of France is a wonderful place to look for your future.

We're all feeling a nice comfort with each other.

"Would you like to take a swim?" Gena asks me. "I can lend you a suit, if you like."

"Great idea," Annette says, and gets up, taking the champagne from my hand. "But why suits? Nobody's looking."

Gena giggles. "I don't think so. . . ."

"Come on." Annette grabs Gena's hands to pull her up from the chaise *longue*. "Are you still shy?"

I'm feeling wonderfully giddy. "I'll borrow that suit, Gena," I say. Still, even with all the champagne, I'm not about to skinny-dip in the bright, unsparing sunlight.

"You can do what you want, Annette, but we're wearing suits," Gena says, and beckons me to follow her to the small poolhouse.

"Don't forget your champagne." Annette hands me my glass, then changes her mind, "I'll carry it for you."

We three go to the poolhouse, where Gena has a suit for me, at least the bottom of one.

"You can hang your things in the closet or on one of those hooks," Gena says, pointing to the brass hooks behind the door with one hand and unbuttoning her dress with the other. Once released, the silk dress slides down her body to the floor. She steps out of it, scoops it up, and drops it onto a chair.

Despite the extra fullness, Gena's body is smooth and soft looking without the dreaded cellulite. On the other hand, once Annette takes off her T-shirt, her body is all muscle, like a young boy's.

Before Gena can reach around and unhook her bra, Annette is there. She unfastens it and reaches around to cup her breasts from behind.

Did I see that? Or have I had more champagne than I realized?

Or is it just as I suspected — Gena has found a man. The only catch is, it's a woman.

But it doesn't matter; in the end the result is the same. No more drifting alone in a sea of unhappiness; Gena has found someone to moor her life to, to strangle with her weight, the way she did the husband who carried her all those years.

I don't want to believe that I must hook up to someone else's life, man or woman, to make mine complete or even just bearable.

Suddenly I'm aware of every glance, every action and reaction, between them. It's a different Gena; this one is flirty, dangling adorable smiles and promises with the lift of her shoulder or the turn of her body as she discards her clothes in a sexy striptease. She does it just the way she would for a man. And Annette responds with the same heat as any horny male, compounded with little attacks of touching and tickling.

"Stop it, Annette!" Gena laughingly pushes her away. Of course, Annette is back in an instant, this time pulling at Gena's panties, playing at taking them down.

"Come on, you don't need those. Look at me," she says, dropping her khaki shorts to reveal her slim naked hips and a full, dark triangle of pubic hair.

Thanks to the many glasses of champagne, I watch them shamelessly, as if I were invisible.

Now they both turn to me.

"No," I say, "but thanks anyway." And they both laugh; neither is offended.

"Perhaps a little more champagne?" Annette says, filling my glass.

"I don't think that will change anything, but I'll take it."

"Come on," Gena says, "let's have a swim before lunch."

A little inlet borders the property. Piles of large rocks jut out of the water here and there, but there is no beach, and the drop is immediate and deep.

The sea off Cap d'Antibes is usually calm and always exquisitely clear. You can see the rocky bottom busy with tiny colored fish that scoot in and out of the rocks and then disappear in the swaying sea grass. Occasionally a school of larger or rascasse daurade will sweep past. Some of the nicest swimming on the coast is right here in Gena's backyard.

I walk down the metal steps into the water while Annette and Gena take shallow dives off the rocks. The water is fresh, instantly cooling the heat of the accumulated sun and champagne in my body but leaving enough of the alcohol lightness in my brain to allow me to pursue what feels like the most graceful underwater ballet outside of Hollywood.

I swim just inches above the bottom, pushing myself past the rocks and into the tall sea grass. I stir up sand and bubbles and small fish that flee in all directions, darting through the lines of sunlight that shoot in sparkles down through the water.

When I come up for air I see Annette and Gena holding on to a rock and talking. They look like lovers.

The thought makes me giggle. Just then a small wave breaks against a rock in front of me and ripples of water hit my face, spilling into my open mouth just as I inhale. Little droplets spray into my throat, catching my breath. I gasp for air, but all that comes is a cough. And the cough makes more coughs, clogging my throat and choking me. I can't swim and cough. In panic I reach out for a rock to hold onto, but none is within my reach.

I see Gena and Annette not twenty feet from me, but I can't call to them. I can't make any sound but the gasping cough of choking. I beat the water to attract their attention. But they don't turn.

I fling my arms furiously against the water, grabbing on to the nothing of it, retching and choking and gagging on more water that splashes up into my face. I can't even see them anymore. I'm sinking into the water. I'm drowning! I'm dying! How stupid! Help me!

And then I feel hands grab me and push me up out of the water. I gasp for air, but I'm too choked to get it. I fall back down and an arm clamps under my chin, and I feel myself being dragged along, then anchored up against a big rock. I wrap my arms around it, but the slippery seaweed and the weight of my body pulls me down. This time the hands behind me grasp my rib cage and push me up again. I dig my fingers into the slime of the seaweed and drag myself higher up on the rock, but I can't stop retching. I feel each cough is going to tear the lungs from my body.

And then the first small wisp of air breaks through, and a surge of water vomits from my throat. Enough of a path is cleared, and more air comes through. My throat is raw, my eyes are stinging with salt water and tears of panic, but I'm saved.

And when I turn around to see, it is Annette who has saved me. Gena is on my other side, but it was Annette's hands and strong arms that pulled me to the rock.

I press my head against the rock, my face deep in the seaweed, still coughing, but breathing and too exhausted to move.

"Are you okay?" Annette asks. I can hear the concern in her

voice. I really almost drowned. "Do you want to try to get back to shore? I can help you."

"Let her rest for a minute," Gena says. "Just stay where you are," she says to me, "we'll be right here."

I shake my head yes, but I haven't the energy to turn to look at them. With my forehead still pressed against the rock, I stare into the seaweed, grateful to be breathing in the strong fresh scent of fish and salt water and life.

Finally my normal breath begins to return and I feel strong enough to try the swim back to shore, a swim of no more than twenty feet. I might have drowned for that simple twenty feet, the same twenty feet from land in one direction and from Gena and Annette in the other. I'd always wondered how it was possible for people to drown a few steps from shore. Now I know firsthand.

Back on land all I want to do is collapse onto a lounge chair. I lie flat on my back with my arm across my face and the sun hot and welcome on my body. Someone sits down next to me, her shadow taking my face out of the glare. I move my arm away from my eyes and see it is Annette.

"Thank-you. You saved my life. I'm not exaggerating. I was drowning."

She smiles down at me. "It was crazy," she says, "so fast. I was just talking to Gena when I happened to look over at you, and I could see right away something was wrong, so I just took off. By the time I got to you, you were starting to go down."

"I was. I really was. I can't tell you how grateful—"

"It's okay, I know," she says, pushing back the wet hair sticking to my forehead, at the same time pulling off a piece of stray seaweed and smiling. "Want to keep this as a memento?"

I close my eyes and feel her hand soothing my forehead. It's soft and cool. For the first time I'm aware of a trembling throughout my body. It's as if the protection of the adrenaline is wearing off, leaving my body emptied and shaking from the shock. And vulnerable to gentle kindness.

Annette must feel me shaking because she puts her hands on either side of my face and asks if I'm all right. I open my eyes and smile and tell her, yes, I'm just feeling the aftermath.

Gena covers me with a towel and tucks it in tight around me. I'm still shivering.

"How about a cup of hot tea?" she asks.

"She could probably use some brandy. I'll get it."

Annette starts toward the house, but I stop her. "I'm okay. I just need a little sun to warm me up."

Gena tries to adjust an umbrella that is shading my body, but it has a cement base that makes moving it difficult. Annette gets up to help her, and together they roll it away from my chair.

They leave me to warm in the sun while they start arranging the much delayed lunch. I watch them from the distance, watch the way they work together, responding to each other. Their intimacy is so obvious, and so touching.

My first impression of Annette was a flip young woman who might even be an opportunist, but now I look upon her with respect.

I watch them being together, and I can tell they've forgotten about me. It's okay, that's the way lovers are supposed to be — insulated, safe in their own perfect world. The way I used to be with Nick. Watching their comfort and ease of touch makes me feel empty. I almost lost my life, but even now I don't really have it. At least not so I can feel it.

Gena laughs at something Annette does. Annette is obviously well out of her expertise in anything resembling the housewife mode. I can see her clumsiness from here. Whatever mistake she's made elicits a gentle, warm laugh from Gena, one that comes from loving delight. From happiness.

I miss so that special indulgence you have for someone you love. When I think of laughing that way, I can think only of Nick.

He could make the most wonderful mistakes because he was so safe with me. And the untried fascinated him. If he fell on his face, so what, he could always get up. And fast, too. Unlike me, whose life rule has been if you even trip, you're out. And everybody's watching, so don't try again.

We, my daughter and I, always loved to be there when he was conquering new horizons. He liked the company, and for us it could have a high entertainment quotient. One time he struggled to hang wallpaper that kept rolling down over his head. Another, our favorite, was when he painted the bedroom. Actually that was boring, until he stepped off the ladder into the paint can.

Gentle laughter. Smiles that warm your whole body. Quick reassuring hugs and floods of good feeling. Where have they all gone? To other lovers, obviously. To Gena and Annette.

I ache watching them. I'll never be able to find my way back into that kind of feeling without Nick. And the sight of it on someone else gives me no pleasure. It makes me want to run.

But I ran away already. And in the end it didn't matter that it was France and all new. If I tricked myself into thinking I could escape, I've been reminded again: you can't break out of the aura of death. It sticks to you.

It stuck to me.

I make my excuses, thank them again, and flee.

KENNEDY AIRPORT

A ir France, right?" the driver said, and Nick snapped out of the fog of his private torture, which was a continuous replay of Anna's mother's conversation with her long-lost friend. The nightmare always ended at the same hideous point, that moment when he should have stood to full height, made himself known. But instead he had slumped away in disgrace.

And with that same air of defeat, Nick got out of the cab, a deep sigh of hopelessness escaping from his heart. He stared at the pile of luggage on the pavement in front of him, not wanting one piece of it, not even his beloved typewriter. Finally, fueled by resignation, he slipped his arms through the straps of the backpack and retrieved the rest of his baggage.

Inside the terminal, the lines to the counters were long and jammed with excited travelers. Silently he took his place at the end of the closest one.

There, waiting at the end of the line, he felt a certain tranquillity, as if he were suspended in an intermission of time where nothing but his physical presence was required and territorial imperative the only operative. Even heartache slipped behind the primitive need to guard your place. Waiting on lines might not hold back time and tide, but it seemed to stop most everything else.

❀

One thing it didn't stop was Anna's desperate charge to the airport. Normally taxis were lined up in front of the hotel; today, of course, there was not one in sight. And when she finally grabbed one on Madison Avenue after unfairly easing out an obviously tourist couple, she was punished by getting locked in a traffic jam on Fifty-ninth for almost twenty minutes. A street fair had forced all the cars to take Sixty-first Street.

She sat trapped in the backseat, sweating from the heat and the panic of the delay. She dared not ask the driver to turn down the hard rock that was blasting from his radio for fear he might ask her to get out. Finally, with her head about to blow off, she chanced asking him to change the station. He said, sure, and flipped the dial.

And there it was. So ridiculous it reduced her to tears, and when the driver asked her what was wrong, she smiled and lied, "It's my favorite song."

And together they listened to the Simon and Garfunkel song, "Mrs. Robinson."

Normally the trip to the airport took about forty minutes, but today they seem to catch every red light on the way to the tunnel and it was almost a quarter to one by the time the taxi got onto the expressway. Nick's plane was leaving at one-thirty. If they didn't hit any unusual traffic, she could be at the airport in time to stop him. She knew absolutely in her heart that he hadn't made that morning plane to Nice.

The only thing unusual about New York traffic is its absence. There were the usual inexplicable traffic jams that clot and clear up for no reason. And just enough of them to add on twenty extra minutes to the trip.

※

Back at the airport, the line moved too quickly for Nick. In fact, he did his job so poorly that two women cut in ahead of him and others would have if an airline attendant hadn't looked at his ticket and insisted he move to the front of the line or miss his flight.

He checked in, got his boarding pass, and began the long walk to gate thirty-seven at the extreme end of the terminal. He walked slowly, mindlessly observing the people along the way. He felt he had been placed on some long, automatic belt of life that would carry him onto the plane, across the sea, and into some unknown he didn't care about. All that without any participation from him.

It was one-twenty, and still he didn't speed up his step.

❀

At that same one-twenty, Anna raced into the Air France terminal and rushed over to the counter, pushing toward the front of the line.

"Excuse me, please," she said, elbowing past the crowd into the space in front of the attendant.

"Hey, lady, you can't do that." A elderly bald man at the head of the line tried to push her back.

"Please," she said to him, "I have to stop someone before he gets on the plane."

Reluctantly the old man grumbled something about manners, but he made room for Anna.

She apologized again, "I'm really sorry, excuse me."

Now she turned to the woman behind the counter. "I need information on the one-thirty to Paris. . . ."

Attendants at airline counters are unimpressed by frantic customers, and this one explained slowly but firmly that Anna would have to wait until she finished punching in the ticket she was working on. And she added, with some pleasure, "There is a line, in case you haven't noticed."

Anna knew arguing would just hold things up. "I have to contact someone who's getting on the one-thirty to Paris. How do I do that?"

"I think you're too late," the attendant said with even more pleasure.

"No, it's only one twenty-three. Please, you don't understand, I have to stop him. Just tell me how I do it."

One of the women on the line overheard and suggested she page him.

The elderly man, his feathers soothed by what he could see was Anna's true desperation, said, "Call him over the loud-speaker."

"Where's that?" Anna asked the attendant.

She pointed up. "On the next level."

"But where on the next level? For God's sake, it's huge up there!" Anna was losing it. "What's it next to?"

"I have no idea," said the attendant, by now turning back to her computer. "Ask information."

"Where's information?"

Without taking her eyes off the computer, the attendant nodded toward the upstairs.

"You're a wonderful person," Anna snapped, and raced away up the stairs to the next level.

Of course, there was no information booth in sight, so she had to ask. And no one to ask save a floor sweeper. But, unlike the attendant, he knew and was helpful and pointed out the counter way down almost out of sight. She took off, flying down the long corridor, cutting in and out of people and carts and babies in strollers.

At the information desk they directed her straight to the paging desk next to the American Airlines desk which, of course, was on the lower level. Precious minutes were ticking by.

※

Meanwhile Nick had finally reached his gate. It was a full plane, more than two hundred people, most of them having waited at least four hours for the delayed flight, were well out of patience. At least half of them were already queued up, ready to board. Nick joined the welcome relief of another line.

There were so many people and so much grumbling and con-fusion that the PA system's announcement for the boarding order could hardly be heard.

Someone behind him said they were boarding from the back first. Nick was in seat fifteen. He had time to sit down but lacked the inclination to move. He just stood there, safely lost in the noisy crowd.

※

By the time Anna, moving at top speed, hit the paging desk, it was almost one twenty-six. There was only four minutes to go.

"Excuse me, please. Excuse me," she said, pushing her way along the front of the counter, squeezing in front of a group of waiting Japanese tourists.

She couldn't have chosen a better group of people to interrupt. With their exquisite manners, they parted instantly to make room for her, bowing and allowing her to pass directly to the center of the counter, opposite the man in charge of the microphone.

"I have to page someone quickly," she said. "He's getting on a plane—"

Without interrupting his message, Bob Walker, the name on his tag, held up one finger to silence Anna, who didn't have time for silence.

"I have to page Nick Devlin—"

"Will the owner of the green Honda civic with license plates—" here Mr. Walker paused to check the numbers on the page in front of him—"40739 J please move your car from the No Parking zone immediately."

By now Anna was pulling at his sleeve in desperation. "Please," she begged, "just page Nick—"

"Madam," the attendant cut her off in midsentence, "you'll have to wait your turn."

"I can't, it's an emergency. Please, Mr. Walker. . . ."

"Very well," he said, irritated at having his routine disturbed but not willing to chance censure in the unlikely event it was a true emergency. But he was certainly not about to make it easy for her. "If you want to make an announcement, you'll have to write it down. That's policy."

"A pen! A pen! Quick!" she said, turning frantically to the group behind her. In an instant at least ten pens were proffered.

She grabbed the nearest one, nodded thank-yous, and searched the counter for a paper. The attendant didn't lift a finger to help her.

The Japanese crowd came up with four pieces of paper. She took one and scribbled down the name *Nicholas Devlin* and shoved it at the reluctant Mr. Walker.

It was one twenty-nine.

※

At the gate the last of the crowd was being herded toward the plane. Nick, deep inside the throng, allowed himself to be carried along.

In the surge forward, he collided with an elderly woman carrying a large overloaded shopping bag. As she knocked into him the edge of his typewriter case caught onto the handle of her bag and ripped it open, sending a cascade of packages tumbling to the floor.

Nick dove down, trying to catch the rest of the bag before it hit the ground. His backpack slipped over his shoulder and into the leg of the man on the other side, who tried to back out of the way, knocking into the people behind him.

After enduring the long wait, these passengers were in such a high state of irritation that the least little thing would have set them off. This minor contretemps did just that. A loud argument broke out, and the man who fell into the people behind him blamed the old woman, who he said purposely pushed into him.

At that very same moment, the PA system announced that a Mr. Ni Colas De Vlan was wanted in the public address office immediately.

Even if his name had been properly pronounced, there was no way, in the noisy confusion of that group at the Air France gate, he would have heard.

※

Back at the counter, Anna shouted at Mr. Walker. "Nicholas Devlin! Not De Vlan, Devlin!"

But Mr. Walker had had enough. This was his domain, and no

one was going to tell him how to run it. He repeated the announcement just the way he'd read it earlier. "Mr. De Vlan, please come to the public address counter." And then he turned to Anna. "We do not repeat an announcement more than two times without waiting five minutes for a response."

That was it. Anna grabbed the microphone from his hand and shouted into it.

"Nick! Nick! It's me! I'm here! Don't go!"

And like the old E.F. Hutton commercials, a silence struck the airport. Thousands of people stopped talking, stopped moving.

"Nick! Please don't go! . . ."

Even Mr. Walker was too stunned to interrupt and retrieve his mike.

At boarding gate number thirty-seven, the people there, too, had stopped in their tracks.

"Nick, please," the voice on the mike pleaded, "I love you!"

Now all heads lifted, searching the crowd for Nick.

Where was Nick?

Who was Nick?

"I'm at the paging desk!" Anna's voice was frantic, "I need you, Nick!"

And then sounds of scuffling over the mike and her voice yelled, "Damn it, let go! Hurry, Nick!"

Suddenly, from out of the crowd a man's voice shouted, "I'm here! I'm coming!" It was Nick. A second later he emerged, jumping up and down and waving his typewriter.

Scores of people turned, pointing and shouting, "It's Nick! He's there!"

"Where?" others shouted.

"Over there! Over there! There he goes!"

By now Nick was running. The crowd pushed back, making a clear path for him.

"Okay, Nick!" they cheered him on.

"Go get her, Nick!"

Meanwhile wails of microphone screeches and grunting and shouting came over the PA system as Anna and Mr. Walker grappled for the mike.

By now others had joined in the cheering. "Go, Nick, go!" they shouted.

And Nick, at top speed, raced along the walkways, running down the center of the terminal, and leaping the steps of the down escalator with his suitcase bouncing off the sides.

"Go, Nick, go!" The crowd was wild with excitement. It was a touchdown, a home run, the French Revolution!

"Nick!" the loudspeaker screamed, "Hurrrrry! Let go, you dumb shit!"

And then there was a loud, popping sound and the system went dead.

But Nick kept going.

Anna could hear the shouting and the pounding of the crowd as they stamped their feet and clapped their hands and chanted, "Go, Nick, go!"

She could see the people beginning to part far down at the end of the corridor and knew he was coming.

And then she saw him racing down the open path, his suitcase and typewriter swinging from each hand.

When he got about fifty feet away he saw her, skidded to a stop, and dropped his luggage.

Even from the distance Anna could see him pulling himself up to full height, could feel the power of his joy as he strode down the aisle toward her. Smiling the smile of the victorious.

The crowd broke into wild applause as Anna ran into Nick's arms.

I'm leaving at the end of this week. Saturday I will make my escape from this failure. And I'll do it fast; I've reserved on a direct flight from Nice to New York. No one knows.

Tomorrow, Thursday, the mason, M. Tonguy, must go to Paris until Monday, and since I won't see him after today (of course, he doesn't know that), I will give him my final instructions for removing the gazebo. I noticed last night that one corner of the ironworks still stands. I hope he doesn't mean to leave it for decoration. I'll deal with that later this morning.

In fact, I'll deal with it right now.

It's the usual scene outside, my enemies all gathered at the worksite, chattering and laughing with loud guffaws, all but slapping their knees. Pleasure running amok until I, the monster patron, make my appearance, and then all goes quiet and they disperse, hostility lingering in their wake.

Only the mason remains, his head down, his shoulders bent; all he's missing are the bales of cotton. I pay no attention.

"That stuff over there in the corner," I say to him, "I want that out, too."

"No," he dares to say to me, "that has to stay." And then he goes on to explain that there is a plumbing line under it and taking off the metal would endanger it. Unfortunately, that is just the spot where the fender of my car hits when I turn. The whole point of removing the gazebo would be lost if I left that protuberance.

Taking a kinder, more reasonable tack, I explain why it must come down.

But he doesn't want to take it down. He doesn't want to be responsible.

"Don't worry," I tell him, "I'll take full responsibility."

No, he's not going to do it.

I want to say to him, What the devil do you mean, you're not going to do it? You're working for me. You do as I say. But, instead, I hold my temper and explain again, reasonably, how I will not hold him liable.

Still he refuses. Now he threatens to leave. Tells me I should get someone else to finish.

"You can't do that in the middle of a job. I'll report you."

To whom I don't know.

Obviously I've chosen the wrong approach because now he's insulted. And as if I've fired him, he begins to gather his tools, loading them onto the wheelbarrow, and without even so much as a glance at me, he wheels them off to his car outside the gate.

I'm trapped in my own threat. What can I do? I can't physically force him to stay. Presently he comes back to get the rest of his things, his small frame stiff with the pride of a winner.

That's when I feel them. *L'équipe.* Even before I see them I know they're there, gathering around for the kill. Like evil Munchkins, they've tiptoed out of the trees, up the stairs, and from the house, to watch and listen and enjoy my humiliation.

I pretend I don't know they're there. I intend to win this one. I will not allow this lowly workman to hand me a final defeat. And certainly not in front of them. I play my last trump card.

"I'm not paying you one more cent if you leave now."

That gives him pause for thought, but then he sees his compatriots. Reinforcements have arrived.

"Did you hear that?" he says to them, but they say nothing.

I expect them to leap at the chance to agree, but strangely enough they remain silent. He, too, expects a positive response, and when he doesn't get it immediately, he explains again. Perhaps they didn't understand.

This time he's stronger, motioning his head to the side, indicating me, and telling them that this woman, with heavy emphasis on "woman," has refused to pay him unless he does the job her way: the wrong way. Having spit that out, he spins around to me with the equivalent of, Ah-ha, now I've told on you.

In triumph he turns back expectantly to his supporters. Now he'll get his response.

I, of course, know exactly what they will say and how they'll say it. First they'll cluck their heads back and forth in sympathy with their fellow worker, their fellow Frenchman, and then they'll smile that smile of eternal forbearance and with a deep sigh gather together all their patience and in baby French explain to me why it will be better to do as the mason says because he knows best, being French and a man.

And when I deign not to agree, they will put up their hands, shrug their shoulders, and say to me in their most patronizing manner, *"Comme vous voulez, madame."* And having shown their French superiority, they will turn to the mason to collect his sympathy. Oh, the burden they must endure with their foolish American patron—worse still, patroness.

But this time I will not be intimidated. Why should I be? I have no future to secure here. Though I was too naive in the beginning to know it, I never had a chance to win their loyalty and affection. Now my fists are clenched in determination. I will not pay this bastard one more penny unless he does what I want.

Meanwhile the mason, with his hands on his hips and cockiness exuding from his stance and his smile, waits to be vindicated. And while he waits, he allows himself one last surge of arrogance and right in front of me tells them how foolish I am to try to make him take off the metal piece when it could endanger the plumbing. Besides, it looks good there. Americans have no taste, he laments to their sympathetic ears.

And then he takes a hard, sweeping swing at the last of the gazebo. "That's what she wants me to do. Break it off!"

The sound of the sledgehammer hitting the metal reverberates in a wave of pings. Everyone watches, their eyes held on the sight of the little piece of twisted metal shuttering from the blow.

But the mason is not finished. With his frustration and anger at me from these last days unloosed by what he sees as their acquiescence, he winds up to take another whack.

But Louis, the gardener, jumps forward and grabs his uplifted arm, holding it back over his head.

"Stop!" Mme. Bareau shouts at the mason. "What are you doing! Show some respect for our patron."

The mason is stunned. And so am I. Another case of faulty translation? But, no. I play it back, word for word, in my head. And that's exactly what she said.

But why?

Can somehow his aggression be a threat to them, too? But why should they care? It's not their property. They just work here.

As I think that to myself, I wince. It's true they only work here, but for how many years? Over twenty for Mme. Bareau and the gardener. Most all of their working lives. It may even be the only job they've ever had. Imagine the attachment that's grown, not to me, but to the villa: this villa by now so deeply installed in their hearts that they probably know it as well as their own homes. How is it that I never saw that? That I never had any respect for that kind of investment?

I step back and listen as each one of *l'équipe* take turns letting M. Tonguy know their displeasure. And as I watch, pieces of understanding fall into place, and all at once it seems so obvious.

The insolent mason's lack of esteem for me, the financial owner, and for the physical property is equally an insult to them as the emotional proprietors, who, in the true measure of feelings, certainly have a greater ownership than I do. All I did was hand over some currency and walk in.

And when I walked in I never even looked at them. And if I did, in my bruised and untrusting state, I saw them only as the enemy, resenting me, the newcomer. Surely there was some of that, but there was also, and more important, great interest in the new mother of their baby. Maybe that was the real reason they all stayed on.

All those years of service and caring that they put in: The water pump that was on its last legs when it was jimmied together five years ago still works. The bougainvillea they started from tiny plants, and trained to walk the wall, is now a magnificent purple splash across the entrance. The chair that was accidentally left out in the rain and then re-covered now looks more beautiful than before. And all the worrying about heavy rains and stone walls that tumble. Those are the things that make up the history of a house. And they were there for them.

And then I, the new owner, took over. And they waited quietly, in the background, for some sign, some recognition of their position.

The cultural dances of tradition are old and fragile. And this time complicated by continental differences. They understood it was not their place to make the first move. But I didn't understand that it was mine. And so they waited to be included.

But that was not possible for me. I shut them out as I shut everyone else out of my life. They took my rejection as personally as I took theirs. We became enemies. And then everything they did seemed hostile to me. I saw myself as the center of their lives, and every time they laughed I knew they were laughing at me; if they whispered, I was certain it was some gossip about me.

Until now.

I turn to the mason, who is still baffled, trying to understand how they could have favored this foreigner over him, a working-class compatriot. "Monsieur," I say to him, secure in my new patron voice, "you have to remove that thing properly, or leave our land."

Our land.

I give them the sign.

Now is the time for them to be stunned. To worry if it was just a grammatical error or if, at last, I am including them.

"What do you think?" I ask Mme Bareau, wiping out any lingering doubts as to my meaning. "It will only be in our way."

Mme. Bareau reads it all in an instant and agrees, taking an even stronger stand with the mason, in my behalf, as if he were the outsider and I the true patron, a respected and intelligent property owner, and she were my top executive carrying out my orders. Am I losing my mind?

Now the others crowd in, and they, too, insist that the mason follow my orders. Some magical door has opened, and they have slipped me inside.

Or I have taken them in.

Who do you think you are? they tell him. If the madame says take it down, then you take it down, and on and on.

My God! They're fighting for me. My people.

Mon équipe.

I'm so touched, I begin to choke up. And then I snap back to reality. Why are they doing this? Have they heard I mean to abandon them? But I know it's not possible. No one knows my plan. All I did was make one phone call to Air France. There are no tickets, nothing written on paper. They can't know.

I stand back and watch them bring their power to bear on someone other than me. It's impressive, and it's working. The mason is backing off. I can hear it in the tone of his arguments. They're getting softer, he's losing heart, and his body language is beginning to read resignation. He's inching back toward the protruding metal, the true villain, and looking at it as if he's trying to figure out how best to remove it.

Now Louis, the gardener, gives him some advice. Something about using the discarded metal to cap the opening.

"Good idea," says the mason. And then he turns to me and tells me how he's going to do it. As if nothing ever happened.

But it did. And Mme. Bareau tells him the equivalent of "Get a move on," and when he picks up his tools in response, she turns and smiles at me.

I've seen her smile before, but never for me. Before I can control it, my own smile, heavy with gratitude, escapes from my heart. Outside of politesse, it's the first genuine one I have ever given her. And it is also the first time I've realized that Mme. Bareau is young. Perhaps younger than I.

Did I never notice before how sweet her face could be? The smile turns up her lips, dances into her gray eyes, and travels to the dimples in her cheeks.

And then it happens; just as I imagine it will be with the language when the revelation comes and everything is at once intelligible, so the revelation comes to our relationship.

Right in front of my eyes a communication, a camaraderie, is being forged, and suddenly, for the first time, all of us—Mme. Bareau, *l'équipe,* and I—see each other as people, insiders, with a common world to share. And the Maginot line dissolves.

They're as stunned as I am. Where have our eyes been all these months? Why were we enemies when we are natural allies? Does it always take an outside threat to unite? Is there such an enormous difference between us?

Not really.

It's in the midst of this discovery that Louis notices that Georgie, the dog, has disappeared. It must have been when the mason opened the gate. Aside from peeing, Georgie's life is centered on two things—his food and his freedom. The part he doesn't spend eating, he spends waiting for the gate to be inadvertently left open. When the mason returned for the rest of his tools, he did just that, and Georgie slipped out. This happens a couple of times a week. Normally Mme. Bareau takes the car to find him. She turns to go, but I stop her.

"I'll go," I tell her. "I think it's better if you wait here with him." I nod my head toward the mason, now deep into the work of prying up the last of the gazebo. Despite the fact that he seems to have accepted his defeat, I think Mme. Bareau will be more effective in case there's any backsliding.

She understands and agrees immediately. We're on the same team now. Besides, the dog is mine, and it's time I took some responsibility for him. Something a little beyond the morning biscuit.

"He usually goes down the rue de Rampe to the yellow villa at the bottom," she says. "They have a puppy there he likes to play with. And the woman is very nice."

I get into the car, and Louis comes after me, carrying Georgie's leash.

"Best to put him on the leash right away," he tells me, "or he might keep running."

I thank him and drive off to look for my dog. "My dog" may be taking it a bit far since Georgie still doesn't know about the rapprochement.

I have no trouble finding the yellow villa, but they haven't seen Georgie. I spend the next fifteen minutes riding around the area looking for him. I shout his name out the window — not that he would respond, but that seems the logical way to look for a lost dog.

It's not like losing a dog in the United States; you don't have to worry about the ASPCA or dog thieves. Here, when they find a dog they check the phone number on a little metal *truc* on his collar and phone you. When you arrive they have fed and watered the dog and he's already part of the family.

The only danger here for runaway dogs is cars.

Since I'm having no success this way, I decide to go home and wait for the phone call. As I drive toward my street, the boulevard Cros Vieil, I see a car stopped in the middle of the road. People are bending over something I can't see. But I know before I see it that it's Georgie and he's been hit by the car. I slam on my breaks, jump out, and run over to the group.

It is Georgie, and he's lying in a heap, blood all over his hind leg. But he's alive.

"Georgie!" I call, and he lifts his head and looks at me. Then he begins to struggle to his feet. I push my way past the people to my dog, who practically throws himself into my arms. One of the men, obviously the driver, is trying to explain how he didn't see him until it was too late. It was on a sharp curve, he tells me, completely blind on this side. I can see he really feels terrible.

I tell him, It's okay, I understand, but could he just help me get Georgie into my car?

I run to open the back door, and Georgie drags himself after me. With the help of the other people, we get him up on to the seat.

Did I never see before how sweet his big face was, with its deeply furrowed brows and worried eyes? I take his head in my arms and press him tight against my breast. Tight enough so that he can feel the beat of my heart, a comfort all creatures know. I can feel his head burrowing in closer, and as I hug him, this warm and alive creature that needs me so, I feel a rush of love released from my body; the force of it spills out, not just for Georgie, but for Mme. Bareau and for all of them.

Just like that, I'm loving again.

The driver is still apologizing when I drive off. Since I've never taken any real interest in Georgie, I don't even know who or where his veterinarian is, so I speed back to the villa to get the information.

Mme. Bareau must see from my face that there's trouble because as soon as I pull the car into the driveway she comes running. One look at Georgie and she jumps into the car and we speed off toward Vallauris, where she directs me to the vet.

Between the two of us we are able to carry the bleeding dog inside. As soon as we enter, everyone goes on immediate alert.

The nurse escorts us directly into the doctor as another nurse lays out a large paper sheet on the examining table. Gently we place poor Georgie on it. The doctor asks us what happened, and Mme. Bareau nods to me to explain. After I tell him about the accident, he asks us to please wait outside.

In the waiting room we reenact the same Hollywood scene seen in hundreds of movies where the reconciled parents wait while the doctors struggle to save the life of the runaway child.

If the small tendrils of a relationship had begun to sprout with the affair of the mason, now they take a deeper root as we wait to know the fate of our dog child.

Another time I would have laughed at the movie cliche of it all, but I'm not laughing now. It feels too real, this aching, this caring. This loving. So much has changed in these last two hours that my emotions are popping out in all directions. Even for Georgie.

And for the first time since I arrived, I find that I'm not alone.

In the forty-five minutes we sit there, our eyes on the door, waiting for the doctor to emerge with news of Georgie, Mme. Bareau and I talk of many things: of changes and improvements in the villa, of making things more suitable to me. And she has suggestions: perhaps if she spoke to our neighbor, he might allow us—*us*—to trim the big eucalyptus that shades so much of my back patio. And would I like her to sew some new cushions for the sun chairs?

Indeed, I would like her to try to get that tree trimmed and implement all the other helpful suggestions she has made. All wonderful changes I won't be there to see.

I say nothing. I am so enchanted with all the affection and interest that our new relationship has engendered that I can't bear to spoil it.

At last the doctor comes out to tell us the good news: Georgie will recover; his leg isn't broken, just badly bruised. The doctor has sewn up the gashes and suggests we leave him there for the night just to make sure nothing else develops.

The ride home is a touch uncomfortable as we search for the new parameters of our infant relationship. If I can lay off the worrying, it will probably find its own shape.

At home, the mason is busy putting the finishing touches on the beautifully empty space that once housed the gazebo. M. Carson has at last been conquered and put to rest.

Happily I manage to fight down a desire to take that extra step and gather my *équipe* around me for some final words of gratitude. Better left for the movie.

When I get upstairs I find a message on my machine from Pierre inviting me to dinner next week at their villa in Opio. Hervé Yeboles, a French poet, will be there. I'm stunned to think they actually remembered what I did.

※

I'm on a roll. What a time to be abandoning it all.

Instead of making myself some mean little dinner, I think I will go out to a restaurant and dine among my new adoptive people.

I dress in the French manner, a little too fancy for the occasion, and drive down to a local fish restaurant in Golfe Juan. The patron is a hardworking, energetic woman who welcomes me with an enthusiastic barrage of friendly chatter.

The good times just won't stop.

Tonight she manages to use every French word I ever learned

attached to all the phrases I have answered dozens of times in my seven months here, and I shoot back my responses like a native. Well, in my head it's like a native.

"Mme. Devlin?" someone calls. I turn and see Mme. Terrier from the bank. Rene's friend. Suddenly all my pleasure dissolves. There's no way I can avoid talking to her. Fortunately she is with a friend, and they're just leaving. I'll keep it to a quick greeting.

But it's been a while, and she's chatty. "I haven't seen Rene lately," she says, "Have you?"

I'm not going to play games, so I tell her I don't see Rene anymore. She loves that and turns to her friend and whispers something. I turn back to my menu. I'll change banks.

Mme. Terrier leans down and whispers, "Did he tell you you weren't pretty enough?" Then she turns back and giggles to her friend. "Actually that would be a little hard in her case."

I can't hold back my annoyance. I tell them both that I don't find anything about Rene amusing. I think he's nothing but a petty criminal.

Now they're confused. And, when I explain, shocked.

Mme. Terrier apologizes. She had no idea that he was a thief and feels terrible for having introduced us. I tell her to forget it. I'll know better next time. And then she explains what she was referring to. It seems that Rene romances the women but has no follow-through and then blames them for his impotence.

Lucky for me, I tell her, I never had the experience. But I do love the story. My evening has been restored, and when they leave I find I have developed a huge appetite.

The small sardines are grilled just right, the turbot is juicy, and the hollandaise is impeccable.

In an afternoon I have found France. Everything I wanted it to be, everything I wanted it to do, it has done.

If death was the enemy, I thought life would be my salvation. But I had limited life to its most primitive form: Break the sexual barrier to freedom. The test of life. I was wrong. Life happened when Mme. Bareau reached out and touched me. Or perhaps she only made an ordinary move and it was I who reached out to her.

Whatever happened, the common spirit between me and the rest of the world has been revived. I am, for the first time in so long, enormously excited to be alive. And without guilt to feel so.

All the pieces seem to be dropping into place. Maybe now I can begin to move ahead. Perhaps I'll decide to stay here for a while.

And then suddenly I know I will. Absolutely. And I don't even need the list to do it.

I feel it again. The wasp of my triumph.

And on and on I dream. No one exists around me. I fantasize. I create. I am four paragraphs into a new poem that will be lyrics for Jake. Won't he be surprised. And happy for me. I hope. It's perfect for that sweet melody he said he had. I call it "Love Song."

It's the first time I've ever written about Nick.

I'm deep into the *framboise* sorbet when I become aware of a little Gypsy girl selling single roses. A far cry from the horrible woman who spat at me in Cannes, these children are a common sight in restaurants on the coast.

This little girl can't be more than eight and very pretty. She goes from table to table without great success until she gets to the table diagonally across from me, where two men and a woman are just finishing their coffee. One of the men, fortyish and slightly heavyset, but not unattractive, beckons the child and chooses a red rose. And looks at me and smiles. Unless he has painted his two front teeth black, they're missing.

My roll is running out. Sevens are coming up roses. Obviously Nick has sent him.

I watch the little girl as she makes her way over to my table with my gift. Panic builds. Is it too late to pretend to be blind?

I call upon my newfound maturity, accept the rose, and nod my appreciation. Perhaps I can discourage him by going back to my dinner. I take a forkful of my dessert, and strangely enough, I'm calm enough to actually taste it.

Without looking up, I can tell he's gotten the message because I no longer sense him looking at me.

Just days ago the threat of such an intrusion, the very prospect of making person-to-person contact, would have put me in a mad sweat, sending my brain soaring high over the scene like a crazed hawk, angry and frightened, and far out of touch.

Tonight I'm comfortable enough to glance around the room, lazily observing the other patrons. Directly in front of me are three older women, obviously English, struggling with the menu, and next to them, alone at a table, is a tall, good-looking man with curly brown hair. His chair is half turned toward me, and I can tell he's tall from the charming way his long legs jut out from under the table. There he sits, pleasant, calm, not spectacular in any way, reading his newspaper, sipping an espresso, and looking like just what he could be — a beginning.

A way to start.

Why not? The timing would be perfect. My decision to stay has already been made. This would be just gravy. Sauce for my new life.

I search the room for the Gypsy girl and find her way in the back, leaning on a table talking to what has to be an American couple. From the earnestness of the conversation, they plan to either report her parents or adopt her.

I signal the child, who drops into her vendor mode, quickly dumps her potential saviors, and speeds to my table.

I give her a ten-franc piece and point to the tall man. And sit back to watch.

She presents herself at his table, and he looks up and is about to shake his head no when she hands him a rose and points to me.

I smile. He smiles back.

Voilà, he doesn't paint his teeth.

My roll is on again.

You see, sometimes beggars do ride, but it takes more work than just wishing.

ACKNOWLEDGMENTS

I would like to thank Joni Evans for her invaluable assistance. My appreciation also to Betty Prashker, Richard Wenk, and Hilary Bloom. And to my extraordinary agent, Amy Berkower.

I am also deeply grateful to James Lee for his expert counsel and help at every turn.

ABOUT THE AUTHOR

Francine Pascal is the creator of the Sweet Valley High series, with more than 90 million copies in print, and the author of five previous novels. Ms. Pascal lives in New York and France.